DEATH BY HOT APPLE CIDER

Unease worked through me. Jimmy and Sidney had fought the day before one of the men was murdered?

I thought back to what I'd seen, how Sidney had thrust the dollar bill at Cindy. Could she have poisoned him then? Did it happen before that? After?

I know those two. Could two people I knew be killers?

"Thank you, Lily. I'll make sure the police know." And I'd hate every second of it.

"Don't give them my name, all right? I don't want to get involved and I don't want to lose my job." Lily shuffled back and forth a moment longer before she turned and ran back into the library.

Not only was Darrin Crenshaw looking like a suspect in Sidney Tewksbury's murder, but now, it looked like I was going to have to add Cindy and Jimmy Carlton to my list . . .

Books by Alex Erickson

Bookstore Café Mysteries
DEATH BY COFFEE
DEATH BY TEA
DEATH BY PUMPKIN SPICE
DEATH BY VANILLA LATTE
DEATH BY EGGNOG
DEATH BY ESPRESSO
DEATH BY CAFÉ MOCHA
DEATH BY FRENCH ROAST
DEATH BY HOT APPLE CIDER

Furever Pets Mysteries
THE POMERANIAN ALWAYS BARKS TWICE
DIAL 'M' FOR MAINE COON

Published by Kensington Publishing Corp.

A Bookstore Café Mystery

Death By Hot Apple Cider

ALEX ERICKSON

KENSINGTON
PUBLISHING CORP.

www.kensingtonbooks.com

KENSINGTON BOOKS are published by

Kensington Publishing Corp.
119 West 40th Street
New York, NY 10018

All Kensington titles, imprints, and distributed lines are available at special quantity discounts for bulk purchases for sales promotion, premiums, fund-raising, educational, or institutional use.

Special book excerpts or customized printings can also be created to fit specific needs. For details, write or phone the office of the Kensington Sales Manager: Attn.: Sales Department. Kensington Publishing Corp., 119 West 40th Street, New York, NY 10018. Phone: 1-800-221-2647.

The K logo is a trademark of Kensington Publishing Corp.

First Printing: November 2021
ISBN: 978-1-4967-2115-0

ISBN: 978-1-4967-2116-7 (ebook)

10 9 8 7 6 5 4 2 1

Printed in the United States of America

1

A deep rumble caused me to pause halfway across the trampled grass. A cacophony of sounds assaulted my ears—shouts, clanks, and bangs—but it was the ominous grumbling that had me worried that things were about to go south very quickly.

Nearly everyone in Pine Hills was at the local park, which was normally little more than a field with an underused walking trail and a couple of old soccer nets, but was now full of tents and activities. The first annual Thanksgiving celebration was in full swing. People were bustling from tent to tent, eating and playing games, all for a good cause. The hope was that by the end of the day, enough money would be earned through the events or donated by the wealthier of Pine Hills' citizens, to make sure everyone in town would have something to eat on Thanksgiving Day.

That hope was now in danger.

A churning darkness could be seen on the horizon. The weather reports had the storm skirting by us, but I wasn't so sure. The day had started out as a seasonally warm mid-fifties, but had quickly plunged into the lower forties. As those dark clouds neared, the temperature would only go lower.

"Come on, hold off for a few more hours," I muttered, forcing myself to look away from the oncoming menace. Maybe if I ignored it, it would go away.

A lot of planning had gone into the event, which was being held a little over a week from Thanksgiving itself. The librarians, Cindy and Jimmy Carlton, were big backers of the festival, and had spent a lot of time going around to all the businesses for support. I, of course, chipped in, pulling my business, Death by Coffee, deep into the frenzy.

I was headed for a tent where I knew the sweets were being sold by the local candy shop owner, Jules Phan, when I saw something—a someone, in fact—that caused me to jerk to a halt once again. My heart leapt into my throat and pounded there, choking me up as I stared at the man talking to Jules.

Dark hair. Skin the color of creamer-rich coffee. Looks that could make any woman drop to her knees and weep.

Will Foster.

My ex.

He was with his family, who surrounded him like a cloud of friendliness. Everyone looked to be in good spirits, and I was glad for it, but a part of me was still sad. Will had left Pine Hills for a job, which in turn, meant he'd left me too. I didn't fault him for it. Our relationship really wasn't going anywhere at the time and it freed me up to turn my attentions to the local hunky police officer, Paul Dalton, but I couldn't help the pang of loss when I saw Will laughing and smiling with a family that, in another alternate timeline, might have become my own.

While I did want to say hi, I couldn't bring myself to do it now, not with his parents and sister there. So, instead, I veered off and headed for the tent where my main contribution to the festival waited.

Warm air blasted from a forced air heater as I stepped beneath the fluttering tent flap. The heat was almost too much with my jacket, but I kept it on since I wasn't going to stay long. A counter stood in one corner. A sign hung from it proclaiming it to be provided by Death by Coffee. I approached it with a smile.

"How has business been?" I asked the two Death by Coffee employees, who were manning the counter.

"Ms. Hancock." Jeff Braun bowed his head and averted his eyes at my approach. He'd worked for me for a long time now, yet still struggled to meet my eye whenever he spoke to me.

"Please, call me Krissy." It would do no good. No matter how many times I told him, he always insisted on calling me Ms. Hancock or ma'am.

"We've been busy," Lena Allison said, nudging Jeff with her elbow. She used a heavily ringed hand to push a lock of purple hair from her eyes. She'd been growing it out lately, and it was in that in-between stage where it would be an annoyance before it became manageable. "You've gotten a lot of compliments on the cider."

"That's good to hear. I was worried everyone would expect us to serve coffee."

"There have been some requests, of course, but after they tried a sample of the cider, all complaints dried right up."

I tried not to let the compliment affect me, but I couldn't help but grin. The hot apple cider recipe was my late mother's own. It seemed the perfect drink for a day that was turning chilly.

"I'll take one of those ciders." Paul Dalton slid an arm around me, causing me to jump. His smug grin told me he'd done it on purpose.

"Aren't you supposed to be on duty?" I asked, playfully shoving him away.

"I am," he said. "But nothing says I can't enjoy myself while doing it."

Paul was in full uniform, and I couldn't help but appreciate the view. His sandy-brown hair was tucked under a wide-brimmed police hat, which was oddly fetching. His uniform fit him rather snugly, which, of course, drew the eye right to his . . . well, assets. When he turned his deep blue eyes and dimples on me, a flash of warmth shot through me that had me near sweating.

Lena was all smiles as she handed Paul a hot cider. He took a tentative sip before taking a much larger gulp.

"This is pretty good," he said.

"You make it sound like you weren't sure it would be."

He shrugged, dimples deepening even more. "Not a big fan of apple drinks. This might make me change my mind about that."

"Rita was by a few minutes ago," Lena said, leaning her arms on the counter. "She was looking for you."

Rita Jablonski was a friend of mine, and was also the biggest gossip in all of Pine Hills. She had to be thrilled with an event like this because it would allow her to people watch to her heart's content. She'd likely come across some new, juicy piece of gossip she couldn't wait to share with me.

"I'll keep an eye out for her," I said. "Do you need me to stick around and help out?" There weren't many people in the tent now, but if the rain were to hit, it could get busy very quickly.

Lena glanced at Jeff, who shrugged. "I think we'll be okay. Beth said she'd be back in an hour, and Vicki and Mason are around here somewhere. Go and have fun." She looked at Paul, and then shot me a sly wink.

A part of me felt guilty for leaving Jeff and Lena to work the booth alone, but it wasn't like there was much to do until the rain did hit. The cider was kept warm—not scalding hot for safety reasons—and looked well stocked for now. I'd need to check back in an hour or so to see if I needed to throw together a fresh batch. If the rain didn't strike first, that was.

"Text me if you need me," I said, patting my back pocket to make sure my phone was still where it should be. "I won't be far."

Paul was waiting a few steps away, sipping his cider. I stepped over one of the many taped-down power cords and joined him.

"Having fun?" I asked him.

"Surprisingly, yeah. I had to break up one argument over by the games tent, but otherwise, everyone is behaving themselves."

"I can't believe we're going to pull this thing off," I said, pausing to watch a man approach the cider booth and deposit a twenty into the donations jar. "We might be able to not just put food on some tables, but stock the food bank for a week afterward."

"You're doing a good thing," Paul said.

"The town is."

We stood silent as we took in our surroundings. Beneath the scent of cider, I could smell hot dogs and fried food and cotton candy. Kids were shouting and running around, often with semi-harried parents yelling at them to be careful. There was a cheer over by the games tent where multiple carnival games were taking place. Someone must have won one of the bigger prizes.

My smile faded as my gaze traveled past the tents and smiling crowds to the horizon. The dark clouds appeared to be a whole lot closer.

Paul saw where I was looking and patted my arm. "It'll hold off."

"It better."

"Come on." Paul started to reach for my hand, but seemed to realize he was still on duty and it wouldn't look professional, because he pulled it back before he could take hold. "Let's walk."

With one quick glance back toward Lena and Jeff to make sure they were okay, I followed after Paul. We stepped out from beneath the tent, into sunlight that was being filtered by far too many clouds for my liking. I swear the temperature had dropped another ten degrees since I'd entered the tent, though it was likely a result of standing next to the heater for so long.

"I saw Will," Paul said. His words were spoken as leisurely as his gait, which was slow and relaxed, but I could hear an underlying current beneath it. I couldn't tell if it was curiosity or jealousy.

"I did too." I refused to look toward the candy tent, just in case Will was still there.

"Did you talk to him?"

"No." I left it at that.

"He seems to be doing good."

"I'm glad." And I was. He might have left me for a job, but we'd parted on good terms. Sure, I still thought about him every now and again. And, yeah, sometimes I got a little melancholy. But I wouldn't trade my life now for anything.

"Robert's around here somewhere too."

Robert Dunhill. Another of my exes. They seemed to be everywhere these days. "I haven't seen him. Was he with Trisha?"

"He was. They seemed to be getting along."

I wondered if Trisha—his girlfriend—had finally accepted his marriage proposal from months ago. Her "maybe" had sent Robert on a downward spiral of self-pity, so perhaps them being here together meant she'd finally said "yes."

I shot a glance at Paul, wondering why he was bringing up all my exes. It made me think of his own ex, Shannon, and I feared he was starting to regret breaking up with her. I didn't know the details on what happened between them, why they broke up, or if it was on good or bad terms, only that Shannon wasn't happy about the arrangement.

Is she trying to win him back? The thought caused every protective instinct of mine to kick in. If she tried, I wasn't going to go down quietly.

I didn't realize it until I heard the "Lordy Lou, that's cold!" coming from ahead that we were headed for the dunking tent. Just hearing Rita's voice brought the smile back to my face and pushed any and all thoughts about ex-boyfriends and girlfriends from my mind.

We entered the tent to find Rita toweling a weak, cold version of my apple cider from her face with one hand. An apple with a bite mark in it was in her other. She'd lost some weight in the last few months, and it looked good on her, but she was still what many considered to be on the plump side. I thought she looked fantastic.

"Congratulations," Cindy Carlton said. The short, round librarian held out a book to Rita, who took it after handing over her towel to Cindy's husband, Jimmy. The muscular librarian could easily have been an army instructor, but instead, he had chosen sweater vests and books over screaming at recruits.

"This your idea?" Paul asked, motioning toward the tub filled with cider and apples.

"No, the Carltons came up with it. I just supplied the cider and some of the books."

A woman handed Cindy a twenty and then lowered herself onto the pillows in front of the tub. She took a deep breath and then dove in after an apple. She fished around for a good ten seconds before jerking her head up with a fling of wet hair, apple caught triumphantly between her teeth. A smattering of applause followed.

"The customers donate whatever they want for a chance to go after an apple," I said. "The books are given out as prizes in the hopes that a few of the victors would take to reading, or at least, give the books to their kids." I was glad to note quite a few teens were queued up in line.

"Sounds like a good cause."

"It is," I said. "A portion of the money earned here

goes to the library for a reading program Jimmy hopes to set up. The rest is earmarked for the food fund."

We watched as Cindy handed out a book to the victorious woman and the next person stepped up to try their hand at the tank. The kid was no more than thirteen, and when he dunked his head, he went all in with a splash.

"There you are!" Rita noticed me for the first time. She walked over, holding her book to her breast. "I was beginning to wonder if you'd skipped the whole affair."

"Nope, I'm here," I said. Behind me, a grumble rolled over the field. I prayed someone had set up a bowling alley next door because otherwise, the thunder was getting a little too close for comfort.

"Well, you won't believe what I have to tell you, dear." Her eyes flickered to Paul. "But it can wait. There's someone waiting on me."

"Oh?" I asked. "Are Georgina and Andi around?" They were Rita's best friends and gossip buddies.

"I'm sure they are," Rita said with a strange smile that caused my eyebrows to rise. *Did Rita have a date?* It would be the first one I'd ever seen her go on, if so.

"Don't let us keep you," Paul said. "Congrats on your book."

Rita patted the back of the book, which turned out to be a lighthearted mystery I'd read last month and donated to the cause. "I plan on reading the whole thing tonight." A gleam came into her eye then. "If I'm not too busy, that is." And then she walked off with a decided bounce in her step.

Both Paul and I watched her go with the same disbelieving expressions on our faces.

"I think she's found someone," I said, still unable to

believe it. Rita was one of those people you couldn't help but think of as permanently single. The idea of her dating anyone was just . . . odd.

"I'm glad for her." Paul turned back to me. "The department is getting a detective."

The abrupt shift in topics threw me off and I sputtered a moment before I managed, "What happened? Did someone die?"

Paul laughed. "No, nothing happened. But there's been more crime around Pine Hills over the last few years than there used to be." Which some people blamed on me, if you could believe it. "The town is growing and the police force needs to grow with it."

"Is this detective from out of town?" I wondered how that would affect me, considering how often I ended up dealing with the local police.

"Actually, there isn't a detective yet." Paul's cheeks reddened. "I'm applying for the position."

"Really? That's great!" And since Paul's mom was the police chief, I found it likely he'd get the job.

"I haven't earned it yet," he said. "There's a lot of studying and work ahead. And I'm not the only one to apply, so there's going to be some competition."

"You'll get it, easy."

"We'll see." Though I could tell he was thrilled about the prospects. "John and Becca are good officers."

"Buchannan is going for the job?" I asked. John Buchannan and I rarely saw eye to eye, and with my penchant for getting myself stuck in the middle of murder investigations, I doubted it would get any better if he was a detective on the case, not just a responding officer.

"He is. And really, I think he'd do a good job. Becca too."

Becca Garrison was another officer on the force who had an up-and-down relationship with me. It seemed like they all did. Other than Paul, of course.

"Well, if there's anything I can do to help . . ."

Paul chuckled. "Let's hope that won't be necessary. I'm not sure your help will benefit my case."

I was about to protest by pointing out how many murders I'd helped solve when a loud "Fine!" pierced the air.

A man stood at the front of the apple-bobbing line, glaring like someone had just called him cheap. He fished into his front pocket and came away with a crumpled one-dollar bill. He shoved it into Cindy's hand like it offended him.

"That good enough for you?"

Cindy scowled as she dropped the bill into the donations bin. One look at the guy and I knew exactly why there was so much friction.

"Oh, no," I muttered to myself, but did so a little too loudly because Paul noticed.

"What is it?"

I kept my voice low. "This could be trouble."

Paul went into cop mode, squaring his shoulders and narrowing his eyes at the man as he stepped up to the tub. "Who is he?" he asked.

"I don't know his name," I admitted. "And I don't know him personally, but I do know he's been causing some trouble at the library and at Death by Coffee."

"What kind of trouble?"

"Complaints," I said. "I don't know all the details, just that he's been demanding we stop carrying certain types of books. He says they're offensive and they're the cause of pretty much every bad thing to happen around town.

We've ignored him, and honestly, I haven't had to deal with him at all. I only know him by sight."

"I see." Paul crossed his arms and watched as the man lowered his head to the tub, but he didn't dunk right away. He swayed there a moment, as if judging the best angle, before he finally lowered his face into the cider. "A drinker?" Paul asked, apparently noting how the man had swayed.

I shrugged. I had no idea. "He's a nuisance, but it's to be expected. There are always people like that around. They complain, but can't really do anything." For which I was grateful. If I was forced to stop carrying romance books and paranormal teen novels, all because of one man's prejudices, Death by Coffee would lose a big part of our business.

Seconds passed. A few bubbles rose from the tub, then vanished.

"Hey, Sidney, you're supposed to grab an apple, not take a nap." A man's voice, but I was too busy staring at the way the man—Sidney, apparently—had gone limp, hands dangling at the side of the tub, rather than gripping it like everyone else did.

The tent fell silent. Then, beside me, Paul cursed, and rushed forward. He jerked Sidney from the tank and laid him onto his back. "Is there a doctor here?" he shouted, even as he pressed his fingers to Sidney's neck.

"I am." To my surprise, a doctor I knew stepped forward. Darrin . . . It wasn't until that moment that I realized I didn't even know Darrin's last name, only that he was a doctor at the office where Will Foster used to work.

Paul moved aside to let Darrin work. Everyone in the tent, including me, stood with bated breath as he performed CPR. Seconds passed, then minutes.

Finally, Darrin leaned back, a defeated slump to his shoulders. When he looked up, his eyes found mine, as if he'd specifically sought me out.

With a heaviness that had my heart sinking straight to my feet, he said, "He's dead."

A crack of thunder accompanied the proclamation and the skies opened up, putting a decidedly final end to not just Sidney's life, but to the Thanksgiving festival.

2

Rain pattered against the tent as Darrin worked over Sidney. Paul hovered over him, face impassive, though his shoulders were tense and his fists were bunched. A crowd had gathered, packing the tent, thanks to the skies opening up. They huddled together with an excited chatter.

"Do you think it was a heart attack?"

"How does someone drown while bobbing for apples?"

"I heard a *boom*. Was he shot?"

"Poison."

The word hung in the air, and cut all other speculation short. It took me a moment to realize Darrin was the one who'd said it.

"He was poisoned?" Paul asked.

Darrin accepted a sheet handed to him by Cindy and

draped it over Sidney's face. Someone actually groaned, as if disappointed.

"I can't be sure until tests are run, but . . ." He frowned as he noticed the crowd hanging on his every word.

Paul nodded and then ran a hand over his face before taking Darrin by the arm and leading him away so they could talk privately. The only uncrowded space put them at tent's edge, with rain sleeting in against their legs.

The once-excited chatter turned panicked as soon as they walked away. Half-eaten apples were tossed to the ground, and one woman started weeping openly. She kept repeating, "I don't want to die!" over and over.

Poison. Fear clutched at my chest. Had I done something wrong? Those were *my* apples and *my* apple cider. And then, remembering someone else who'd taken a bite of one of the apples, I joined in with the panic. *Rita!*

I turned, thinking to go in search of her, but one look at the crowd at my back and the rain falling outside, kept me from doing it. When I'd seen her, she'd seemed fine. The apple-bobbing had been going on throughout the day and no one else had fallen ill, so I was guessing they weren't the cause.

I took a deep breath to calm my nerves. There was no sense in panicking and running all over the park when I didn't actually know what had happened. A man was dead, yes, but that didn't mean it had anything to do with my apples or apple cider. Darrin could have been mistaken.

Paul returned a moment later, looking grim. He'd called in the other cops who'd been prowling the festival and they were now in the process of securing the scene. "All right, everyone," Paul said, raising his hands to draw the crowd's attention. "There's nothing to worry about here. I'm going to talk with each of you and then send you on your way."

This time, the groan went around the tent, and I'm pretty sure a few people took the opportunity to slip out into the rain while it was still too packed to notice. Or stop them.

"Hang tight. This will be over soon." Paul's eyes found mine. I'd seen that look before, and knew what it meant.

Sidney's death wasn't an accident.

We were dealing with a murder.

The next hour was an exercise in patience. Paul did his best to talk to everyone, but it was impossible to keep track of the crowd. People came and went, and as the rain petered out and the sun peeked out from behind the clouds, more and more people slunk away.

I hovered at the back of the tent, certain Paul would want to talk to me about what little I knew. But when he finally did notice that I was still hovering, he merely told me to go home.

With some trepidation, I did.

To say I wasn't happy about it would be an understatement, but it wasn't like I had any new information to offer him. I only knew the victim by sight, had donated the apples and the cider, but hadn't set anything up myself. And Paul was with me when Sidney had died. He saw everything I did.

By the time I pulled into my driveway behind the wheel of my new-to-me orange Escape, the only dark clouds were the ones shadowing my thoughts. I went inside and immediately scooped up my orange, long-haired kitty.

"It's been a long day," I told him, cooing the words. "I need some cuddles."

Misfit withstood my attentions for about ten seconds before squirming to be let down. As soon as he hit the floor, he fluffed out his tail and pointedly looked toward his empty food dish.

"That's all you see me as," I said. "Your personal waiter."

Still, I filled his dish with a half a scoop of dry and then sank down into a dining room chair. Exhaustion tried to overwhelm me, but I wouldn't let it.

Poison. The word kept flittering through my mind. It reminded me of my first days in Pine Hills, when a customer at Death by Coffee—my best friend's husband's brother—ended up dead after drinking one of my coffees. He hadn't been poisoned by actual poison like Darrin implied Sidney had, but it was close enough for me to draw the parallels.

Irrationally, I checked the news to make sure Brendon Lawyer's killer hadn't been set free and had come back to town for revenge. I'd almost forgotten that Mason—the aforementioned brother—had suffered so much in the short time I'd known him.

No articles hinted at a release. In fact, the news was pretty light and fluffy, all things considered. *That'll change the moment Sidney's death hits the airwaves.*

I spent the next two hours puttering around the house, waiting for Paul to call. I knew he was going to be busy, but he wouldn't leave me hanging like this. I vacuumed the carpet, ran a lint roller over the couch where Misfit liked to sleep, and then went through my new purse, as if I thought I might find something interesting buried at the bottom.

When all of that was done, I glanced at my phone.

Still no call from Paul.

I went to the window and peered outside, hoping to catch a glimpse of his car pulling into the driveway. Instead, I noticed a car sitting in the driveway next door.

Interest piqued, I went outside to investigate.

The *For Sale* sign was still standing in front of the house that had belonged to Eleanor Winthrow before her recent death. My neighbor had passed only a few months ago, and I still wasn't used to not having her watching me from her armchair by the window.

The car in the driveway looked old and well-used, but not decrepit. I'd never seen it before, and it wasn't accompanied by the Lexus of the woman who was selling the house; a grouchy Realtor by the name of Vanna Goff.

The murder must have triggered my paranoia because I immediately wondered if a thief had broken into the empty house, though what they could steal was beyond me. The only thing left were dusty shelves and appliances that were so old, they probably broke some sort of housing code.

I crept across the yard, hand poised and ready to snatch up my phone the moment I saw a masked face. The dark clouds were long gone and the sun was shining brightly, which should have been a clue that no one was trying to steal Eleanor's dust bunnies. I'd just stepped up beside the older car—a Toyota—when a couple rounded the house from the far side.

"Oh!" the woman said, hand shooting to her mouth in

surprise. She was a tiny woman, built like a dandelion. A stiff breeze could have blown her away. "I didn't know anyone was here."

The man beside her looked guilty as he stepped forward. Like the woman beside him, he was thin and wispy, and when he spoke, his voice matched the visual. "We're sorry if we intruded."

"No, you're fine." I relaxed, mentally reprimanding myself for being so paranoid. "I saw your car and was curious." I smiled. "I live next door. Krissy Hancock." I held out a hand.

The man took it. His grip was surprisingly strong for such a small person. "Eli Tuttle. This is my wife, Helena."

She flashed me a smile. "Pleasure."

"We're looking to move to Pine Hills," Eli went on. "I wanted to see the house before contacting the Realtor, get a feel for it and the neighborhood, you know?"

"Totally understandable," I said. "Are you from nearby?"

"Cleveland." Eli left it at that.

"Have you lived here long?" Helena asked.

"A few years. I was nervous coming to such a small town, but now that I'm here, I can't imagine going back to the bustle of a bigger city."

"I see." The Tuttles shared a look I couldn't decipher before they turned back to regard me. No one spoke for so long, I started to get fidgety.

"Well, if you have any questions about the town, feel free to stop by," I said, breaking the uncomfortable silence. "I live right over there." I gestured toward my house. "Everyone in the neighborhood is friendly and wouldn't mind visitors or questions, if you have them."

"That's good to hear," Eli said.

"If you do decide to move in, you'll find Pine Hills a serene, quiet place. It's as peaceful as it gets."

Paul chose that moment to pull into my driveway. His lights weren't flashing and the siren wasn't blaring, but he *was* in his police cruiser. He stepped out, still in full uniform, looking like a man who'd just come from a murder scene. He saw me standing next door and waved me over, with just a hint of impatience.

The Tuttles watched him, a slow frown creeping across each of their faces. So much for peaceful and serene.

"He's a friend," I said. "I'd better go. Feel free to stop by anytime." I hurried over to where Paul stood.

"New neighbors?" he asked.

"Possibly." When I glanced back, both Eli and Helena were sitting in the Toyota. They hadn't yet backed out, but the engine was running. I turned back to Paul. "What did you learn?"

His gaze flickered toward my door. I got the hint.

We went inside and I put on coffee for the both of us. Paul looked exhausted and I needed the comfort. He took a seat at the counter and removed his hat. I gave him the time it took for the coffee to finish percolating to gather his thoughts before I sat down across from him with a, "Well?"

"Dr. Crenshaw stands by his original assessment of poison," he said, taking a sip from his coffee. "I don't know the details, but he noticed something about the victim's face that gave it away."

It took me a moment to realize Dr. Crenshaw was Darrin. I felt silly for not knowing his last name, despite having seen him in the office multiple times over the years.

Heck, he was one of Will Foster's best friends, so I *should* have known it by now. What did that say about me?

"Was it the apple?" I asked.

Paul shook his head. "Initial tests found the apples and the cider in the tub to be clean."

I sagged in relief.

"We're running on the belief it was the hot cider."

"What?" I very nearly leapt from my chair. "That can't be right. You drank it! You weren't poisoned." Or was he? Would Paul collapse at any moment, foam bubbling from his lips? The image was so vivid, I just about hyperventilated.

"It looks like the only drink affected was the victim's. No one else has shown any symptoms, but we can't be sure just yet."

"It was my apple cider," I said. "My employees were serving it." My eyes widened. "Are Lena and Jeff in trouble? What about Beth? She was helping out, but wasn't at the booth when we were there. And Vicki. What about me? Am I a suspect?"

"Calm down, Krissy." Paul laid a hand on my own. "No one suspects you of anything. And while I talked to your employees, I don't think any of them killed that man."

"Could it have been an accident?" My head was spinning. Another murder in quiet little Pine Hills and, once again, I was going to be thrust in the middle of it by no doing of my own.

Paul spread his hands. "I won't know until more tests are run. Right now, we only have Dr. Crenshaw's early assessment. There's always a possibility he'll be wrong and this will turn out to be an accident."

I found it unlikely, but hoped Paul was right, nonetheless.

"Is he sure it was poison?" A new thought. "He came to that conclusion awfully quickly."

Paul's expression darkened, making me wonder what I'd just put into his head. Before I could ask, he hit me with a question of his own.

"You said you knew the victim?"

"Barely. His name was Sidney. I heard someone call out to him while he was—" I blanched, thinking about him facedown in the tub.

"Sidney Tewksbury," Paul confirmed. "I got his name from a friend of his who was there."

"I only knew his first name," I said. "Other than that, I know little about him. Vicki was the one who'd always dealt with him whenever he showed up at Death by Coffee. Did you talk to her?"

"Not yet." Paul sighed and pushed his coffee away. "I should get to the station. There's going to be a boatload of paperwork to take care of, on top of the interviews I still have to do. I really hope this turns out to be an accident."

"Me too." I rose with Paul. "I wish I knew more about the victim so I could tell you." Though that would mean I'd have known him better, which would have made his death hit me even harder than it already had.

"I'm glad you don't," Paul said. We stopped by the front door. "Take a day or two to think about it. If you remember anything about Mr. Tewksbury, call."

"I will." I paused, and decided to try to lighten the mood. I hated parting with him on such gloomy terms. "I guess you'll have a chance to test your detective skills."

"Unfortunately." He managed a weak smile that faded almost as soon as it appeared.

Paul didn't make a move for the door. He searched my face for a long couple of seconds. I knew what he was looking for, and did my best to keep any hint of interest off my face. *I'm just an innocent bystander in this. I have no intention of investigating myself.*

At least, investigating outside my own circle of friends. Talking to Vicki would be natural. If we happened to bring up the victim, well . . .

Paul sighed in a way that told me he'd deciphered my attempt at an innocent expression and knew there was no way he could dissuade me from asking questions. It just wasn't in my nature to sit back and do nothing when there was something I could do to help.

"Be careful, Krissy," he said. "We don't know what really happened yet, and there might be a lot more to this than it appears right now."

"I know. I'll be careful. Promise."

After a brief hesitation, Paul leaned forward and kissed me on the cheek. He then put his hat back on, adjusted it, and then walked out the door.

I watched him until he got into his car and pulled away. Then, I closed the door and immediately pulled my phone from my pocket. My finger hovered over the Facebook icon; my favorite investigative tool when I wanted to know something about someone.

But I didn't press it.

Instead, I set my phone down on the counter and turned my back to it.

"I'm not getting involved," I said to Misfit, who was

watching me from the couch. "It might have been an accident." How someone managed to poison themselves in the middle of a Thanksgiving festival, I'd never know, but for now, I had to be content with the hope that somehow, someway, Sidney Tewksbury hadn't been murdered.

3

I stood, hands on my hips, staring at the books in Death by Coffee, the bookstore café I'd opened with my best friend Vicki Lawyer, back when she was Vicki Patterson. A man with a gut overhanging his belt sidled down the aisle sideways. He could have walked normally, but the fit was tight enough that he must have found it safer to sidestep.

That, to me, was a problem.

The morning rush had come and gone, and I was alone upstairs, looking over the layout of the books. Trouble, the store cat, wasn't in attendance yet since he didn't arrive until Vicki or her husband, Mason, did, and that wasn't going to be for a while. It gave me a chance to survey the area without the often-troublesome feline getting underfoot.

Not much had changed in the years since we'd opened

Death by Coffee. We had the same shelves, the same general layout. There was a seating area in the corner where customers could sit and read. I'd looked over the space before, hoping to find a way to open it up so customers had more room to move, but nothing had been done to correct the issue. Every time we considered it, something got in the way and the project was put on hold.

The big man pulled a pair of books off a shelf and headed for the counter, still sidestepping his way along. I checked the prices on the books—they were both steamy romances with heroines with their clothes half torn off and the men shirtless—and rang him up. He was reading the first even before he was down the stairs and out the door.

Of course, seeing the romances made me think of Sidney Tewksbury and his murder. He'd complained to Vicki more than once about such material, deeming it unsuitable for children and a hazard to the mental health of adults. Now, it wasn't like grade-schoolers ever came in, browsing the romance section, but I could see a teen or preteen giving them a look, if for nothing more than a laugh.

For a heartbeat, I wondered if maybe Sidney was right and we were corrupting the youth of Pine Hills by allowing them access to such books.

Common sense prevailed and I shook off the thought. People gravitated toward books that they *wanted* to read, books that interested them. Why deprive people of their enjoyment, their fantastical getaways, just because a handful of spoilsports didn't approve?

I turned my attention back to the problem of space, and spent the next hour working out solutions that were better than my last attempts at it. If we could open the area up more without reducing the number of books our customers could buy, then it would be a win. I just wasn't sure how we were going to pull that off without adding square footage somehow.

"I finished up in the back and the tables are all wiped down."

I turned to find Lena at the top of the stairs. "Great." I wasn't sure why she thought it important to inform me of her progress. She knew I trusted her with the store and making sure everything got done.

"Beth is handling the counter right now, but we're pretty dead."

I glanced downstairs to see a pair of twentysomethings leaning across a table, staring into one another's eyes over their cappuccinos. They were the only customers in the store.

"Anyway, I was wondering, since Jeff is due in about an hour, and there aren't many people here, if maybe I could take off a little early." Lena's face reddened and she refused to meet my eyes. "If not, that's completely fine," she added in a rush.

"Is everything all right?" I asked her.

"Yeah. Totally cool." She scuffed one neon pink Converse on the floor. "It's just that, Zay . . . you remember Zay?"

I nodded. I knew he was Lena's friend, and that she might be interested in him romantically, though she'd never admit it to me. I didn't know much about the guy, other than how he was like a quiet, male version of Lena. "How is Zay doing?"

"He's great." She flushed, cleared her throat. "Well, he's got this thing and he invited me to it and I said maybe since I had to work, but since it's dead in here, I thought that I could, I don't know, pop on in and check it out."

A smile crept onto my face and refused to relent. I'd never seen Lena so flustered in all the time she'd worked for me. It was nice to not be the one too embarrassed to speak in proper sentences. "Sounds like this is important to you."

She rubbed at the back of her neck. "Nah. Just figured it would be cool to show up and support him is all." She glanced back toward where Beth was cleaning the cash register and studiously not looking our way. "I can stay if you need me."

"No, go." I wanted to reach out and hug her. Lena deserved to be happy, and to do it with someone who got her. Because of her colorful hair, her piercings, and her penchant for scraping up her arms and knees on her skateboard, a lot of people prejudged her as some sort of hoodlum. She was a genuinely good person, and I was happy she might have found someone who accepted her for who she is. "Beth and I can hold down the fort until Jeff arrives."

"If you're sure . . . ?" I could see the pleasure spread from her face, all through her body. She was practically dancing with it.

"Yes. Go!"

"Thanks, Ms. Hancock! I mean, Krissy." She bounded down the stairs and headed for the back for her things.

I followed her down at a slower pace, mood lifted. It felt good to make someone's day, even if all I did was allow her to beg off work an hour or two early. It was the first time I could remember her ever asking for time off, other than when she'd broken her arm. And then, I'd practically had to shove her out the door when she'd shown up with a fresh cast and a determination to work, despite the pain she was in.

The couple at the table rose, leaving their empty coffee cups behind. Beth hurried out to clean up after them, paying them only a quick, annoyed glance as she did. I had half a mind to ask them to pick up, but seeing how they were so lost in one another's eyes, I decided to let their good mood continue. Our little town needed some good cheer right about then.

I slid behind the counter just as Lena emerged from the back.

"I'll make this up to you," she said.

"No need. You earned a break." I paused, and knowing it might drag down the mood, but needing to know, I asked, "Do you recall if you served apple cider to the man who died yesterday?"

As expected, Lena's smile faded. "Yeah, I remember him."

"Did you notice anything odd?" I wasn't sure what I was asking, but I really wanted to know what had happened. I mean, it was *my* apple cider that did him in.

"Not really. I only remember him because he wasn't all that happy when he bought his cider. He wanted it cold, I guess."

"Was he with anyone? Did he say anything else?"

"If he was, I didn't notice. Jeff was the one who'd served him, if I'm remembering right. I only caught part of the exchange. Sorry."

"That's all right. Go. Have fun."

Lena's smile returned. "Oh, I will." She practically skipped out the door.

I started to turn away when the door opened again. Thinking Lena might have forgotten something, I turned back, but found myself frozen to the spot, mouth hanging part of the way open with an unasked question on my lips. The man who opened the door was definitely not Lena.

William Foster. My ex. The man who almost broke my heart. He smelled as good as he looked, and some of the old flame tried to flare at seeing him up close again.

He entered Death by Coffee, stepping back into my life as if he'd never gone.

And he wasn't alone.

The woman was blond, her hair pulled up off her neck in a messy bun. She wore glasses that made her look like she could rival Will in smarts, which was saying something, considering he was a doctor who was moving up in the world. She was dressed just as smartly as he was, and when she looked at him, her blue eyes filled with love that could be felt clear across the room.

This time, it was jealousy that tried to rear its ugly head.

Will immediately saw me and guided the woman my way with a hand on her back. His smile was hesitant, almost frightened, when he said, "Hi, Krissy."

I snapped my mouth closed and reined in the swirl of emotions threatening to overwhelm me. "Will. It's been a long time."

"Too long." He took a deep breath. "I'm sorry I haven't called. I've been so busy at work and getting used to my new surroundings, I let a lot of things slip by me."

But not her. I stomped down hard on the jealous thought. I was with Paul now. Sort of. I mean, we'd gone on a few dates and saw each other nearly every day, but I'm not quite sure our relationship was official. I suppose, technically, it was. But now, standing there with Will again, it made me wonder if I was making a mistake not forcing Paul to come right out and declare me his one and only.

Stop it, Krissy! You're acting irrational.

"I'm glad you stopped by," I said, and then let my gaze slide over to the woman. "I'm Krissy Hancock, by the way." I held out a hand.

She glanced at Will before taking it. Her grip was surprisingly strong. "Deb Foster."

I couldn't help it; I erupted into a coughing fit as I nearly choked.

"We're not married!" Will was quick to assure me. "It's just a coincidence."

The look Deb gave Will was part amusement, part annoyance.

Will took a deep breath and the uncertain smile returned. "Deb and I met shortly after I arrived in Arizona. It took some time, but we've grown on one another."

Deb leaned briefly against him before she noticed the books upstairs. Her eyes lit up and she straightened. "I'm going to go see if I can find something to read for the trip back home. You two should catch up."

Both Will and I watched her go. She walked with an assuredness that told me she wasn't intimidated by me, or anyone, in the slightest. I instantly liked her for it.

I turned back to Will, eyebrows raised in question.

"I wanted you to meet her," he said. "I felt I owed it to you. We've been dating for . . ." He did mental math. "Three and a half months now."

"I'm happy for you." And I was. Just because we'd broken up, didn't mean I held any ill will toward him. We'd both moved on, which was the adult thing to do.

Though seeing him *did* bring back all sorts of warm

and fuzzy feelings that I'd thought I'd tucked safely away for good.

"I saw you yesterday," Will went on. "I wanted to say hi, but I was with my mom, and well . . ."

I got it. Maire Foster was an opinionated lady who thought Will had made a mistake in leaving me for his job. I'd tried to assure her we were both better off for it, but she refused to listen. I could only imagine what she would have said if she'd gotten us both in the same space together.

"Does she like Deb?"

Will chuckled. "They tolerate one another. Deb is a psychiatrist. Mom thinks *she's* one. They've come to a compromise when it comes to me, but they disagree on pretty much everything else. Dad thinks she's fantastic and Deb gets along great with Jade." Jade was Will's sister.

"I'm glad it's working out." I debated on leaving it at that, but ended up blurting out, "I'm seeing Paul Dalton."

If I expected shock, I didn't get it. "I figured you two would finally get together." Was that sadness in his voice? "Mom made sure to call me the moment she found out."

"She didn't!"

"She did." He laughed. The sound was comforting, despite the uncomfortable topic of conversation. "Told me I missed my chance." Will sighed. "I get where she's coming from. When I first left, I was a wreck. I almost came back home three times that first week."

I didn't know what to say to that, so I said nothing, though my heart swelled in size. *He really did care about me.* It was hard to remember that sometimes when sitting alone in my house.

"Deb talked me down a few times, back when we were just friends. It's not too much of a stretch to say that you kind of brought us together. If I hadn't been so torn up about my choices . . ." He shrugged, looked away, clearly embarrassed.

I fumbled for something to say, and settled on, "Well, I'm glad I did my part."

Seconds passed as we shuffled our feet and looked anywhere but at each other.

Will broke the silence. "We can't stay long, but I did want to stop in and apologize."

"You have nothing to apologize for."

"I do," Will said. "I made a lot of mistakes in my last days in Pine Hills, and I'll always regret that. I'm glad to see you're doing good, and I hope it continues. And I'd like to extend an offer for you to come down to Arizona some time. Deb is perfectly okay with it. In fact, she insisted."

"I'd like that." Though I'm not sure I'd actually be able to go through with it. I wasn't big on traveling and then I'd be alone with an ex and his girlfriend, with no one else to turn to. Time would tell, I supposed.

"I hope we get a chance to speak again before Deb and I leave," Will said. "We're here until the day after Thanksgiving, so we've got time. I really would like to talk."

Deb came down the stairs, a couple of books tucked under her arm. Beth Milner, who'd completed the sale, was staring thoughtfully at her retreating back. I noted both the books she carried were true crime.

"Ready?" Will asked her.

"I am." She turned to me. "It was a pleasure to meet you, Krissy."

"You too."

"We'll see you around." Will put an arm around Deb, who snuggled in close, even as she opened a book about a serial killer.

They left and a sense of rightfulness washed over me. Sure, a part of me wondered, "What if?" but it was a small part. I was happy. Will was happy. There was nothing to feel bad about.

"You all right?" Beth was standing behind me, at the bottom of the stairs. "I know you two had a history."

"I'm good," I said, smiling to prove it. "Better. I'm great."

Beth nodded, but didn't appear convinced. "I heard what you talked to Lena about."

"About Zay?"

"No, about the man who'd died: Sidney."

"You knew him?"

"No, not really." Beth fidgeted with her nails, which were polished, yet somehow not chipped, despite working all day. I couldn't get polish to survive putting the bottle away, let alone leave the house with it intact. "But I knew his brother."

Thoughts of Will fled from my mind as I gave Beth my full attention. "He had a brother?" Stupid question, but I couldn't help it.

"I think Lena knew him too, but I'm not sure she'd know it." Beth looked around, though we were the only ones in Death by Coffee at the moment. "His name is Kevin Tewksbury. He's a teacher at the high school."

"A teacher?" The dumb questions kept slipping out.

Beth nodded. "He started the same year I graduated, which was a lifetime ago."

I ignored that. Beth was still young, and if she thought she'd been out of school for a long time, what did she think of me?

"I take it you were his student?" I asked when Beth didn't continue.

She bit her lower lip before answering. "I was, but that's not how I knew him." Another furtive glance around the room. "We kind of dated."

"You dated your teacher?"

She winced as if she'd taken my question as an accusation or a condemnation of her character. "It was after I graduated. He was only a few years older than me, so it wasn't weird or anything. And it lasted only a month, maybe a month and a half."

"I'm not judging," I said. "I was just surprised. What does his brother have to do with his death? Did you see him at the festival?"

"No," Beth said. I could tell she was having some sort of internal debate, and I let her work through it at her own pace. After a few seconds, she blurted out, "I don't think they liked one another."

"Really? Do you know why?"

"I don't," Beth said. "This was at the end of our relationship, and honestly, I hadn't thought about Kevin in years. If Sidney hadn't died, I might not have remembered him at all."

The door opened and a customer walked in. I moved closer to Beth and urged her to go on, knowing I only had a second or two more before I had to take the woman's order. I feared that if I left the conversation now, Beth might not bring it up again.

"What happened between them?" I asked.

For a moment, I didn't think she was going to answer. Then, voice pitched at barely above a whisper, Beth said, "I don't know the details, but after a particularly short phone call, Kevin got really agitated, and wouldn't talk to me. When I asked him what was wrong, I remember, clear as day, him saying, 'I don't care that he's my brother. If he keeps this up, I'm going to kill him.'"

4

I stopped at home after work for a quick shower, since I planned on spending the rest of my day out and about and didn't want to do it smelling like sweat and old coffee. I noted Vanna Goff's Lexus sitting in the driveway next door as I pulled in. After my shower, I checked to make sure the car was still there before heading over.

I'd only met Vanna twice since she'd taken on Realtor duties for the house, and both experiences were less than pleasant. Normally, I would have avoided her, but I was curious about the Tuttle family and the prospects of them moving in.

Vanna's car was the only one in the driveway, telling me she was there alone. I knocked on the door and plastered on a friendly smile, though I was already gritting my teeth in anticipation of the Realtor's unpleasant personality.

The door opened, revealing Vanna in her tried-and-true skirt and suit jacket. Her hair was a curly mess atop her head, and was streaked with gray I wasn't entirely convinced was natural. She looked as if she could be in her fifties, but knew she was only pushing forty. I supposed the artificial age increase made her look more knowledgeable. Or, at least, that was what she was hoping.

"Ms. Hancock," she said by way of greeting. "Is there something I can do for you?" Her gaze flickered to my house. "Planning on making a move of your own, perhaps?"

"I'm perfectly happy where I am, thank you," I said. "I don't anticipate moving for a long time."

"Pity."

An inward cringe that was only visible by the twitch of my lips shot through me. I was already regretting coming over. "I met some people interested in the house yesterday. The Tuttles. Do you think they're going to buy?"

Vanna narrowed her eyes at me like she suspected me of spying on the Tuttles before she answered, "They are interested in a possible purchase, yes."

"Good. They seem nice."

A careful, "They are." Followed by, "I do hope you don't plan on harassing them."

"I haven't harassed anyone," I said, suppressing the urge to scream it. Vanna had accused me of scaring off her first prospective buyer when they abruptly stopped taking her calls. I think it had more to do with Vanna's personality than the fact that I'd been singing along to music while mowing—and not realizing how loud I was being because of the noise of the mower and my earbuds.

When they'd arrived, they'd taken one look at me—and listen—and climbed right back into their car.

"I would appreciate it if you kept to your own property until the house is sold, Ms. Hancock," Vanna said. "Not everyone appreciates a nosy neighbor."

"But they would like friendly ones, rather than stand-offish people who can't be bothered to get to know the family that they might be living next to for the foreseeable future."

Vanna sighed and stepped out of the house. She closed and locked the door behind her, taking great care to do so in a way that showed she was doing it for my benefit.

"I will be showing the Tuttles the house tomorrow at six. I do hope you won't be here." And with that, she headed for her Lexus.

The urge to shout something—anything—at her tried to overwhelm me, but I remained civil. I'd honestly tried to make nice with Vanna Goff, but the woman flat-out refused to be swayed to returning the favor. Last I heard, she even had a problem with Lance Darby and Jules Phan on the other side of me, and no one disliked those two.

Refusing to let Vanna's foul attitude disrupt my day, I walked back over to my own yard and climbed into my Escape. It wasn't a Lexus like Vanna's, but I felt it was just as fancy. It had one of those backup cameras and remote start-up and all the bells and whistles I could ever want. Compared to my old, now scorched Focus, it was a massive upgrade. And it was eco-friendly to boot.

I guess I was still a bit salty about Vanna's clipped tone, and pushed all thoughts of her away as I backed out of my driveway. It wasn't like I had to deal with her for long. Once she sold the house, I would never have to see her again.

By the time I reached the Pine Hills library, I'd just about forgotten about Vanna Goff and her Lexus. The library was an older building just outside the downtown area. A blue tarp was pinned down over one half of the roof. It had been there for the last four months, placed after a pretty bad thunderstorm that had sounded like a tornado had ripped through the town. There was no sign that anyone had begun to work on repairs, but at least rain wouldn't get inside with the tarp in place.

It was disheartening to see and to make matters worse, there were only a few cars in the parking lot. I made a mental note to spend a little more time supporting the library as I got out of my vehicle and made for the door.

The smell of old books and rotting plaster hit my nose the moment I was through the door. A chunk of the floor to the left had been torn up and was blocked off so someone wouldn't trip over the uneven footing. Where there used to be trophy cases converted to display artwork of local kids, now stood an empty wall showing some pretty severe water damage.

Thankfully, the rooms on that side of the library were used for storage and study. That meant very few books were damaged in the leak.

I turned to my right, where the main entrance to the library stood. The first level was where a majority of the books were kept. A second level, half the size of the lower, held all the DVDs and magazines. It was also where the reference books were stored.

A woman who appeared to be no older than twenty sat at the children's desk to my left. Two kids were sitting at a nearby table, headphones on, playing a numbers game on the ancient computers that clicked and whirred as they struggled to keep up with the simple processes.

Both Cindy and Jimmy Carlton were at the checkout desk to my right. The librarians managed the building the best they could, but lack of funding and a seemingly worldwide disinterest in libraries had made the task nearly untenable. Both looked grim as they sorted through recent returns and placed them on a book cart to be shelved.

Jimmy saw me first. "Krissy," he said with his nasally voice, which sounded strange coming from such a muscular man. He set aside a book and rounded the counter. "It's good to see you."

Cindy raised her head and sniffed before quickly looking away. There was a redness to her eyes that told me she'd been crying.

"How are you two holding up?" I asked, shaking Jimmy's hand. I knew the librarians mostly as mere colleagues. I often donated books to them whenever we needed to replace stock, and I helped with a few things here and there, like the Thanksgiving festival, but we didn't really *know* one another. I was regretting that now.

"We've been better," Jimmy said.

"Funding has been cut again," Cindy said, joining us. "I don't know how we're going to get repairs done if the town keeps cutting our funding."

"That's the point." Jimmy's tone was bitter. "They drive us out, and then use the space for apartments."

"I'm sorry to hear that," I said. "Is there anything I can do?"

Cindy leaned against the counter with a sigh. "Talk to anyone you can. If we can get more people in here, it'll go a long way to getting the place funded. We can't even get anything on the ballot anymore. I'm sure there are lots of people who'd be willing to throw in a few extra dollars a month if it meant keeping this place open, but you know how it is."

"Politicians," Jimmy said with a shrug.

I almost asked them about using money from the fundraiser, but realized they wouldn't hear of it. That money was to go to hungry kids. There was no way they'd use it for themselves, and I didn't blame them. You'd think more people would want to chip in to help keep the library afloat since the Carltons did so much good for town, but I guess some people didn't think that hard about how they could help their struggling neighbors out.

"Oh!" Cindy stood upright. "You're here for your things."

I'd donated a few items, including books for the festival. It was why I was there, but after seeing the library's condition and hearing the distraught tone of the Carltons, I changed my mind. "Actually, you can keep the books if you want. Sell them if you think it will help."

Cindy's eyes softened and I thought she might cry again, but she held it in check. "Thank you. Every little bit goes a long way."

"We do appreciate what you've done for us over the years," Jimmy added. "I fear it won't matter in the long run, but we'll keep fighting."

Of course, the word *fighting* made me think of the murder and the problems the Carltons had with the victim before his death. "It's terrible what happened to Sidney."

Cindy's expression tightened. "It was. I'm just glad we made a decent amount before he . . . well . . . ." She scowled.

"He wasn't a popular man around here," Jimmy said. "A part of me feels like he died where he did just to spite us."

"He'd be thrilled to see this place closed, and he very well might get his wish." Cindy huffed and jerked open a drawer beneath the counter. She removed a handful of recently returned books from the book drop there and stacked them on the counter with force.

"I knew he was making a nuisance of himself," I said. "I didn't realize it was that bad."

"It was more than just bad," Jimmy said. "He came in here at least once a week, sometimes daily, and demanded we drastically change our book selection."

"It was awful," Cindy said. "There was this one time when he blocked off an entire section of books, refusing to let anyone in to browse. We very nearly had to call the cops on him."

"Wow," I said, wondering if he'd done the same at Death by Coffee and Vicki had never told me. "Why was he so adamant about it?"

Jimmy shrugged. "Who knows? He claimed we were corrupting the youth of the town by allowing them to read books with 'questionable content.'" He made air quotes.

"You know those murders over the last few years?" Cindy asked.

I nodded. Of course, I did. I was involved in every last one of them.

"Well, Sidney blamed our books for them. He said that the murder mysteries caused those deaths, as if the killers had come in here to research methodologies or some nonsense."

"And then there was the constant badgering about our romance novels," Jimmy said. "He said that every affair, every premarital coupling, were because we allowed people to check out filth for free. He claimed children were reading them and were looking to re-create the scenes in the books."

"Most kids won't even go near those racks," Cindy said. "They see the covers and giggle or turn so red in the face, they look sunburned."

"Sounds like he would make a lot of enemies harassing people like that," I said, wondering if Sidney Tewksbury's anti-book stance had somehow gotten him killed. How? I had no idea, but it was somewhere to start.

"Oh, I know quite a lot of people who didn't like that man," Cindy said. "He wasn't the only person to make complaints, but he sure was the most vocal."

"Do you think it might be why he was killed?" I went ahead and asked them. There was always a chance they'd seen or heard something during one of Sidney's rants.

"Who knows," Jimmy said. "I'm still not convinced it wasn't an accident. You can't just look at someone and declare them poisoned like that doctor did. It makes me wonder if he made such a bold statement so quickly so he could snatch up the limelight."

I almost pointed out that Paul had confirmed the cause of death, but held my tongue. Tests still needed to be run, and Jimmy could be right. Perhaps Sidney had died of an allergic reaction to something in the apple cider. It would explain why no one else was affected.

"Dr. Crenshaw wouldn't do something like that," I said. "I know Darrin. He's a good guy."

"Maybe," Jimmy said. He didn't sound convinced.

"Either way, it's made things tough on us," Cindy said. "Sidney's death might make life around here a little easier, but it really did hurt the amount we pulled in for char-

ity. I'm afraid we might not be able to get food to everyone who needs it."

"It's a shame," Jimmy said. "I'm not going to miss
Sidney Tewksbury, but I wish he would have chosen to
die sometime, and somewhere, else."

The conversation petered out after that. Since I wasn't
going to take my things back home with me, I decided to
spend my time doing what I could to add some business
to the library. Twenty minutes after I'd entered, I left with
a book tucked under my arm and a new library card in my
pocket. I saw why Jimmy and Cindy might not be upset
about Sidney's death, but couldn't imagine either of them
hurting him. For one, I didn't think they had it in them,
and secondly, they wouldn't have done anything to hurt
the fundraiser.

"Hey. Ma'am?"

I turned to find the young woman who'd been sitting
at the children's counter coming my way.

"Call me Krissy," I said.

"Oh. I'm Lily." She glanced back toward the library,
and then hunched her shoulders and lowered her voice
like she was afraid someone might overhear whatever she
had to say.

"Hi, Lily." I gave her a reassuring smile. "What can I
do for you?"

"I heard what you were talking to the Carltons about.
The dead guy."

I nodded for her to go on.

"They . . . um . . ." She cleared her throat and glanced
back again. She was clearly uncomfortable talking to me
about whatever it was she had to say.

"It's all right," I told her. "If you know something, it
doesn't have to get back to Jimmy or Cindy."

Lily ran a hand through her hair. "It's just . . . they didn't tell you everything."

"Okay? What didn't they tell me?"

"It's Mr. Carlton. Jimmy. I saw him with the murdered guy the other day."

"At the festival?"

She shook her head. "No. The day before that. It was here at the library and I was just about to get off work and go home when I saw them." She pointed to the corner of the lot. "They were over there, arguing."

I glanced at where she pointed, but all I could see was an empty parking space and some weeds that had grown up through the pavement. "Did you hear what they were arguing about?" I asked.

"No. But it was pretty heated. Jimmy ended up shoving the guy, knocked him on his butt. I thought it was going to come to real blows, you know? Jimmy shouted at the guy to stay down, and the guy did what he was told, so Jimmy turned and headed back inside. By then, I was by my car and he didn't see me. The other guy did." She shuddered. "The look he gave me scared me."

Unease worked through me. Jimmy and Sidney had fought the day before one of the men was murdered? And not only that, but Sidney had died but a few feet from where Jimmy was standing.

I thought back to what I'd seen, how Sidney had thrust the dollar bill at Cindy. Could she have poisoned him then? Did it happen before that? After?

I know those two. Could two people I knew be killers?

"Thank you, Lily. I'll make sure the police know." And I'd hate every second of it.

"Don't give them my name, all right? I don't want to get involved and I don't want to lose my job." She looked down at her feet. "But I don't want to see someone's death go unsolved, and figured it might be important."

"You did the right thing." Though, telling Paul this directly would have been better. "I won't give the police your name."

"Thanks." Lily shuffled back and forth a moment longer before she turned and ran back into the library.

"Great," I muttered, returning to my Escape. Not only was Darrin Crenshaw looking like a suspect in Sidney Tewksbury's murder, but now, it looked like I was going to have to add Cindy and Jimmy Carlton to my list.

All people I knew. And my own apple cider was involved, meaning I couldn't completely rule out my employees. Beth *did* know the brother, Kevin. Could she have killed Sidney for him, despite no longer dating him? Or were they still secretly together?

I pressed my head against the steering wheel, hating that I was even remotely entertaining the idea that someone I knew, people I worked with, might be involved in a murder.

But if one of them didn't do it, then I had no idea who did.

5

A soft purr rumbled on my lap where Misfit lay, contentedly snoozing as I stared at my library book, which I'd been doing for the last twenty minutes. Four pages in and I was beginning to realize reading wasn't on tonight's agenda. Every time I started to turn my attention to the words on the page, my mind would drift.

Who killed Sidney Tewksbury?

Could the librarians, people I've known for years, be killers? Darrin?

Why did Will come to see me?

I wanted to call Paul and ask him to come over, partly because I craved his company, and partly because I was curious to know if the police had made any progress on the investigation. But, unfortunately, he was busy working on said investigation. It might be days before I saw him again.

That thought soured my mood further. I closed the book and set it aside, choosing instead to stroke Misfit's soft, orange fur. If my mind wanted to run wild, there was no stopping it.

Lights flared across my window, briefly illuminating my living room beyond the single lamp I had on. Misfit opened one eye, huffed, and then jumped down to saunter into the bedroom where his nap wouldn't be disturbed.

I rose, heart thumping. The car had pulled into my driveway. Had Paul decided to call it an early night and stop by to check on me?

I hurried over to the door and waited for the knock, not wanting to appear too eager. Our relationship was still in the fledgling phase, despite how long we'd known each other. I wasn't even sure you could call it a relationship yet. It was more like a friendship that was finally breaking into romantic territory one excruciating inch at a time.

The sudden hammering that followed caused me to jump back from the door in surprise. That wasn't Paul's knock. The thumps were quick, almost frantic in pace. They were soon followed by a whiny voice.

"Hey, Krissy? You there?"

I groaned. Robert Dunhill. My other ex.

There was a moment where I considered hunkering down and waiting him out. This was a man who'd cheated on me and, in some ways, was part of the reason I'd moved to Pine Hills in the first place. I'd thought I'd seen the last of him when I'd moved here from California, but it wasn't long before he popped up, begging for me to take him back.

I'd declined. Many times.

We were well past that now and his unwanted advances had stopped. I'd even forgiven him. Mostly. Robert now acted as if we were the best of friends, despite our less-than stellar past, taking my grudging acceptance of him as an invitation to invite himself over whenever he pleased.

"I can hear you breathing."

I slapped a hand over my nose and mouth, but it was already too late. With a sigh, I opened the door.

"Hi, Robert. What do you want?"

He didn't wait for an invitation. He pushed past me and barged into the house. Already, I could tell this was going to be one of *those* visits.

"She still hasn't said yes!" he said, throwing himself down onto a stool at my counter. "I could use a cup of coffee."

I glared hard at the back of his head before closing the door and walking over to the coffeepot. Call me gullible, but coffee *did* sound good. When I turned to face him, he started up again.

"I'm worried Trisha is stringing me along." Trisha was his girlfriend, one he'd proposed to months ago. She'd given him a firm "maybe," which was more than I'd expected. "She's cool when we get together, but whenever I bring up us getting together permanently, she goes all coy on me. What if she's seeing someone else?"

"You're giving her space, right?" I asked.

"Yeah, sure." His eyes slid from mine.

I crossed my arms. "Robert?"

"Okay, fine. I might have tried to nudge her into an answer." A quick look at me, then, "And I suppose I might have subscribed her to a few bridal newsletters. But if she wants to marry me, then she'll need those anyway! It's not like I'm forcing her into anything."

"But you're pressuring her." I knew he wouldn't be able to help himself, but had hoped. "Marriage is a big step. And you do have a past."

"She knows all about it, and says she trusts me." It came out almost petulant.

"Trust is one thing," I said. "You need to understand that this is her life. You might be ready to spend your days cleaning up after her, cooking for her, and waking up to smeared makeup and bed head every morning, but she might not be ready to take that step quite yet."

"I know."

The coffeepot beeped. Robert sulked as I filled two mugs and carried one over to him.

"Give it time. You two haven't been dating one another for too long."

"Long enough," he grumbled. "I know someone who got married to a girl after dating her for four days."

"And they're happy?"

He shrugged. "Last I heard, he was dating someone else and she was engaged to a guy she met online."

"Does that sound like the kind of relationship you want?"

"No."

"Then don't force it. If you allow it to happen naturally, you're going to be far happier than if you pressure her into something she's not ready for."

"But I got a tattoo!"

I nearly choked on my coffee. "A what?"

Much to my horror, Robert stood and pulled off his shirt. Tattooed on his chest, right at his heart, was Trisha's name with a heart around it. The artwork looked new, the ink bright and stark against his skin, but it was past the healing stage, so the skin wasn't red and angry. "She loves it."

"I . . ." I was at a loss for words.

Robert plopped back down, sans shirt. "It was spur-of-the-moment, and it hurt. Do you think I made a mistake? What if she dumps me? What am I going to do? It's not like I can change it to say something else. Frisha? Trisba?"

Frisbee.

A knock at the door saved me from having to continue to give relationship advice to my ex. Or come up with alternate names for his tattoo if it came to that.

Robert took a drink from his coffee, shoulders slumped. Despite there being someone at the door, he didn't look like he had any intention of leaving. Or putting his shirt back on.

Somebody please save me.

The knock came again. I left Robert to stew in his own misery so I could answer it. If there was one good thing about Robert showing up to dump his relationship troubles on me, it took my mind off of murder and my other ex, Will.

Can my life get any weirder?

I opened the door and was surprised to find Rita Jablonski standing on my stoop. She was looking back toward Robert's car, a speculative expression on her face.

"Rita?" I asked. She didn't normally stop by unannounced. "What's up?"

She turned back to me, or, well, in my general direction. Her gaze slid right past me, into the house, likely searching for my mysterious guest. When she saw Robert sitting there without a shirt, her eyes widened.

"Oh, my Lordy Lou!"

"He's just visiting." I could feel a blush coming on. "And he was just leaving. Right, Robert?"

He glanced back, puppy-dog eyes in full effect. "Yeah, I guess." He stood, flung his shirt over his shoulder, covering his Trisha tattoo. "Hey, Ms. Jablonski." And then he trudged past us, to his car. Rita watched him the entire way.

"He wanted to talk about his soon-to-be fiancé," I said.

Rita turned back to me. "Uh-huh. I'm sure that's all it was, dear."

I could tell she didn't believe me, but wasn't sure if trying to dissuade her of the notion that something untoward was happening between me and Robert would make things worse or not. Rita had a tendency to gossip, and the more anyone tried to deny rumors she'd heard, the worse she could get.

"You'd best come in," I said with a sigh. Tomorrow was going to be fun. "Is there something you needed?"

Rita took one more look back toward Robert, but he was already driving away, before she entered the house. The moment she was through the doorway, she started in.

"Well, it's about what I was going to tell you yesterday before that nasty business with the apples." She visibly shuddered. "I can still taste the one I bit into. I even ate half the thing! And they're saying poison? What if I got some in me? Should I go to the doctor?"

"It wasn't the apples," I assured her. "And it wasn't the apple cider." At least, the apple cider in the tub. "You're safe."

She gave me a skeptical look before going on. "Anyway, I thought you might want to know about that former boyfriend of yours."

"Robert?"

"No, the other one. William Foster."

I could already see where this was going. "I know about him," I said. "He brought his girlfriend to Death by Coffee to see me."

Her eyes widened. "Did he now? And I missed it?" She tsked. "But that's not what I wanted to say. I just happened to overhear him talking to his mother, Maire. She's a hoot. I could listen to her all day. Anyway, I heard the two of them talking, and you won't believe what I heard."

I wanted to tell her that I didn't need to know, that Will was in the past, and that his business was his business, but curiosity got the better of me. "What was that?"

"He's looking to get back together with you!"

I opened my mouth, but nothing came out. Once more, I had no idea what to say.

"Now, he didn't say that outright, and I suppose it was Maire going on about it more than he was, but I could tell he was interested. And since you've gotten together with Officer Dalton, I knew it might cause all sorts of problems for you." That speculative look was back. "That is, unless things aren't going so well between the two of you. Are you two dating other people?"

"We're not," I said, though I wasn't 100 percent sure Paul was only seeing me since we weren't officially official. "And Robert and I . . . No. Just, no."

Rita waved a hand at me, though I knew I wasn't making any progress in keeping her mind from going places it most definitely shouldn't. "I won't be surprised if you hear from Will Foster soon about rekindling that flame of yours. You'd best be ready for it."

"I will be, but I doubt it's going to happen. He's happy with . . ." My mind blanked on his girlfriend's name.

Subconsciously? On purpose? Was I really as over him as I thought?

"Do you think he helped Dr. Crenshaw?" Rita asked before I could flounder any more.

I blinked at the sudden shift. "What?"

"Will? He's still a doctor, isn't he?"

"As far as I'm aware."

"And he used to work with Dr. Crenshaw before he moved away?"

I was struggling to figure out where she was going with this. "He did."

"I heard from Andi that there's a rumor that Dr. Crenshaw was the one who did poor Sidney Tewksbury in."

"He just happened to be there," I said, carefully. My own concerns about Darrin's possible involvement did *not* need to become public knowledge. "Nearly the entire town was there, actually."

"And you believe it to be a coincidence that the doctor wasn't just at the festival, but in the same tent as the murdered man?" She sniffed as if disappointed in me. "Those two men had a history, one that could quite easily lead to murder."

I was about to jump to Darrin's defense when what she'd said fully hit me. "They had a history?"

"Didn't you know?" Rita feigned surprise, though it was obvious she was pleased to be telling me something I didn't already know. "Dr. Crenshaw was once Sidney's doctor. They had a falling-out when the doc prescribed Sidney with a medication to help with his anxiety or whatever it was. It turned into a pretty big spat, though, honestly, I never did learn what the big fuss was about."

My mind raced. Sidney and Darrin had fought? It

wasn't looking good for the doctor. "How long ago did this happen?"

"Oh, I'd say three, four months ago? It might have been longer, but who's keeping track? All I know is that Sidney threatened to sue. He was smearing Dr. Crenshaw's name every chance he got. Why, I once heard tale that Sidney had an online show, or whatever they call those things where people talk like they're on the radio, but it's on the internet instead. He used his platform to tear down the doctor and anyone else he saw fit. I never listen to such things, so I can't be certain as to exactly what he said, but I heard it was pretty bad."

I'd listened to a few podcasts in my time, though they'd been focused more on coffee, and had turned out not to be very useful. I didn't know anyone in Pine Hills had a show of their own. I made a mental note to go in search of Sidney's podcasts later; if they were even still available.

"Well, I'd better let you go," Rita said. "As much as I'd love to stay here and keep talking about this, I can't keep Johan waiting."

I was still churning over the information she'd dumped into my lap, so it wasn't until she was halfway out the door that it registered what she'd said.

"Who's Johan?"

Rita's grin just about split her face in half. "Oh, just someone I know." She winked and with a final wave goodbye, she hurried over to her car, leaving me to stand dumbfounded at the door.

Johan? It looked like she *had* found herself someone. At least someone's love life seemed to be moving forward without a hiccup.

Or an ex or two popping up every time she turns around.

I closed the door and resumed my seat on the couch, mind a jumble of information, and very little of it good.

I looked at my book, wishing I could dive into someone else's fictional mess of a life—and the mystery they were trying to solve—but knew it was a lost cause. I wasn't going to be reading—or sleeping—for the rest of the night.

"Well," I said as Misfit peeked around the corner to make sure everyone was finally gone. "I suppose I could do some research." My cat turned, flipped his tail, and headed for bed without me.

With a put-upon sigh, I picked up my phone and, alone, began my search.

6

Needles pressed into my cheek as a heavy weight pushed the air from my lungs. Gasping, my eyes flashed open, arms flailing. The weight vanished and a thump sounded at my bedside. A moment later, there was a meow from beside the door.

Heart pounding, I touched my cheek to make sure it wasn't bleeding. I sat up with a yawn that seemed to last forever. My eyes were crusted and I had to blink several times before I could see.

"I'm up," I muttered as Misfit meowed again. One of these days, the cat was going to suffocate me.

It took twice as long for me to go through my morning routine, which started with feeding my cat, who thought he was starving if he wasn't being fed every ten minutes. By the time I was showered, dressed, and sitting at my table with a cup of coffee and a bagel, I was mostly awake, sifting through what I'd found last night before I'd headed for bed.

It had taken me right up until I was too tired to think before I found Sidney Tewksbury's podcasts. Thankfully, they were archived or else my search would have been in vain. The website was simple, titled *Sid's Thoughts*, and had very little in way of description of what I was getting myself into. I'd been too tired to listen to them last night, and the thought of what they might contain haunted me until Misfit unceremoniously woke me up.

Now that I was more awake, with fuel in hand, I took the time to really look through the site, and found that my original assessment was correct. There were no photographs, no diatribe berating the library or anything of that sort. Just a short bio claiming that Sidney Tewksbury was an educated man with a deep understanding of the human psyche. He didn't go into detail about where he got that education, or if it was all simple boasting.

And then there were the podcasts.

The archive was set up as a dated list. I found there was no other information listed that told me what I was about to listen to. I couldn't simply jump to a rant about the library or one about how Sidney feared for his life. If I wanted to get a complete picture of the man's thoughts, I'd have to listen to all 123 of them.

There was no way that was happening.

"I guess we could start from the beginning," I told Misfit, clicking on the link. There was no download, just a stream, which meant I didn't have long to wait before Sidney's voice came through my tiny laptop speakers.

"This is Sid Tewksbury, and these are my thoughts."

I stood and refilled my coffee as Sidney spoke. He rambled on a bit about his day, then complained about the state of the world, how most of us had lost our way. It was pretty standard stuff, really. I heard much the same at Death by Coffee when some of my older customers got together and were talking about how they preferred the world when they were kids and so on. It wasn't anything to be killed over.

I returned to my seat and stopped the current podcast. I scrolled down the list to the more recent ones. If Sidney *was* afraid that someone was after him—a theory I had no evidence for—I figured I would find it there.

I clicked *play* and got up again, this time to clean up.

Sidney rattled on like before, though his voice was pitched at a near-shout. He didn't have guests or callers or anything like that. It was just him and his mic, ranting about the state of the world.

"You turn on the television these days and what do you see? Naked flesh paraded around. Men shunning women in order to perform evil pleasures with other men. They flaunt these things in our faces, and whine when we speak out against their deviant lifestyles."

I bristled, but kept listening despite my distaste. Sidney was obviously very opinionated, and seemed to think his opinion was the only one that counted. I mean, if you didn't like something you saw on TV, why not turn it off?

"I see their agenda everywhere every day," Sidney went on at a near-shout. *"Deviancy. Debauchery. It makes me sick, and I, for one, refuse to stay silent. We, as a people, must rise up and fight for our rights. Go to these people, tell them they aren't wanted. They have no place here. We should round them all up and—"*

I cut it off before he could finish.

"What a jerk," I said, pacing away from the laptop so I wouldn't throw it across the room.

It was no wonder someone wanted to see Sidney dead. The man was so full of hate, it spilled from him every time he opened his mouth. I'd only ever heard him say about six words in person, and they had been spat with venom.

I paced for a good five minutes, my own blood boiling from listening to Sidney's rant. I could only imagine how someone who believed in what he was spewing felt. The guy was instigating violence with his words, and it made me wonder if his anger had ever caused someone to go out and hurt others. It wouldn't surprise me if it had—if he even had enough listeners to matter.

Jules. I stopped. My openly gay neighbor. Could Sidney have come after him?

I didn't know if he was home, but that didn't matter. I needed to find out if he'd ever been the target of one of Sidney's threats. I headed straight over and knocked on the door.

Barking met my knock. It was followed by the sound of claws on the door, and then a voice.

"Settle down, Maestro," Lance Darby said. He was Jules's partner, and lived in the house with him. I didn't know if they were actually married, or just cohabitating, and honestly, didn't care either way. They were two of my best friends and were fantastic neighbors. They could do whatever they wanted, as far as I was concerned.

The door opened and I was met with Lance's wide smile. He was holding Maestro, their excitable white Maltese. "Krissy! What do I owe the pleasure?"

A flash of heat washed through me, which happened often when I saw Lance. Blond hair, muscular, fit build. He was every woman's dream, though he wasn't interested in anyone but Jules. My heart might belong to Paul

Dalton these days, but there's nothing wrong with appreciating a well-made man.

"Hi, Lance," I said, clearing my throat. "Is Jules home?"

"No, sorry. He's at Phantastic Candies." Jules owned and operated the candy store downtown, and could often be found there in an outlandish outfit, entertaining the children.

"Oh." All wasn't lost, however. "Maybe you can answer my question."

"I can try. Come on in." Lance stepped aside.

I entered the house, giving Maestro a quick rub behind the ears as I did. The dog licked my wrist and squirmed to be let down. Lance held on to him until the door was closed, and then the bundle of fur rushed me.

After giving Maestro a sufficient petting, I followed Lance into the living room. A suitcase was standing by the couch with a pillow leaning against it.

"I'm heading out this evening," Lance said before I could jump to an incorrect conclusion. "Three days in Belize. Jules is going to close early today so we can spend a few hours together before I go. I'll miss everyone here, but, well . . ." He chuckled. "I hope you don't take offense, but I'm not going to miss you all *that* much."

"I don't blame you," I said. I'd never been to Belize myself, but knew it was a beautiful place. "Work?" I didn't know exactly what Lance did for a living—oddly, I never pried—just that it sent him out of town often.

Lance nodded. "I'm so spoiled." He sighed and then turned serious. "What was it you were wanting to ask Jules?"

My mind drifted away from sunny skies and soothing water, back to the vitriol I'd just heard. "Do you know a man named Sidney Tewksbury?"

Lance frowned. "He's the man who died, right?"

"That's him."

"No, I can't say that I knew him."

"Did Jules ever talk about him?"

"Not that I recall. Why?"

I debated on what to tell him. If Sidney hadn't confronted Jules or Lance about their relationship, then was it my place to inform them of his thoughts? He was dead, so why bring it up?

But I did want to know if he'd been making a nuisance out of himself publicly—more than his demands at the library and Death by Coffee—or if Sidney Tewksbury was indeed all talk.

"It's just something I'd heard," he said. "Sidney had very . . ." I considered what to call it, and settled on "conservative views. I was wondering if he'd ever come to you or Jules and made a scene."

Lance took a moment to consider it before shaking his head. "I can't say that he did. At least, he never said anything to me."

It was no wonder, I supposed. Lance had proven himself more than capable of taking care of himself. I'd even seen him use old football skills to tackle someone who'd tried to run from an interrogation. A man like Sidney would likely look for easier prey.

"Did Jules ever complain about someone saying something to him?" I asked. "Something derogatory, I mean."

"There's always someone of that mindset around," Lance said. "Pine Hills has been pretty accepting of us, but there are still people out there who don't approve of our lifestyle. I don't hold it against them. Some people simply don't understand."

"So, it's possible that Sidney said something?" I asked,

not wanting to delve too deep into how people could be mean to others, simply for being different. I didn't want to think badly about my customers and neighbors.

"It is," Lance said. "I can call Jules if you'd like?" He pulled his phone from his back pocket.

"No, that's okay," I said. I didn't want to ruin their day, since it was going to be the last one they'd have together for a few days. "I'll talk with him about it tomorrow."

"If you're sure?"

"I am." Maestro had plopped down at my feet and was looking up at me with adoring, puppy-dog eyes. I gave him the petting he craved before heading for the door. "Thanks, Lance. Have a safe trip."

"Thanks. I'll be sure to send you pictures."

"You're trying to make me jealous, aren't you?"

He laughed. "Maybe. Is it working?"

"Yep." I paused just outside the door. "You'll be back for Thanksgiving, right?" It was still a week away, but I didn't know if the three days Lance would be gone were all in Belize or if they counted travel as well.

"I will be."

"Did you get my invitation?" I'd mailed them out last week, which, yeah, is short notice, but I hadn't thought of having a big dinner until then. Since I wasn't going to California to spend Thanksgiving with my dad, and I had no other family here in Pine Hills, I'd decided to have a big get-together with many of my friends.

"We did. Jules and I still plan on being there."

"Great. See you then!"

Misfit was waiting by the door when I returned home. He sniffed me once, smelled dog, and then ran under the table to glare at me.

"Hey, at least it's not a cat."

I was about to sit down and resume listening to the podcasts, but my phone rang. It was my best friend—and co-owner of Death by Coffee—Vicki Lawyer.

"Hi, Krissy," she said when I answered. "How are you holding up? I heard you were there when that man died."

"I was." I glanced at my laptop. "I'm doing okay, but it came as a pretty big shock."

"I bet." She paused. "I should have been there with you. I mean, I was at the festival, but not in the tent."

"I'm glad you weren't. It wasn't a pleasant experience."

"Yeah, well . . ." She trailed off. Something in her voice caused my anxiety to spike.

"What's wrong?" I asked. I knew she knew who Sidney Tewksbury was, and that she'd dealt with him, but it would surprise me if his death hit her hard enough to upset her more than what was natural.

"Nothing's wrong," she said. "It's just . . . we don't really get to spend much time together anymore."

"I'll see you at work," I said. "And then there's Thanksgiving."

"No, that's not the same. We used to go out and get coffee or ice cream. Would sit and watch movies on the couch for hours. Now, we only see each other at work and during holidays."

I opened my mouth to object, but closed it before I could speak. She was right. It had happened so gradually, I hadn't even noticed it happening. I'm admittedly bad at relationships—and not just the romantic kind—but hadn't realized it had gotten so bad.

"It's not your fault," Vicki said, as if reading my mind.

"I got married, and with Death by Coffee, life had come at me kind of fast. I should have made a better effort to keep in touch."

"I don't hold it against you," I said. "Really, you have nothing to feel sorry about. I should have—"

"No, it's me. Let me take this one."

I frowned, but didn't object. If I tried to tell her it was my fault, or that we should both share the blame, her stubbornness would kick in. I would never win this fight.

"We're both going to be really busy right up until Thanksgiving," Vicki said. "I get that, and there's not much either of us can do about it."

"I could make time."

"I probably could too, but we both know that with Sidney's death, you're going to be extra-busy." I could hear the smile in her voice. "You can't help yourself."

She had me there.

"What I propose is, we make time, post-Thanksgiving. We pick a day of the week, and we make that *our* time."

"Mason—"

"No." She cut me off before I could finish the thought. "No Masons or Pauls or anyone else. Just us. We get away from work, from life, and we relax. Have fun. Like we used to."

It sounded nice. Really nice. "Deal."

"Good." She sounded relieved, like I'd helped lift a great weight from her shoulders. "Sometimes, I could really use your shoulder."

"Same here."

"All right." The perky, happy Vicki was back. "Then it's settled. We don't need to rush to come up with the when right away, but soon." A voice in the background caught her attention briefly. "I've got to go. Work calls."

As if I needed another example of life intruding. "Maybe I'll stop in later," I said. "We can talk about this more then."

"Good deal. See you later, then."

We clicked off.

I set my phone aside with a sigh. Vicki might have wanted to take the blame for our drifting apart, but I knew it was just as much my fault as it was hers—more so, even. I'd been so focused on my budding relationship with Paul, I'd let everything else slip away.

"I'll do better," I promised her, though she could no longer hear me.

I returned to my laptop and, pushing thoughts of Vicki aside for the moment, I clicked the next podcast link. I wasn't all that excited about listening to more of Sidney's drivel, but I was still hoping to hear something that would tell me why he'd been killed.

While I listened, I began checking my cupboards to make sure I had everything I'd need for baking later. I wanted to have a wide selection of pies—pumpkin being predominant among them—and other treats for when I had my get-together. I was both worried and excited about it. My house wasn't big by any stretch of the imagination, and I was afraid I wouldn't be able to comfortably fit everyone inside.

At least Paul will be here. The thought of being forced to stand close to him would make the stress leading up to dinner so worth it.

"Maggie has been scouting that place downtown, Death by Coffee."

I came to an abrupt stop, nearly dropping my flour in the process. Did I hear that right?

Sidney went on, *"She assures me they are just as irre-*

sponsible as the library and schools. I'd already talked to one of the owners twice about it, but she hasn't done a thing. Maggie keeps telling me that more drastic measures might be required. I'm beginning to think she might be right."

"What?" I slammed the flour down onto the counter and rounded the island in a flurry, intent on stopping the podcast to fume. The sudden movement startled Misfit from beneath the table. He shot from his spot and made straight for the hall.

Which put him directly into my path.

I saw the cat at the last possible second and tried to halt my momentum, but it was too late. My foot swung forward, just as Misfit darted in front of me. I almost managed to step over him, but I hadn't been high-stepping my way to the table. My foot clipped him, just enough to throw me off-balance.

Arms flailing, I tried to catch myself on the back of my chair as Misfit vanished around the corner and into the bedroom. My hand slapped the wood and I managed to grab hold, but I was already going down. Only now I was dragging a chair down on top of me as I fell.

With only one hand to brace myself, I hit the floor hard. My elbow buckled and my chin hit the floor with a solid impact. Pain lanced up my wrist, straight through my elbow, and into my shoulder. Stars danced in front of my vision and my mouth felt as if I'd been struck by a concrete ball.

"Ow," I managed, rolling over onto my back. Thankfully, there was no blood, and I'd missed biting my tongue as I went down. I closed my eyes and lay there, holding onto my wrist as I waited for the pain to subside.

It didn't.

Above me, Sidney's voice continued unabated, an angry drone that added to the buzzing in my head.

"We won't remain silent!" he shouted. *"These people corrupt our youth. They defy us at every turn. I will no longer stand for it. We will do everything in our power to enact change and return this town to its proper glory. A bomb has been placed within their walls, and if things don't change, if they do not heed my righteous fury, I will set off that bomb, and those who oppose me will be buried beneath the rubble."*

7

Every bump in the road caused a hiss of pain to slip from my lips. My wrist was cradled in my lap, and I knew I needed to get it looked at, but I couldn't let Sidney's words slide. What if his mention of a bomb was more than just a metaphor? Could Death by Coffee be minutes from an explosion?

I pressed down on the gas, praying I would be in time.

Paul was already waiting for me when I arrived. Alarmingly, he was alone.

"Where's the bomb squa—ow!?" I asked, nearly doubling over from pain. My wrist felt like it was broken, but I could move my fingers and it wasn't *too* swollen. I just had to take it slow.

"We don't have one," Paul said, hurrying over to me. "And what happened to you?"

"I fell. I'm fine."

"You don't look fine. You look pale. Krissy—"

"Let's focus on the fact that someone made a bomb threat involving my store. We can worry about me afterward."

The concern never left Paul's face, but he turned away to face Death by Coffee, which looked the same as it ever did. The large plate glass windows were clean. The big sign with the open book and cup of steaming coffee with *Death by Coffee* written in froth looked as new as the day we'd put it up. A pair of women dressed in business attire exited, chatting amicably between them.

"How serious was this threat?" Paul asked.

"Hard to say. The man who made it is dead."

He turned an incredulous eye my way. "Sidney Tewksbury threatened to blow up your store?" I hadn't had time to inform him on the details when I'd called, mostly because I couldn't drive, let alone get into my Escape, with one useless hand. I'd told him that there was a threat and then hung up so I could focus on the road.

"Kind of." I explained the podcast and how Sidney ranted and raved, spewing his hate all over the internet. "He didn't say there was definitely a bomb inside, but he implied there might be."

Paul sighed and ran a hand over his face. "So, this might have been someone boasting on a radio show in order to boost ratings?"

"It was a podcast." Paul gave me a warning look. "Okay, okay. Yes, he might have been boasting, but it worried me." I took a step toward Death by Coffee, but the movement jarred my arm enough that I hissed in a breath and came to an abrupt stop.

"Here's the deal," Paul said, putting a hand on my shoulder to keep me from walking away. "I'm going to go in and have a look around. Buchannan is on his way to help. I'll talk to Vicki if she's in and have her check places we might not think of. We'll do this quietly and cautiously as not to scare anyone. If I feel it necessary, I'll have customers leave and close the store down until we're sure it's safe."

"Then, let's do it." I tried to stride forward, but his hand remained firm.

"I said *I'm* going to do this. *You* are going to the doctor."

"But—"

"No buts. You're hurt. You won't do me any good getting in the way and panicking and injuring yourself further."

"I'm not panicking."

Another look, this one flat and unamused. "Get checked out. I'll even have someone go through records to make sure Mr. Tewksbury didn't have a history of blowing things up. I'm pretty sure he didn't, but for you, I'll check."

"Thanks." It came out grudgingly.

"Now, go. I'll handle this. You get that looked at."

I didn't want to go, but knew he was right. If I went in there yelling about a possible bomb, I'd start a panic that might end up with someone else getting hurt. I never wanted to see that happen, and especially not so close to Thanksgiving. If I was the cause of someone getting trampled and not being able to spend the holiday with their loved ones, I'd never forgive myself.

With only a slight pout, I eased my way back into my Escape, and pressed the button to start the engine. And then, with worry gnawing at my gut, I headed for the doctor, leaving Paul to make sure my livelihood wasn't about to go up with a *boom*.

* * *

There were no hospitals in Pine Hills, but I'd been to the small private practice many times in my years in town. Stepping through the doors always gave me a twinge of nostalgia since Will used to work here. When I walked through the doors this time, the nostalgia of a boyfriend lost turned into a face full of ex-boyfriend chest.

"Krissy?"

My eyes were watering so badly, I couldn't see, and the pain that had shot through my arm when I'd walked directly into Will had me mute.

"Are you all right?"

Gentle hands guided me to a plastic chair just inside the door. Blinking away the tears, I was thankful to note the only other person to see my clumsy entrance was Bea at the reception window. Her bifocals were perched at the end of her nose, a paper of some sort in her aged hand. She gave me an unconcerned, flat look, before turning her attention back to the page.

"I'm fine," I managed. "Or, I will be. I fell." I held up my arm to show him, which sent all sorts of new painful sensations shooting through me.

Will immediately went into doctor mode as he took hold of my wrist. "Does this hurt?" My face must have turned an alarming shade of red because he followed the question up with, "Never mind. Let's get you to a room so I can look you over."

I let him guide me to my feet, but no further. "Go ahead and go. You were on your way out."

"I'm in no rush."

"I'll be okay," I assured him. "Dr. Lipmon will patch me up."

"Paige isn't here," Will said. "I can do this. Please, let me do this for you."

As nice as it would be to have Will fawn over me again, I didn't want our reconnection to turn into something more. I didn't think it would, but sometimes, when we least expect it, mistakes are made. I so desperately didn't want to make a mistake with Will that would cause me to lose Paul.

"Maybe next time," I said. "Really, Will, I'm okay."

He gnawed on his lip, but before he could insist, the door opened and Dr. Darrin Crenshaw peeked out.

"You're still here?"

Resigned, Will handed me off. "I ran into her on my way out. I think it's a sprain," he said. "Take care of her."

"Thanks, Will," I said, though I wasn't sure what I was thanking him for. All I knew was that as soon as the words were out of my mouth, Darrin touched my wrist and I nearly blacked out.

Okay, okay, maybe I'm exaggerating, but it *hurt.*

Will nodded once, and then waved to Bea before he walked out the door. I wondered if it would be the last time I ever saw him, and the thought didn't sit well with me. I needed to make some time for him, even if it was coffee at the shop with all my friends surrounding us.

"Come on, let's get you a room."

Darrin led me through the hallway, to one of the exam rooms. I eased up onto the table with his help. "All right," he said, even as he typed something into the computer in the room. "Tell me what happened."

"I tripped over my cat." I left it at that, not wanting to bring up anything having to do with Sidney, at least until he'd checked me over. If Darrin truly did have a history with the dead man, I didn't want to agitate him until he made me better.

"I see." Darrin scanned something on the screen—my chart, most likely. "You have a history of minor injuries. Broken toe. Sprains." He glanced at me. "Same wrist?"

"Nope. The other one this time." My sprains and breaks were almost all a result of my poking around in murder investigations, and this one was no different, I supposed. Though, this injury *did* hurt a whole lot worse than the last couple.

Darrin spent the next five minutes checking me over and making me want to punch him in the face for causing me pain. By the time he was done, I had tears on my cheeks and a headache had started to form.

"It's definitely a sprain," he said. "No break. It'll need to be immobilized so you don't reinjure yourself, but you'll be fine. I'm going to prescribe you something for the pain, and we have a sample at a lesser dosage here I can give you now to tide you over until you can pick it up."

"Thanks." My wrist was throbbing in time with my heartbeat and it was making me sick to my stomach.

"Give me a minute and I'll get you all squared away."

Darrin left the room and I spent the next few minutes mentally going over what I wanted to say to him. I refused to let a golden opportunity like this pass. Dr. Crenshaw might have valuable information that I could pass along to Paul—if he didn't already know about it, which was entirely possible. If nothing else, I hoped to ease my own mind.

He returned a moment later. He set me up with a sling and handed me a pill sample for my pain. I downed the pills and then opened with a tentative, "I see Will stopped by." That wasn't what I'd wanted to say, but I wasn't sure how else to begin.

"He did," Darrin said. "He seems to be doing good." He eyed me out of the corner of his eye as if gauging my reaction.

"I met his girlfriend. She's nice." And then, blurted, "How did you come to the conclusion of poison so quickly?"

Darrin opened his mouth, but nothing came out but an extended, "Uh."

"Sorry," I said, feeling like a dope. I blamed it on the pain. "I saw what happened and it was my apples and apple cider that were in the dunking tub. You were quick to diagnose Sidney."

"I studied poisons when I was younger," Darrin said, speaking slowly. "It was sort of my thing." He then seemed to realize how that sounded and added, "I wanted to find ways to counteract them quickly, not use them."

"Do you know what kind of poison was used on Mr. Tewksbury?"

"I can't divulge that information."

No surprise there. I might know Darrin through Will, but I didn't know him well enough to get him to break protocol and, well, the law for me.

Still, I didn't let it stop me.

"I was told Sidney was your patient."

"He was."

"And that you two got into an argument."

"We didn't come to blows, if that's what you're implying. And, I'm sorry, but my interactions with Mr. Tewksbury are protected. I can't talk to you about them. I've told the police everything they need to know."

"I'm not trying to pry," I said, knowing I was doing just that, "but I've heard rumors that Sidney had anxiety or some sort of condition and that he didn't like the medication or diagnosis." Come to think of it, Rita had been pretty vague on exactly what was the argument was about.

"I can't . . ."

I waved him off with my good arm. "I know, I know. I don't know if you were aware, but Sidney did podcasts and posted them on the internet." Darrin nodded; he knew. "In one of them, he mentioned blowing up Death by Coffee, and I was just wondering if I should take the threat seriously. I know he's dead, but if he'd already placed a bomb . . ."

"You needn't worry about that," Darrin said. "Sidney had issues, as do we all. And, yes, he could sometimes get paranoid, but he wasn't dangerous. I had my own issues with him. Many people did. But I wouldn't say he was a violent man. Misguided, sure. And he did have a bad habit of running his mouth, but he would never blow anything up."

"Are you sure?" I asked, but I was already relieved.

"Positive." He pushed his way to his feet. "Now, if you experience any increased pain, or if the swelling gets worse, don't hesitate to call me. You'll be sore for a few days, but as long as you don't go falling down again, or overusing your arm, you'll be fine."

Effectively dismissed, I headed out and paid my copay with Bea before returning to my Escape. I debated on calling Paul or heading to Death by Coffee to tell him what Darrin had said, but decided it would be best to let him make doubly sure that Sidney hadn't grown a violent streak since Darrin had last treated him. Better safe than sorry.

Besides, while Darrin might not think Sidney dangerous, there were other people who were closer him who would know him better and might be legally able to give me some insights to the man who'd threatened my store.

A quick Google and I had a number, along with an address. I had some time before I could pick up my prescription, so I figured, "Why not?" and dialed.

"Hello?" Cautious.

"Hi, Mr. Kevin Tewksbury?"

"Speaking. Who is this?"

"My name is Krissy Hancock. I was hoping we could talk."

There was a moment of silence before, "Is this about a student? If so, you should try the school. I'm taking a few days off."

"No, I'm not a parent. This is about your brother."

No response.

"I was there when he died," I said, and then added, belatedly, "I'm sorry for your loss."

"Thank you." Flat.

"I was wondering if we could meet somewhere and discuss Sidney."

"I'm not so sure that would be a good idea. What happened was a tragedy and I'm content to leave it at that."

"I talked to Beth." It came out in a rush. I hadn't meant to bring Beth into it at all, but I didn't want Kevin to hang up on me. "Beth Milner. She was your student." *And girlfriend.* But I decided not to mention that part quite yet, just in case it was a sore spot.

"I remember Beth." It came out just above a whisper. I

couldn't tell if he was happy about hearing her name, or if I'd angered him.

"Please, Mr. Tewksbury, I just need a few minutes of your time. I didn't poison it, but it was my apple cider that was used against your brother. And . . ." Quick mental debate. "Sidney threatened to blow up my shop in one of his podcasts. I sell books."

A heavy sigh rattled the phone speakers. "All right," he said. "I'm at home." He gave me his address, which I already had, thanks to my Googling. "Just be warned: I don't think you're going to like what I have to say."

8

Kevin Tewksbury lived in a quiet cul-de-sac not far from where I lived. Most of the yards were fenced, many with a couple of trees providing shade for patios, and in one instance, a hot tub that was currently covered. I saw three inflatable turkeys decorating front yards, and more Thanksgiving window decorations than I could count.

I parked in Kevin's driveway, but didn't get out right away. Doubts were creeping in about my involvement in the investigation. I mean, I was there to further gauge Sidney's personality so I knew if he truly might have planted a bomb at Death by Coffee. At least, on the surface, I was. Deep down, I knew I was sniffing for clues as to who might have wanted him dead.

Back when Paul and I were just friends, I found it easy to go poking around, prying into lives I probably shouldn't have. He'd be annoyed at me for snooping, would warn me off, but would never actively get in my way. Now that we were kinda, sorta dating, I didn't want to see that disappointment in his eye, or make him think I didn't care about what happened to me.

The smart thing to do would be to go home and let Paul deal with everything.

I got out of my Escape.

A chilly breeze caused me to pull my fleece jacket tighter around myself as I approached the door. I pressed the doorbell, noting it was one of those security ones with the camera built in. I fought down the urge to wave.

A man built like the Stay-Puft Marshmallow Man opened the door. He had a kindly smile and an aggressively retreating hairline. He was soft and round all over—that included his fingers and nose—and he stood at least seven feet, if not a smidge over.

"Kevin Tewksbury?" I asked, craning my neck back to look him in the eye.

"I am. I take it you are Krissy?"

"In the flesh."

"Come on in." He stepped aside, but kept his hand on the door. I was easily able to duck under his arm to enter the house.

If the giant who answered the door defied my expectations of a short, pudgy English teacher, the house corrected it. Bookshelves were everywhere, each and every one overflowing with books. The living room had three, the connecting hall another. I could see another pair in the dining room. The house smelled of paper and mothballs.

"Sorry for the mess," Kevin said. He closed the door and lumbered into the living room. He cleared a stack of papers off a chair and indicated I should sit. "I might be taking some time off to grieve, but the grading is still there. Essays." He dropped the stack on an already–over-packed coffee table.

"A teacher's work is never done," I said, taking the proffered chair. It was old, soft leather, and when I sat, it tried to swallow me whole.

"No, it's not." Kevin eased down into a chair the twin of mine. It sank in dramatically, but he still looked to be too large for it. "We get told how we only work half a year and get paid for sitting on our butts the rest of the time. And then there's the complaints about working only until three or so and spending the rest of the day relaxing while 'real people'"—he made air quotes—"are still working."

"It must be frustrating."

"It is. What these people don't seem to realize is that we work while at school, then spend our 'free hours'"—another air quote—"grading and planning for the next day. Our contracts also pay us for time spent working, but it's paid out over the entire year; so, no, we don't get paid for sitting at home during the summers."

I could tell I'd hit a sore spot without trying and wondered if it tied back to Sidney. "Well, I'm glad you do what you do," I said. "Not many people could do it, no matter what they say."

"Thank you." He leaned back and rested his ankle across his knee. I tried not to stare at his shoe, which looked as if it could serve as a canoe. "Are you all right?" He nodded toward my arm in its sling.

"I'm fine." I even smiled to show him how fine I was. "Took a spill and sprained it. Should be healed up in a day or two." Or, at least, I hoped. My last sprain took nearly two weeks to heal and this one felt worse.

Kevin drummed his fingers on the armrest of his chair before saying, "You mentioned Beth Milner on the phone. How is she?"

"She's good. She works with me at Death by Coffee. I'm part-owner."

"I've never been."

"You should stop in sometime. We serve coffee, of course, but we also have a bookstore." I glanced around at the sagging shelves. "If you need any more books."

Kevin chuckled. "There's always room for more. I keep shelves of books in my classroom stocked for the kids and could always use new ones. The school won't pay for it, so it comes from my own pocket, but I don't mind." A pause. "It's still Milner, then?"

"It is."

"She never married?"

"Not as far as I'm aware."

"I see." The canoe bounced up and down. "Perhaps I should pay her a visit sometime."

A quick glance at his finger told me Kevin wasn't married. I didn't know if he'd gotten divorced, or just never found the one, but had a feeling Beth would soon be finding out.

Kevin's expression hardened. "You were here about Sidney, were you not?"

"I am."

"He threatened you?"

"Not me, directly," I said. "But my shop. I found his archived podcasts and he alluded to setting a bomb at Death by Coffee. It's worrying."

"Honestly, there's nothing to worry about," Kevin said, with a wave of his massive hand. "Sidney was always all talk. Admittedly, he did talk a lot; more than most of us liked. But he would never actually go out and hurt someone."

"I don't know," I said. "He sounded pretty . . ." I wasn't sure how to put it. Insane? Angry?

"Trust me, I know all about Sidney and his penchant for playing the victim. Everything was offensive to him in one way or the other. Most of it was a put-on, a show for anyone who would listen, though some of his bluster was legitimate."

"I take it you have firsthand knowledge?"

Kevin's laugh was bitter and not the least bit amused. "I did. I don't know if you've noticed, but while I'm not happy Sidney is dead, I'm not too broken up about it."

I shrugged noncommittally. It did bother me that the man's brother was dead—murdered, even—and he looked as if he'd never shed a tear over it, but I knew nothing about the family's history. As far as I knew, Kevin was the one who'd killed Sidney, and had just finished celebrating it.

"Sidney was . . . troubled. I don't know what the medical term for it might be, but he was paranoid, which caused him a great amount of anxiety. When we were younger, he used to sit in his room and refuse to come out, claiming our stepmother was out to poison him."

"Poison him?" I asked, instantly making the connection.

"I know what you're thinking, but no, she didn't do it. She was unkind to us, and neither of us were too upset when she drank herself into an early grave, but she never would have tried to kill us intentionally. Indirectly . . ." He shrugged. "Our dad found out how deadly a verbally abusive alcoholic could be."

"I'm sorry," I said. I'd lost my mother, but still had a

loving father. And the only memories I had of my family—both before and after my mother's death—were happy, so I couldn't imagine what it would be like to live in an unhappy household.

Kevin waved off my condolences. "It's ancient history now. We'd both moved on." He looked wistfully over my shoulder, out the window, before continuing. "I guess I should say, *I* moved on. The paranoia never left Sidney, and only increased over the years. His friends didn't help."

A memory flashed through my mind: the man who'd called out to Sidney while his head was in the tub of apples, and wondered if he was one of those friends. "They fed into his paranoia?" I asked.

"They amplified it." Kevin's hands balled into fists the size of boulders. "One in particular caused the most problems. Maggie Reed." He practically spat the name. "I've only met her a few times, but that was enough."

"He mentioned a Maggie in his podcasts."

"He would. I don't know if they were dating, or if she was merely a friend. By this time, Sidney and I were barely speaking. She would often wait for him outside the school whenever he made a nuisance of himself."

"He came to the school?"

Kevin nodded. "Let's just say Sidney didn't approve of the books I was teaching. He complained to the board more than once and tried to get nearly every book I taught banned. If he would have settled solely on targeting me and my books, I think he might have succeeded, but he went after everyone else too. Science shouldn't teach evolution. History shouldn't teach about our less-than stellar past when it comes to race. If he could attack it, he did. He was well-known in those halls, let me tell you."

I knew Sidney had it out for books and that he didn't approve of Jules and Lance, but I never realized he was against . . . well, everything. "That sounds bad."

"It was. And since he was my brother, it put a spotlight on me. He nearly got me fired at least twice. I could have strangled him . . ." Kevin's face flushed red and his fists relaxed. "I'm sorry; I shouldn't have said that."

"I understand." Though it did make me wonder if Sidney's constant badgering had finally pushed Kevin over the edge and he'd decided to do what Sidney accused him of. I couldn't help but notice the collection of fairy tales on the shelf behind him, and wondered if Snow White was among them.

Kevin pushed his way to his feet with a groan and a popping of knees. Moving a body that size around had to be exhausting. "I really do need to get back to work."

I stood. "Thank you for your time. And thank you for talking to me about Sidney. It couldn't have been easy."

Kevin walked me to the door. "It's all right. I hope I eased your mind about your store. Sidney could be trying in the best of times, downright frustrating the rest, but he wasn't a violent man. An instigator, maybe, but he would never hurt anyone on purpose."

My mind wasn't at ease, but I didn't want to show it. "I do feel better," I said.

"Good." Kevin reached out a hand and gripped my good one with a somewhat squishy handshake. "It was nice to meet you, Krissy. I'll be sure to stop in at Death by Coffee and check out your books."

"You do that," I said, though I knew it wasn't the books he was interested in.

We said our goodbyes and I climbed back into my Escape. I'd turned my phone to silent when I'd gone in to talk to Kevin, so I checked it, hoping to find an update about my store. I had a missed call and a voicemail.

"Hey, Krissy, it's Paul. We checked the store and both John and I agree that you have nothing to worry about. The place is clean. If Mr. Tewksbury planned on placing a bomb inside, he never got around to it. I'll check in with you tonight. Got to run."

I sagged back into my seat, a wash of relief passing through me. Death by Coffee was pretty much my life. I didn't know what I'd do with myself if something were to happen to it.

I backed out of Kevin's driveway and hit *dial*. Paul was likely busy at work, and I doubted he would answer, but wanted to try him anyway.

Much to my surprise, he answered.

"Krissy," he said, sounding oddly relieved. "Are you all right?"

"Yes." Fear made my stomach muscles clench. "Why do you ask?"

There was a long stretch of silence, which only caused my worry to skyrocket.

"Paul?" I just about screamed his name.

"I'm here," he said. He sounded tense. "I tried to call you."

"I know. I got the voicemail. No bombs." The fear leapt to absolute terror. "There were no bombs, right?" If they'd missed it and Death by Coffee had gone sky-high . . ." I felt light-headed and pulled off to the side of the road so I wouldn't wreck. "Paul?"

"No, there were no bombs." He sighed and I could hear a scratchy sound, like he was rubbing at his cheeks.

"Then what's wrong?" I asked.

"Nothing." It didn't sound like nothing.

"Paul, please. Did something happen? Is Vicki okay?" Another thought, this one completely unfounded. "Misfit?"

"They're fine."

I closed my eyes and leaned my head back. "Out with it. I don't think I can take any more stress right now."

"I just . . ." He cleared his throat. "It's stupid. No, *I'm* stupid."

That didn't sound like Paul at all. My concern shifted from my place of business and friends to him. "Are you okay?"

"Yeah." He huffed and chuckled. "I ran into Rita."

A new dread seeped through me. "What did she say?" Though I was pretty sure I already knew. *Darn Robert and his need to show me his tattoo.*

"She showed up at Death by Coffee, looking for you. When she saw me, she started acting cagey. I pressed her, thinking you were out snooping into the murder and had recruited her to help out. It didn't take long before she said something about you having shirtless men at your house."

"Men?" I squeaked. I was so going to kill Rita when I saw her next. "It was Robert."

"That doesn't make it any better."

"No, I mean, he was there and he took his shirt off . . ." I smacked myself on the forehead, and then winced when it made my headache flare. "He wanted to show me his tattoo. He was upset about Trisha. There was nothing to it."

"She wasn't very clear about it, admittedly," Paul said. "I don't mean to sound like I'm jealous or overly possessive, but after what else I was told, I—" he cut off abruptly.

"What else were you told?" I asked.

"It's nothing. Look, I should get back to work. We can always talk about this later."

"No, now," I said, sitting up. I'd gone from frightened to steaming mad, and the light-headedness and headache wasn't helping matters. "Did someone say something about me?"

"I got a call," Paul said. He was speaking carefully, as if he was choosing his words to cause the least impact. "Anonymous."

"About me?"

"And Will."

It took me a nanosecond to put it all together. "Someone told you he and I were together." Flat.

"And since Rita wouldn't name names, my mind took off on its own. Ex in town. Shirtless man in your house. You fainting in Will's arms."

"I didn't faint!"

"That's not what I was told. The man on the line claimed Will practically carried you into the clinic and took you into one of the private rooms to tend you himself. Said you didn't come out for a long time."

"He didn't tend to me at all," I said. "Darrin Crenshaw did."

"I see."

"He should be able to verify that. You say it was a man who called?" The only men I saw at the doctor's office were Darrin and Will. Who would have called and told Paul that I'd fainted in Will's arms? It didn't make sense.

"Forget it," Paul said. "I didn't recognize the voice,

and I probably should have dismissed the accusations out of hand, but I guess, well . . ." I could imagine his flush and it caused much of the anger to bleed away.

"If you want, I can stop by and show you my fancy new sling," I said. "My wrist is sprained, but otherwise, I'm okay." That did remind me that I needed to stop by and pick up my prescription before the pain meds wore off.

"No, I'm pretty busy here. Are you sure you're okay? I was concerned you were far more injured than you let on. You were so pale and, well . . . I was worried."

"I'm fine. I should be as good as new in a few days, maybe a week."

Someone called Paul's name in the background. It sounded a lot like his mother, who was also the police chief.

"I really do have to go," he said. "Talk to you to-night?"

"Count on it."

We disconnected.

I took a relieved breath, and then pulled back out onto the road. I desperately wanted to know who called Paul and made up that story about me and Will, but had no idea where I could go to discover that information. I figured it would be best to give it a few days to see if the anonymous caller would strike again before I started accusing people of slander.

Though, I did wonder. Darrin wasn't happy I was asking questions about Sidney. He knew poisons and had a history with the victim. Could he have called Paul because he feared I was getting too close?

My phone dinged and a quick glance told me my prescription was now ready and waiting for pickup at the downtown pharmacy. Just the thought of the pain pills made my wrist start to ache, so I decided that before I did anything else, I needed to pick up my prescription.

As I drove, a new worry gnawed at my gut.

Sidney Tewksbury was poisoned. Darrin Crenshaw studied poisons as a student in medical school.

And he was the one who called in my prescription.

9

The pills looked like standard pain pills, yet I couldn't bring myself to take one. I doubted the pharmacy would fill a prescription for poison, but what about one for a high dose of an addictive drug? My wrist was beginning to throb again, and I desperately wanted to stop it before it became unbearable.

But should I risk it?

Gritting my teeth, I decided I could take the pain for a little while longer.

I was sitting in the parking lot of Pine Hills High. School was due to let out for Thanksgiving break in only a few minutes, which meant this would be my only chance to get inside the building and, I don't know, look around. Maybe something would become evident once I was inside.

Honestly, I wasn't entirely sure why I was there. Kevin

had mentioned how Sidney had come to the school to make a nuisance of himself, and Kevin himself worked inside the building, so there *was* a connection. I supposed I was still a little worried about the possibility of a bomb at Death by Coffee, and talking to a few more people who'd had to deal with Sidney might help ease my mind.

And, hey, maybe I'd be lucky and someone here would know who had reason to kill the guy.

The bell rang loud enough for me to hear from inside my vehicle, though it was a distant sound. A few minutes later, kids started spilling from the doors, a few toward cars, while most of them toward the buses lined up at the side of the building. I had a brief flashback to my time in school. The naivete. The bullying. While I'd made friends, there were always kids whose sole purpose in life was to ruin the happiness of others. I knew my fair share of them and briefly wondered if they'd ever grown out of the pettiness.

I waited until the stream died down to a trickle before deciding it was time to go. Shoving the bottle of pills to the bottom of my purse, I got out of my Escape and headed for the large glass doors that fronted the school.

Security precautions had been put into place, requiring anyone who entered the building to go in through a specific set of doors that funneled visitors into the main office. I considered bypassing them and sliding in through a door swinging shut after a group of chatty teens barreled their way through, but to do so would immediately put me on the bad side of anyone who saw me do it.

Waving to the teens, who rolled their eyes at me like I was a total moron, I entered through the designated entrance and found myself in a cramped room taken up by a long counter. Stacks of papers sat atop it, one promoting an upcoming drama production, another for a dance. I perused them while I tried to come up with something to say that wouldn't make me sound like I'd shown up on a whim—which, honestly, I had.

"Can I help you?" the secretary asked when I didn't immediately say anything. A nameplate on the counter in front of her named her as Naomi Pratt. "Are you here for a student?"

"Hi, my name's Krissy Hancock. I was wondering if I could talk to some of the teachers."

Naomi peered over her thick glasses at me and amended her second question to, "Are you here *about* a student?"

"No." I leaned in closer to her. "It's about Sidney Tewksbury."

The scowl that hit the woman's face was so sudden, I stepped back in surprise. "What about him?"

"I just finished talking to his brother, Kevin. He's a teacher here."

"I know who Kevin Tewksbury is." Annoyed.

"He told me about how Sidney treated the teachers here. I was hoping I could talk to someone who might have had reason to dislike him."

"We all had a reason," Naomi said. "Take your pick." She gestured toward the door, as if indicating I could talk to anyone in the building and get a negative review of Sidney.

With what I knew of the man, I wasn't surprised.

"Is there anyone who was really angry with him?" I asked. I really didn't want to wander the halls, hoping to bump into the right person. "Maybe someone Sidney targeted more than others?" I was fishing, but I didn't know what else to ask.

"There are a few who meet that criteria." She leaned forward, narrowing her eyes. "What is it to you?"

I would have joined her lean, but my injured arm prevented it. "I'm close with the investigating officer," I said, keeping my voice low on the off chance someone who knew Paul was within earshot. "I help him talk to suspects whenever he's busy elsewhere."

The doubt on Naomi's face was as easy to read as a large-print book. "Really now?" she deadpanned.

"Really." Now that I'd started, there was nothing to do but dive in headfirst. "I've assisted on quite a few murder investigations here in Pine Hills, and one out of state. If you want, I can call someone who'll verify it." I prayed she wouldn't take me up on the offer, because I wasn't quite sure who I could call without having to explain what I needed from them first.

Naomi's expression changed from annoyance to interest. "Sidney Tewksbury was murdered?"

"Poisoned," I said, surprised she didn't know. "The best guess is that it was intentional, and by someone he knew." And then for emphasis, "And by someone who might have had a problem with him."

Naomi's eyes flickered toward the door. "Huh." She glanced behind her, where a closed door to the back had a plaque on it declaring it the principal's office. A window showed no one inside, yet Naomi lowered her voice as if there was. "And you think someone at the school might have killed him?"

I shrugged in a "You tell me" way.

"Jeez." She drew out the word. "I knew a few of the teachers were at the end of their ropes when it came to Sidney, but didn't realize one of them might go so far as to kill him. I thought old Sid drowned or something."

"Nope." And then, whispered. "Murder."

Naomi bit her lower lip and then removed one of those *Hello, my name is . . .* stickers. "Krissy, wasn't it?"

"With a K."

She wrote my name in the blank and handed it to me. "For security reasons," she told me.

"Thank you." I slapped the sticker to my shirt.

"You'll want to talk to Mr. Alvarez and Ms. Carmichael. He's in room one-oh-four and Ms. Carmichael is in two-thirty-two, right across the hall from Mr. Tewksbury's room. If anyone would have a reason to go after Sid, they would."

I thanked Naomi again and exited through the door leading deeper into the school.

By now, most of the students had fled the building for freedom, but there were still a few teens milling through the school. The gym was across the hall from the office. I could hear the squeak of sneakers and the shouts of kids shooting hoops. Another group of teens sat on a stage built into the cafeteria down the hall. They looked glum as their teacher talked to them, but I couldn't hear what was being said.

Room 104 was on the first floor, which I was already on. I followed the room numbers until I found it. The door was hanging open and a man stood at his desk, packing papers into a briefcase. He looked the part of a teacher, to the point it was almost sad. His brown slacks were old and his shoes were scuffed. He had a comb-over that didn't look all that bad considering, and he had small, round glasses on a bulbous nose that looked as if he'd once been a fighter who'd taken a few too many to the snout.

"Mr. Alvarez?" I asked from the door.

He glanced up. "Yes?"

"Hi, my name's Krissy. I wanted to ask you about Sidney Tewksbury, if that's okay."

At Sidney's name, his jaw tightened and he glanced at his watch. "I have a few minutes, I suppose."

"Thank you." I entered the classroom, and after a brief consideration, I closed the door. "I'm sorry to interrupt. I'm sure you're anxious to be heading home."

"You'd think so, but no. There's nothing there but Edgar."

He didn't extrapolate, but something about the man and his sweater made me think Edgar was a cat, not a roommate or partner.

Not sure how to bring it up gently, I decided to dive right in. "I was told you might have had an issue with Sidney Tewksbury. Would that be an accurate statement?"

Mr. Alvarez worked his jaw a moment before he found the words to answer. "*Issue* would be an understatement. He came in here demanding I change my curriculum because he didn't believe in the type of science I taught. I'm not sure he believed in science at all, to be honest."

A quick glance around the room told me that the science Mr. Alvarez taught was biology. Charts hung on the walls and a line of microscopes sat on a table at the back of the room. An open cabinet in the corner had spaces for them.

"What did he think you should be teaching?" I asked.

"He simply called it *facts*." His laugh was bitter. "He said evolution can't be factual because religion precluded it. He'd filed numerous complaints with the school, all focused on his personal beliefs. And while I understand that some students hold the same beliefs themselves, there's no reason they can't learn something that might help them better understand the world around them."

As he spoke, Mr. Alvarez's cheeks turned red. He managed to keep from shouting, though it was obvious he wanted to.

"What did the parents say?"

"Some agreed, most didn't. You might believe that vaccines cause other illnesses, or that they are used to implant tracking devices." He scoffed. "But isn't it better to understand what else they do? You can't make an informed decision without learning all the facts, right?"

"Right."

"The same goes for everything else in this world. Too many people want to hide from anything that doesn't fit perfectly in their little world. The world isn't a perfect place. These people want to protect their children from their fears, while instead, all they're doing is making sure those children are unprepared for what awaits them once they get out into the real world. These kids end up—I'm sorry. I didn't mean to rant."

"That's all right. It's understandable."

"Just mentioning Sidney's name is enough to get under my skin. I swear that man only lived to make other people miserable, Kevin most of all."

"Do you think Kevin would have harmed his own brother?"

Mr. Alvarez shrugged and picked up his briefcase. "Honestly, if he did, I congratulate him. The rest of us didn't have it in us to do it." He strode toward the door, giving me no choice but to follow him.

"Are you saying there are no other teachers who would have gone as far as to kill Sidney?"

Alvarez pulled open the door, but hesitated before stepping into the hall. He considered the question carefully before answering. "I'm saying that many of us hated that man. Kevin had reason to despise him to the point of murder, though if he'd go so far as fratricide . . ." Another shrug. "That's all I have to say on the subject."

He waited until I left the room before he closed the door, which locked the moment it was shut. A bow of the head my way, and then he was gone, quickly striding away.

As if he was running from something? I thought, none-too kindly.

Other teachers were making for the doors as well. If I wanted to catch Ms. Carmichael before she left, I needed to hurry.

I found the stairs leading up to the next floor down the hall, tucked away in a sort of cubby that hid them from casual view. I took the stairs quickly, and hurried down the hall to room 232. A tiny woman was leaving the room as I approached.

"Ms. Carmichael?"

She glanced back at me as she closed her door. "Yeah?"

The rough voice coming out of such a petite woman had me stuttering over my words.

"I, uh—I wanted to ask you something."

She didn't pause. She started walking down the hall. "I'm late."

"It'll take just a second," I said, hurrying after her.

"If you have a complaint about your son or daughter's grades, you'll need to call it in."

"I'm not a parent."

She glanced back at me, but didn't slow her stride.

"I'm here about Sidney Tewksbury."

She stopped at the top of the stairs. "I have nothing to say about him."

"I was told you had a problem with him."

"I have nothing to say." She turned as if to go.

"I'm trying to figure out who killed him."

Ms. Carmichael spun on me. "Look, I didn't kill the guy if that's what you're implying. He got on me a few times for teaching a book that he called smut. Then one he said attacked white people." She rolled her eyes. "He was a troublemaker that no one will miss." She paused. "Well, almost no one."

"You mean Kevin?"

"No, Kevin and I were of the same mind." Ms. Carmichael ran her fingers through her short, red hair. "It's Irv who kissed Sidney's hind end every chance he got."

"Irv?"

"Irving Barrow. The guidance counselor at the school, if you can call him that." She looked as if she wanted to spit after saying his name.

"You don't get along?"

She barked a bitter laugh. "He's an ass."

The bluntness in the middle of a school caught me off guard and left me speechless.

Thankfully, Ms. Carmichael filled the silence. "Irv has been guiding students away from my class, as well as Kevin's, for the last year, year and a half. He's championed change, as he put it. Every time a book comes under scrutiny, Irv is quick to call for its removal. He somehow managed to get *The Lord of the Rings* books removed from the school library because the magic promoted pagan ways and the mystical creatures somehow devalued reality." Another eye roll.

"Wow."

"And then he—" She suddenly smiled. "Mr. Barrow, how nice to see you."

I turned to find a stunningly good-looking man heading our way. "Ms. Carmichael." His eyes flickered to me. "And you are?"

"Krissy Hancock." I presented him a hand to shake, but he merely glanced at it and dismissed it. "I'm here talking to people about Sidney Tewksbury."

"His death is a shame," Irv said. "A real shame. Why are you bothering the staff about him?"

I turned to Ms. Carmichael for assistance, but she was already retreating down the stairs. I returned my attention back to Irv. "Well, he was murdered," I said, lamely.

"And the killer should pay for that."

"They should," I said, and meant it. Sidney might have gotten on a lot of people's bad side, but that didn't mean he deserved to die. "Which is why I'm here."

Irv crossed his arms and looked me up and down. "You don't look like a cop."

"I'm not, but I—"

"If you're not a cop, then you have no business here."

"It's not a crime to talk to people." I started to cross my own arms to match his stance, but was quickly reminded of my sprain at the flash of pain that shot through my wrist at the motion.

"I can always call the police and have them sort it out if you'd prefer?" Irv said. "This is a school, Mrs. Hancock, not a public place to talk about murder. These children shouldn't be exposed to such things."

I wanted to point out that nearly all of the students were long gone, but realized I would be wasting my breath.

"There's no need to call the cops," I said. "I'll go."

"And where did you park?"

I had no idea why that mattered, but answered anyway. "Out front. I'm the orange Escape."

"In the student lot?"

I shrugged; I had no idea. "I guess."

"Well, you'd best make sure not to hit anyone. The next time you decide to show up, park in the guest lot or else I *will* have to call the police."

And with that, Irv Barrow stormed down the stairs.

That man is supposed to be guiding students? I couldn't imagine it. I had a feeling his office door was rarely shadowed by a student seeking help. He probably told any of them that asked that they weren't good enough for college, just so he could keep them from being "exposed" to it.

I shook off the bitter thought and took a step toward the stairs.

And then I stopped, a new plan forming.

The hallway was empty. I could hear voices in one of the classrooms, but otherwise, I had the space to myself.

I turned and hurried down the hall until I was outside room 233; Kevin Tewksbury's room.

The door was, of course, locked, but I tried it anyway. Frustrated, I peered into the dark room, using my hand to shield the glare coming from the lights behind me.

The desks in the room were set up in a circle. Bookshelves lined the back wall, and they were just as overstuffed as the shelves at Kevin's home. His desk was a mess of papers and books, telling me the clutter at his house wasn't simply because of his grading, but that he was a messy man.

"What are you doing?"

I jumped and then whimpered as I jarred my sprained

wrist. A tall, dark-skinned man in a suit was giving me a disapproving look.

"I'm sorry," I said, mind scrambling for a lie, though I doubted I needed to have done so. "I was looking for Kevin Tewksbury. Is he in?"

"Mr. Tewksbury is taking a leave of absence. He'll be back in a few days. You should call the office if you wish to speak to a teacher."

"I'll do that." I gave him my best innocent smile.

The tall man nodded toward the stairs. I complied.

He followed me all the way to the doors before he entered the principal's office. He remained by the window, apparently making sure I left.

The parking lot was empty of all but a few cars as I crossed the lot to my Escape. I imagined more kids would remain after school on a normal day, but since this was the last day before break, most of them hightailed it out of there.

I was about to climb into the driver's seat when I noted a flash of red on the pavement beside my back tire. Curious, I went back to investigate.

The back bumper of my Escape was dented on the left side, and the rear-light casing was shattered, exposing the bulb within.

I stared at the damage, dumbfounded, before hurrying to the front. I checked the windshield wiper, but no note had been left. Whoever had hit me had fled the scene.

I stood in the lot, hoping someone would show to apologize and offer me insurance information, but my hopes were in vain. Not wanting to leave a mess in the school parking lot, I picked up the biggest chunks of plastic and put them in the back before I slid into the driver's seat with a sigh.

I could probably go back inside and ask if they had cameras targeting the lot—these days, it was likely—but I doubted they would jump to my request. For one, I had no right to look at the footage and secondly, I'd just made a nuisance of myself. Calling the police would amount to a report, followed by a "There's not much we can do." Even Paul would struggle to find the culprit. My only real option was going to be checking with the insurance company, and we all knew what kind of nightmare that could be.

With my wrist pounding in time with a building headache, I put the Escape in gear, and headed for home.

10

"Thank you. All right." I breathed a sigh of relief as I clicked off. The insurance company was going to cover the damage to my Escape, but the woman on the line had explained that my rates were going to increase despite it not being my fault. I merely needed to take the vehicle in to an approved location for an estimate and I was good to go.

It wasn't ideal, but at least I wasn't going to have to come up with the money out of pocket—outside the deductible, of course. I'd left a message with Paul, letting him know what had happened, and hoped that he'd have another solution, one in which my insurance company wouldn't jack up my rates, but I had yet to hear back.

I sank down onto the couch, thoroughly exhausted. The insurance company had tried to give me the run-around, as expected. Perhaps it was time I swapped to someone a little more local. The rates might not be as good, but at least I could talk to them face-to-face if need be.

And maybe I'd get a sympathetic ear.

It made me wonder what kind of insurance Mason's father, Raymond Lawyer, specialized in. Thinking of having to deal with such a grumpy man over money made me change my mind pretty quickly, however. I'd rather go broke.

Misfit sauntered into the room, rubbed against my leg, and then left again. I could have used more cuddle time with my cat, but didn't have the energy to chase after him.

Glancing at the clock, I was surprised to find it was already nearing six. My stomach complained loudly, reminding me I had yet to eat. I didn't feel like making anything, and while a part of me hoped to hear from Paul and possibly have a romantic dinner somewhere, I wasn't counting on it. Instead, I picked up my phone, found the number for the local pizzeria, and placed an order.

While I waited, I fished out the pain medication Darrin had prescribed me. He wouldn't have called in anything that would hurt me; it would be too obvious. My wrist was screaming, and I knew Tylenol wasn't going to cut it. When it comes to pain, I'm a wimp.

"Well, here goes nothing," I muttered. I tried to twist off the cap.

Pain shot up my arm and I instantly stopped. I moved the bottle to my injured hand and tried to grip it tight enough to twist it off with my other. No go.

Tears leaked from my eyes as I sat back. Who gives childproof caps to people with only one good arm?

I was debating the merits of using a hammer to open the bottle when there was a knock at my door.

"Coming!" I called, rising with some difficulty. It's amazing how often you use your arm to push off when attempting to stand. I was forced to wiggle from side to side until I was in a position to get both feet under me. Still, I very nearly tipped over as I rose. A wave of dizziness washed over me—likely a product of missing lunch—as I carried a twenty to the door. When I opened it, however, it wasn't the pizza guy waiting.

"Jules?" I asked. "Where's Lance?"

"Gone." He fluttered a hand to his chest and looked to the sky. "I am now alone." He looked back down and transformed from lovestruck man into a concerned neighbor. "Krissy! What happened to your arm?"

"I had an accident. Let's just say my cat was involved and leave it at that."

"Been there. Maestro has a tendency to get underfoot at the worst of times."

"Hear! Hear!" I paused. "I thought you and Lance were going to spend the evening together?"

"We were," Jules said. "But he was forced to move his flight up and had to leave today."

"That sucks." A car pulled into my driveway. A kid popped out, pizza in hand. "One sec."

Jules stepped aside and waited while I paid the pizza guy. He accepted the box in my stead. "I didn't mean to interrupt your dinner," he said as he carried it to the island counter. "We can talk later."

"No, I could use the company." I started to hold out the pill bottle for Jules to open for me, but changed my mind. I fished around in my purse until I came up with a likewise childproofed bottle of Tylenol. "And a little help."

Jules twisted the cap off with ease, and shook two pills into my palm. I grabbed a water and downed them gratefully. "Thanks. I was afraid I might have to chew my way in." My stomach chose that moment to growl angrily.

"You sound hungry enough to do it too," Jules said, laughing. He moved into the kitchen. "Plates?"

I pointed to the correct cabinet and he retrieved a plate for me. "Feel free to grab one for yourself," I said. "It's pepperoni and mushrooms."

Jules took a deep breath. "It's tempting, but I just ate."

"More for me."

I dragged a pair of slices onto my plate and dove into the first. It wasn't pretty, but I was ravenous. Jules watched with an amused expression on his face. Once I finished with the first slice, I paced myself for the second. No sense making myself sick by eating too fast.

"Lance said you stopped by earlier."

I swallowed before answering. "I did." Thinking back to the topic of our conversation, my appetite abated somewhat. "Did he tell you what we discussed?"

"He did. It's why I'm here." Jules's expression grew troubled. "I knew Sidney Tewksbury. Well, I mostly knew him through someone else; a woman named Maggie Reed."

I set my pizza down. "Sidney mentioned a Maggie in his podcast and his brother said something about her as well."

"I wish I never had the pleasure," Jules said. "I normally try to see the best in people, and honestly, I get along with pretty much everyone in town these days."

"But not Maggie?"

He shook his head. "She never attacked me directly, so don't get that impression. She was sneakier with it.

She would show up and make snide comments about Lance or me while others were around. Some of the things she said . . ." He tsked. "It wasn't fit for children."

"Was Sidney a part of that?"

"He was there on occasion, but he never participated. I swear I caught him giving me sympathetic looks every now and again, but if Maggie were to look at him, he would change like that." He snapped his fingers. "I always assumed they were an item and he went along with her antics to support her, but he never actually supported her, if you know what I mean?"

Interesting. The Sidney I heard on his podcasts, and what I'd heard about him from others, didn't quite jibe with Jules's impression of the man. Could Maggie have run his podcasts and coerced him into saying what he did? Or was he one of those men who have no problem tearing people down in private, but as soon as anyone is looking, they wither.

"They eventually moved on to greener pastures," Jules went on. "I hadn't seen Maggie or Sidney in months. If it wasn't for what happened at the festival, or you stopping by earlier, I might not have thought of them at all."

"Do you think Sidney was targeted because of his beliefs?" I asked.

Jules shrugged. "I couldn't say. But if you'd asked me who I could see getting themselves murdered, I would have put money on Maggie Reed over Sidney."

Before I could delve further into Jules's impression of the—couple? Friends? I wasn't sure what they were other than possible coconspirators—there was a hammering at my door. My mind instantly went to Robert and I wondered if he was still having troubles dealing with Trisha's indecision over his proposal.

Already annoyed and mentally calculating what I was going to say to him, I rose to answer as the hammering increased.

"I'm coming!" I shouted, but if the person trying to knock my door down heard, it didn't make them stop.

I jerked open the door, angry now. I opened my mouth to yell at Robert, but it wasn't his furious face that met me.

"What did you do?" A polished nail nearly jabbed me in the nose. "The Tuttles canceled on me and don't plan on looking at the house at all!" Vanna's face was flushed with anger. "I know you had something to do with it."

"Me?" I asked, taking a step back. "I wasn't even home!"

"You talked to them," she said. "What did you say to convince them to look elsewhere?"

"Nothing." I looked to Jules for help. He had an amused smirk on his face, one that said he was thankful I was the target of her ire, not him. "If anything, my conversation with them would have made them want to move in. I said only good things."

"You expect me to believe that?" Vanna huffed. "They found themselves a new real estate agent. They're looking at a place on the other end of town. You can't tell me that doesn't mean something."

Maybe it means they were tired of dealing with you. I wisely kept the thought to myself.

"The house *is* kind of small," I said. "And Eleanor didn't keep up with the maintenance in her later years." Thinking of my former neighbor, a flare of melancholy washed over me. She might have been a nuisance at times, but I did miss her. "They might have wanted something a little more modern."

Vanna sniffed. Some of her anger had bled away, but she wasn't going to let me off the hook. "Well, I suppose it was to be expected," she said, turning her back to me. As she walked away, she finished the thought loud enough for me to hear.

"This used to be a nice neighborhood."

I didn't bother to respond. I closed the door and turned to Jules. We stared at one another for a long moment, and then we both burst into laughter. My mirth was short-lived, however, as the motion caused my arm to ache, despite the pain meds, which were starting to kick in. I returned to my pizza, as Jules dried his eyes.

"You make all the friends," he said.

"Tell me about it." I took a big bite of my pizza and was disappointed to find it had grown lukewarm. I prefer my pizza piping hot and considered nuking it, but didn't have the energy for it. "I don't know what she has against me."

"Trust me, it's not just you." Jules rose. "I'm going to let you eat in peace. I just wanted to stop by and let you know what little I knew about Sidney Tewksbury and that woman, Maggie Reed. I hope it helps."

"It does," I said. "Thanks for stopping by. And if you get lonely while Lance is gone, feel free to come over. I have a feeling I'm not going to be doing much running around in the coming days." I lifted my arm in its sling.

"Will do. Get some rest and try not to move it too much." Jules strode to the door. There, he paused. "And be careful. Something about this whole thing smells wrong. I'm not sure what it is, and I know murder is never pleasant, but I'm worried." And with that, he made his exit.

I chewed on my nearly cold pizza, but had lost the

taste for it. Jules was right; something did smell fishy about the whole situation. There was the murder, of course. But what he said about Maggie seeming to be in charge, when everything else I'd heard up to that point pointed at Sidney being the ringleader. Was that by design?

Shoving the remains of my pizza away, I fetched my laptop and brought up the podcasts again. If there was some evidence hinting at Maggie as the driving force behind Sidney's attempts at censoring the entire town, I figured it would be there.

I scrolled through the list of podcasts, and then decided to start somewhere in the middle. I hovered the mouse pointer over the link, considered whether or not I actually wanted to go through this again, and then went ahead and hit *play*.

It wasn't any easier to listen to than the last time I'd tried.

I would start on one podcast and Sidney would begin to rant and I'd grow agitated. I would skip ahead, hear more of the same, and then move on to the next.

It went on like that for an hour. Misfit came in, sat at my feet for a few minutes, and then he left, obviously just as annoyed by Sidney's unfounded accusations and fact-light rants as I was.

But the exercise wasn't in vain.

The more I listened, the more I began to note inconsistencies in what Sidney had to say. He would be dead set against something in one podcast, but would ease up on it in the next. He would then reaffirm his original statement in the following, as if the middle one hadn't happened.

I skipped ahead to the podcast that had led to my fall and listened to his threat again. He *sounded* angry and determined. That twinge of fear that he wasn't making idle threats against Death by Coffee returned. Sidney had one of those voices that struck a nerve, albeit a bad one. It was the kind of voice that inspired people to violence. He was a pro at propaganda.

Once he finished his rant, I moved on to the next podcast. It sounded much the same. But the one after it was . . . softer? I wasn't sure how to put it. He was saying much of the same things, but was doing so in a less dramatic, threatening way.

"The institutions we've come to rely on have failed us." His recorded voice droned from the speakers in an oddly calm manner. *"We cannot go out to eat anymore without confronting that which defies our beliefs. But what can we honestly do about it? Perhaps reflection is needed."*

That sure didn't sound like the Sidney Tewksbury I'd come to loathe.

I checked the date on the file, and realized it was the last podcast posted.

And it had been posted two days before his death.

11

Easy. Easy.

The tray wobbled as I pulled it from the oven. I desperately wanted to use my right hand—the dominant one—but that wasn't happening. I bit my lower lip as I backed slowly from the oven, and then turned to slide the cookie tray onto the table to cool. I breathed a sigh of relief as they settled into place without a cookie lost.

"I think that deserves a reward," I said, plucking a hot cookie from the tray. The melted chocolate burnt my tongue and I had to do the open-mouthed breathing thing to cool it down, but it was oh, so worth it.

My wrist was doing a lot better now that I was a day out from the sprain. It still hurt, but not nearly as much as it had. Tylenol helped, obviously, but I was sure I'd be doing a lot better if I trusted the stuff Darrin prescribed me. A part of me hated the fact I suspected him at all, but with a murderer running loose, I couldn't be too careful.

While the cookies cooled, I debated how best to get them to the front. I was determined to do it myself, even though Jeff Braun was in the dining area, readying the rest of the store for opening. Lena was due to join us once we opened the doors, but for now, it was just the two of us.

I'd just decided on risking taking the entire tray up front one-handed when the door opened and Jeff peeked in. His cheeks were red and he refused to look at me as he spoke.

"I . . . um." He cleared his throat. "There's someone here for you."

Before I could ask who, Jeff vanished and both Vicki and Mason Lawyer strode through.

"What happened to you?" Vicki asked, planting a hand on her hip. She was as perfect as ever, and while that might have annoyed me, she never flaunted it. "And why didn't you call me?"

"I fell," I said. "And there was no reason to call. I'm fine."

"You could have asked someone else to come in for you," Mason said with the faintest of smirks. "You *are* co-owner. It's not like anyone will fire you for taking a day or two off."

"I know," I said. "But I'm doing okay. As long as I take it easy, I'll be able to work without too much trouble." I slid on the oven mitt and reached for the cookie tray.

"Nope." Vicki swooped forward and plucked the mitt from my hand. "I've got this. You. Rest."

"But . . ."

"No buts." Mitt on hand, she picked up the tray and gracefully spun on her heel and out the door to fill the display.

"You really should rest," Mason said. "We've got this."

"There's no need for me to go home." I was close to pouting and forced myself to relax. "Jeff and Lena can handle the heavy lifting. I can stick to the register and easy jobs. I can't sit at home and do nothing."

"Sure you can." He leaned against the table. "Vicki and I can handle the store in your absence. We weren't planning to do much today. Besides"—he grinned—"don't you have a murderer to catch?"

"That's Paul's job," I said. I'd decided early this morning to stop poking my nose where it didn't belong. "They're creating a detective's position at the police station and Paul's going to go for it. If he solves Sidney's murder, I'm sure it'll make him a shoo-in for the job."

"Can't his mom just give it to him?" Mason asked.

"She could, I imagine. But I doubt it would look good if she were to do so. I bet she'll have to make a show of considering other candidates, just to keep the peace, even if she does intend to choose Paul."

"Guess you're right." He sighed. "I wonder what it's like having a parent who thinks like that." Mason's dad, Raymond, wasn't known for his—shall we call it—tact. Or friendliness. Or, well, anything nice.

Vicki returned then. She deposited the tray in the sink to be washed, and then moved to stand beside Mason. "So, exactly how did that happen?" she asked, indicating my wrist.

I briefly went over the story. She already knew about the bomb threat since she was here when Paul showed up to check the place over, but she didn't know how I'd come to discover it.

"He plastered it all over the internet?" she asked.

"On his site, anyway," I said. "I'm not sure how many people actually listened to him."

"Even one is too many," Mason said. "If he made threats like that about other places of business, it's no wonder he ended up dead."

"Why not just turn him in to the police?" I asked. "I mean, if I'd heard the podcast before he'd died, I would have called Paul and that would have been that."

"He'd probably claim freedom of speech," Mason said.

"And he'd quickly learn that freedom of speech doesn't extend to threats and incitements of violence," Vicki said.

"Did you ever suspect him of wanting to go that far?" I asked Vicki. "I know you'd dealt with him before."

"To bomb us? No. Sidney was an annoyance, sure, but I never suspected him of being a violent man."

"I never actually met him, but after what happened, Vicki told me all about him." Mason snaked an arm around his wife's waist. "His complaints were unfounded, and honestly, were going nowhere. I'm not sure we'd have a reason to want him gone."

"It was like he knew he would never succeed, but kept at it anyway," Vicki said. "I always took him for one of those guys who liked to complain about things, just to create drama. It wouldn't surprise me to find out he never actually believed what he spouted, but was doing it for clicks."

I wondered if she might be right. After listening to the other podcasts, I was beginning to suspect a lot of Sidney's complaints were for show.

"Have either of you heard of a woman named Maggie Reed?" I asked.

Mason shook his head and looked to Vicki.

"I don't think so," she said. "Why?"

"Sidney mentioned her a few times in his podcasts and a few other people brought her up when I talked to them about Sidney. I think she might have been the muscle behind his bluster."

"You think she pushed him into it?" Mason asked.

"That, or he was trying to impress her."

Mason sighed. "What we men do for the women we love."

Vicki rolled her eyes and shoved him away. "If you want to get on my good side, you'd better get to washing the morning dishes then."

"Yes, my love." He laughed as she smacked his arm. Then, he went and did as she requested.

"You should go home." Vicki and I drifted through the door to the front. The tables were set and ready, the coffee had just finished percolating. Death by Coffee smelled like bliss.

"I'm okay to work," I said. "Really."

"I know, but there's no reason to push it. If we need you, I can call."

"I suppose I could get some of my baking done," I said, warming to the idea just a little. "My big Thanksgiving dinner is coming up fast and I'm nowhere near prepared for it."

"You know you could always ask for help."

"I know, but—"

"What did we say about the buts?" Vicki brushed a strand of hair out of my face for me. "I miss hanging out. I wasn't kidding when I said we need to get together more."

"Yeah, me too." I sighed. "There's just so much going on that it's hard."

"Let's both promise that after Thanksgiving, we'll try harder to make time for our friends. Just because I'm married, doesn't mean I don't need some time away. Mason's great and all, but he's not *you*."

"It would be kind of weird if he were."

She laughed. "Yes, it would be. Promise me you'll call if you need help for Thanksgiving? I can always put Mason to work for you so we can sit back and laugh at him together."

"Sounds great."

"Perfect!" Vicki all but shooed me to the door. "I can't wait to see what you have planned. But until then . . ."

"I need to get my things," I said, veering off to the office. The closet-sized space was in serious need of a remodel. The desk was now just a catchall, filled with junk. Whenever one of us needed to do any sort of paperwork, we carried it out front where there was more space. My purse sat among a mass of papers, boxes, and supplies. I plucked it up, already mentally cataloging what we might need to do to spruce the place up.

When I returned to the front, Jeff scurried back upstairs as if fleeing a war zone. I watched him go with a growing certainty that I knew why he was keeping well away from me.

"Vicki?"

"Hmm?" All sweetness.

"How did you know I was hurt?"

There was a pause that reaffirmed my suspicion.

"What do you mean?"

"Jeff called you, didn't he?"

Her face contorted as she tried to keep the smile from cracking her lips. "Maybe."

"Ugh!" If I could have, I would have thrown my arms in the air in frustration. "He shouldn't have done that." I made sure to pitch my voice at a volume that would carry.

"He did the right thing," Mason said, coming from the back with a dish towel thrown over one shoulder. "Get the door; we have a guest."

I would have liked to plead my case, using Jeff's betrayal as ammo for why I should just go ahead and stay, but when I turned, I saw Paul peering in through the glass door and the fight melted right out of me.

"Hi, Krissy." He hesitated as the doors opened, and then leaned forward to give me a quick peck on the cheek. He was in full uniform and looked ready to start the day. "Vicki. Mason."

"The usual?" Vicki asked.

Paul nodded, and then turned to me. "How are you feeling?"

"I'd feel a lot better if my friends stopped treating me like an invalid." I gave both Mason and Vicki the stink eye, which only caused them to laugh. When I turned back to Paul, he was grinning. "Not you too!"

He cleared his throat and stuffed the smile back where it belonged. "Of course not." Vicki handed him his coffee. He thanked her and we moved away from the counter. "I'm glad I caught you. With everything that's happened, I've been pretty busy."

"You have a murder to solve," I said before he could

apologize. "I can't wait to start calling you Detective Dalton."

He tried to wave it off, but I could tell the thought pleased him. "Nothing is certain yet. Buchannan is making a strong case for himself, and Garrison is no slouch."

"But you're the best cop I know." I nudged him with my good shoulder.

"Yeah, well, we'll see." He took a drink, glancing around the empty store. "If you aren't busy tonight, I thought perhaps we could have dinner."

Any complaints I might have had about Vicki and Mason kicking me out of my own place dried up. "I'm free," I said, already making plans for my outfit. "Where do you want to go?"

Paul adjusted his hat on his head and took another drink of his coffee before answering. "I thought that instead of eating out, you might like to come to my place tonight. I could cook."

I gaped at him. The next words just sort of slid out without my brain being a part of the conversation. "You cook?"

He laughed. "Yeah, I cook, but rarely. It's a lot easier to swing over to J&E's than to find time to throw on a few steaks."

The idea of steaks at Paul's was almost too exciting for me to comprehend. It was a new step, one we had yet to take. Paul had been over to my place numerous times, and we'd gone out to eat together before, but I'd never actually been to his home. He was almost always stopping by my house after work, or was picking me up there instead.

"What do you think?" he asked after a few moments

of me daydreaming about the possibilities. And standing there silent like a dope. "You up for some of my famous— well, I can't promise it'll be good, and I'm not sure what I'll cook yet, but it'll be food."

"I'd love to," I said. And unable to suppress the urge, I leaned forward and gave him a real kiss—none of this peck-on-the-cheek crap.

Despite being on duty, Paul accepted the kiss, and re-turned it in a way that made the pain in my arm flutter away. I could have stayed like that forever, but the door opened and Rita's voice tore right through the bliss.

"Lordy Lou, am I here early or what?"

Reluctantly, I pulled away from Paul. "Hi, Rita. Vicki and Mason are taking orders. I'm heading out."

"Oh, well, that's fine, dear. I'm only stopping in for a quick drink." She started toward the counter, but paused. "I didn't know you were allowing people to stick flyers to your windows. Perhaps I should get a few made up for the book club or writers' group. We could always use the extra promotion."

"Wait, what?" I glanced at Paul, who shrugged. "What flyers?"

"The ones outside," Rita said. "Didn't you see them? I swear, you need to pay closer attention to what's going on around you, dear. It's no wonder it's taken you this long to get with that cop of yours."

Normally, I would have flushed and sputtered out de-nials, but my attention was fixated on the papers stuck to the plate glass window that fronted Death by Coffee. They hadn't been there when I'd arrived, and I sure didn't recall seeing them when I'd let Paul in.

I couldn't make anything out from inside the store,

other than a faint outline of text, so I headed outside to investigate. Paul followed along behind me.

The first thing I noted was the book with the red circle and slash through it. Below that, the text I'd noted.

Books of violence begets true violence. Stories of murder, from a place that revels in death, led to the death of our own beloved Sidney Tewksbury. Ban the books, and save lives.

There was no signature beneath the message, but I already knew who had planted it.

"Maggie Reed," I grumbled, tearing the page from the window. Chunks of it remained, and when I tried to remove what was left, I realized she'd used some sort of super-sticky glue. I tried picking at it, but it was stuck fast.

"What is it?" Paul asked as I moved to the other side of the door. Another page was stuck there. It was identical to the first.

"She's trying to implicate me in Sidney's murder," I said, tearing the page off. Like the first, it left behind remnants that refused to be easily removed. "Or insinuate my store led to his death."

"Maggie Reed did?"

I dug a nail into the glue and yanked. It gave a little, but not before my nail bent back painfully. I sucked on the wounded finger as I steamed.

"How do you know she did this?" Paul asked. He took one of the torn pages from my hand and read it. "It doesn't have her name on it."

"Sidney mentioned her in his podcasts, as did some other people who knew them both." At Paul's look, I hurriedly explained my talk with Kevin Tewksbury and the teachers at the school. "I'm positive she's involved in this. She probably goaded Sidney into doing something that got him killed."

Paul didn't look convinced. "I'll look into her, but don't jump to conclusions. Someone else might have placed the flyers."

I doubted it, but I nodded. I was already worked up and if I started throwing ideas around, I'd end up in my car, seeking Maggie Reed out to tell her to lay off.

Honestly, that wasn't such a bad idea . . .

The doors opened and Rita came out, carrying a to-go cup. She looked at the windows and tsked. "You should be more careful, dear. There's easier ways to stick those things on."

"I didn't do this."

"Well, either way, you should pay more attention. If you let them, half the businesses in town will be over plastering their flyers all over your store; just you watch." She tsked once more, and then strode away with a shake of her head.

"You should listen to her," Paul said, taking the other page from my hand. "I'll give these a look, and see if I can learn anything from them. You, go home. I'll see you tonight."

More people were filing into Death by Coffee now. The morning rush had begun, and I was only in the way. I nodded grudgingly. Even thoughts of visiting Paul's house weren't enough to lift my sudden gloom. "I'll see you then."

Paul carefully folded the pages and carried them, along with his coffee, to his cruiser. He waved to me once, and the look in his eye was one of concern. I waved him off, hoping that he wouldn't decide to check in on me throughout the day because I wasn't so sure what I was going to do as of yet, and it might include having some words with Maggie.

Once Paul was gone, I trudged my way to my own vehicle. I really wanted to find Maggie and demand she explain herself, but the more I thought about it, the more I knew it would only lead to bad things.

"This is Paul's case," I reminded myself once safely behind the wheel. "He can deal with it." Besides, I had baking to do.

12

The smell of pumpkin filled the kitchen. The pie wouldn't be ready for another ten minutes, yet I was itching to pull it from the oven and grab myself a slice. I would have to bake another pie before my big Thanksgiving dinner because this one was mine.

I tried not to watch the timer, and instead focused on the apple cider in front of me. It was my mom's recipe, the one I'd donated to the ill-fated festival. Drinking it used to bring to mind fond memories of my mom, of time at home in California when she was still alive, laughing and goofing off with Dad. I used to love to sip the cider, slowly reliving all those memories. It kept her alive.

But now those memories were marred by Sidney Tewksbury's death. While my apple cider hadn't killed him directly, it was used to poison him. There was no way to scrub that memory away.

With a sigh, I pushed the cup away. Eventually, I thought I'd be able to drink it again without thinking about murder, but not until the killer was caught.

The timer dinged and I rose to check on my pie. I always set the timer a few minutes early so I could eyeball the final minutes myself. I'd burned enough desserts to know that sometimes it's better to do things yourself than to rely on a machine.

The color was just the right shade of scorched orange, so I pulled the pie free, thankful I had set the timer short. I carefully lifted the tin up to the stovetop and deposited it there, hand shaking the entire way. I apparently needed to work on my left hand's strength because this was ridiculous.

Not bothering to wait for the pie to cool, I carved myself a slice, transferred it to a small plate, and carried it over to the counter where I'd left my cider and book.

The next fifteen minutes were a too-hot-to-eat bliss.

There was just something about fresh-from-the-oven treats that didn't last once they cooled. Cookies were the same way, which was why I tended to eat them after they'd soaked in freshly brewed coffee. Maybe it was the melty goodness. Maybe it was the comfort of the heat. Either way, I was able to focus on the last few pages of my book as I ate, and forget about death and murder for a little while—at least, the real kind of death and murder. The mystery I was reading was full of the imagined, and I was okay with that.

Once I scraped my plate clean, I debated on whether or not to grab another slice of pie, but decided against it. I'd learned my lesson the last time I'd made chocolate chip cookies and ate half a dozen before they'd cooled. My poor tummy didn't feel right for the rest of the evening, which I'd spent sprawled across the couch, groaning in both misery and contentment.

While I waited for the rest of the pie to cool so I could put it away, I busied myself around the house. I planned on cleaning the place from top to bottom before the first guest arrived in a few days, and would need to do some rearranging to make sure everyone fit. Not for the first time, I questioned the wisdom of inviting my friends here, but it felt too—I don't know—rude to ask if Vicki and Mason might be able to host the dinner in their bigger home.

"I'll make it work," I told Misfit, who was watching me from his spot on the couch. That was another thing I was going to have to figure out: What to do with the cat? He wasn't too keen on strangers, not unless they were giving him treats. And I didn't want him to use those claws of his on someone's dinner clothes. He'd ruined more than one pair of my jeans.

Once the pie was cool, I covered it and slid it into the fridge. I had hours of baking and cooking ahead of me, and while a part of me was intimidated by doing it all myself, I was looking forward to it. It would keep my mind occupied and it was for something that, despite my trepidation on location, was going to be good for my soul. I hoped the Thanksgiving dinner at my place would be the start of a long-standing tradition.

Now that my hunger was sated and my kitchen was clean, I had one more task I wanted to accomplish before my date with Paul later that evening.

I snatched up my finished library book, grabbed my purse and keys, and headed out the door.

On the way, I called Paul, not expecting an answer and

not getting one. I was curious to know if he'd found any-thing out about the flyers plastered to Death by Coffee's windows, but it could wait. I was *not* going to pester him. I was going to let him do his job, earn his detective's badge, and cheer him on all along the way.

The thought carried me all the way to the library, where it died a horrible death at what awaited me.

A group of five people stood outside the library doors, blocking the entrance. All five—three men and two women—wore white shirts with *Freedom from Filth* splashed across the back in red, white, and blue. Two of them were holding signs, but currently had them turned away from me since everyone was facing the front of the library where Jimmy Carlton stood, red in the face.

"You killed Sid!" one of the women shouted, jabbing a finger at Jimmy's face. "Murderer! Murderer!"

The others took up the chant.

I eased from my vehicle, book clutched in hand. Jimmy's accuser was a short, pixie-like woman, with a voice like a rottweiler. Jimmy wasn't a small guy, yet he recoiled from her at every finger jab. I wondered if I was looking at Sidney's friend, Maggie Reed.

"This is a library," Jimmy said, doing his best to keep his voice respectful, but there was an angry edge to it. "We don't kill people here."

"The filth you distribute to impressionable minds does," the woman I thought might be Maggie shouted. "If you would have listened to Sid, he'd still be alive today."

"Murderer!" the others shouted.

I approached the group, not quite sure what I was go-ing to do. My main goal was to return my book and pick up a new one, possibly the second in the series, but now, the book felt more like protection than anything. If one of those finger jabs came my way, I planned on using it as a shield.

"I don't want to have to call the cops," Jimmy said. "Please, just leave us be."

"Our freedom is in jeopardy. We will not stop until our children once more have the ability to enter your library without being subjected to vile, hateful materials."

Hateful materials? I wondered. The only hateful thing I was seeing were the protestors.

Instead of pushing through the small gathering, I decided to go around. No sense antagonizing them more than they already were.

"Stop!" The woman spun on me like a snake before I'd made it past her. "The library is closed until further notice."

"I'm just returning a book," I said, keeping it well hidden behind my back. If she was anything like Sidney—and from the looks of it, she was—she'd use the murder mystery as a weapon against me.

Two of the protestors moved to block off my path. Jimmy threw his hands into the air and retreated through the doors, leaving me to fend for myself.

"I know you," the woman said, turning her full attention to me now that Jimmy was gone. "You're one of the owners of that coffee shop downtown." Her eyes narrowed and she took a threatening step my way. "The books you sell are part of the reason our society is crumbling."

"Murderer!" one of the men shouted, hand pumping the air. When no one else joined in, he dropped his arm, face turning crimson.

"I take it you're Maggie?" I asked, not backing down.

We might not be in front of Death by Coffee, but we might as well have been. An attack on the library was an attack on me. "You're the one who stuck those flyers to my store windows?"

She grinned as if it was some sort of big accomplishment. "I did. The public must be informed of the danger you represent."

"There's nothing dangerous about books," I said. "They're entertainment, an escape from reality. They're not how-to guides." At least the fiction ones weren't.

"Those books teach children with impressionable minds evil things. They teach adults who should know better that it is okay to fornicate with people other than their spouses. If you and the media were to stop glorifying violence with your 'stories,' then we'd finally have world peace."

I gritted my teeth to keep from snapping at her. "You can't blame books and TV for violence. The people who commit crimes would likely do so regardless of what they see and read. It's already a part of them."

Maggie snorted and looked back at her companions. Two of the men frowned, while the one who was so fond of shouting "murderer!" chuckled. The only other woman there looked like she wanted to be somewhere else.

"Sid died because of your so-called innocent stories," Maggie said, turning back to me. "All he wanted was to cleanse Pine Hills of evil. He used his rights to protest, used his freedom to speak his mind, and someone silenced him. They want to take our freedoms from us!" Her voice rose to a shout. It was followed by a half-hearted cheer from her four companions.

There was no reasoning with Maggie or her cohorts, not while they were in protest mode. I might not agree with her point of view, and she had the right to believe what she wanted, but I wished she realized she didn't have the right to push those views on everyone else, or interrupt people's livelihood.

"I'm sorry you feel that way," I said. "But I didn't kill anyone."

"Your books convinced someone else to do it for you," Maggie said.

"Yeah? Like who?"

Maggie glanced behind her, and oddly, lowered her voice from a shout to something approaching a normal tone. "Kevin Tewksbury."

I blinked at her. "You think Kevin killed his own brother?"

"He was influenced by the filth he surrounded himself with. He may have done the deed, but I hold all of you responsible." She flung an arm toward the library, obviously adding Jimmy and Cindy in with the accusation.

I heaved a sigh. I didn't have time for this. "I'm going to return my book," I said as calmly as I could manage. "And I'm going to ask you to stop leaving flyers at my store. Customers can choose what they want to read, just like you can choose not to buy those same books." I took a step forward, toward the doors.

Maggie's finger felt like a steel rod as it jammed me hard in the chest. I rocked back, wincing, hand going reflexively to the spot she'd poked. The sudden movement caused me to drop my book.

Pages fluttered as the book hit the ground. The word *Murder* screamed from the cover, almost an accusation. I started to reach for the novel, but Maggie snatched it up before I could.

"A book about murder," she sneered, holding it up for

the others to see. "From a woman who revels in it, who names her store after it. Why am I not surprised?"

And then, much to my horror, she opened the book up and ripped out a handful of pages.

"You can't do that!" I shouted, vainly trying to catch the pages as they fluttered toward the ground, as if by keeping them from touching the pavement, I could somehow put them back as if it had never happened.

Maggie's only answer was to tear more pages from the book and throw them in my face.

The anger that shot through me then had me rocking forward on my toes. I'd always heard the expression—and probably had used it many times myself—of seeing red, but had never actually experienced such a thing before in my life.

Now, I finally knew exactly how the expression came about.

I'm not sure what I would have done one-handed. I might have ripped the book from her hands, or I might have struck her with my good, weak arm. Who knows, maybe I would have actually thrown myself at her and tackled her to the ground in the sudden flare of rage that washed over me like scalding water from the shower.

I'll never know for sure because at that moment the *whoop-whoop* of a siren sounded behind me as a police cruiser pulled into the lot.

Thinking that Paul had somehow found me, I turned with a savage grin. If Maggie thought she could get away with attacking me and my book, she had another thing coming.

But it wasn't Paul who stepped out of the police cruiser.

Officer John Buchannan unfolded himself from the

seat, a grim scowl spread across his face. He took in the scene, eyes lingering on me a few seconds too long, before he strode forward. Behind me, the library doors opened and Jimmy stepped back outside.

"Time to break it up," Buchannan said, deep voice rumbling. "Go home. Cool down."

"It's in our rights to protest corruption," Maggie said.

"You're on public property, yes, but you're also disturbing the peace." Buchannan wasn't swayed. "Please disperse." He glanced at the scattered pages on the ground. "After you clean up this mess."

Maggie tossed the remains of the book at me. I fumbled with it and dropped it. "It's hers. Come on, let's go." She strode past me, close enough I could smell her perfume.

The three men followed her without question, though I noted one of them looked concerned. The woman appeared undecided about what to do. She looked from me, to Buchannan, then with a "Sorry," she hurried after the others.

As soon as they were gone, Buchannan heaved a hefty sigh. "Why am I not surprised you're involved in this?"

"I just showed up," I said, crouching to pick up the torn pages. I managed to gather a handful before half of them slipped through my fingers again. I made a frustrated sound and closed my eyes.

Buchannan knelt beside me. "Let me." He quickly gathered the pages and carelessly shoved them back into the book. They were filthy, bent, and stuck out at all angles, but he'd gotten them all. He handed the ruined novel back to me.

"She destroyed it," I said. "It belongs to the library. Can't you arrest her for that?"

"No, but she can be fined for destroying someone else's property." He took the ruined book from me and carried it to Jimmy. "Do you want to press charges? I can file it, but doubt it'll come to anything."

Jimmy took the book and shook his head. "Not at this time, but if she keeps it up, something is going to need to be done. Cindy is inside, trying to remove the stickers from the books."

"Stickers?" I asked.

"They have that *Freedom from Filth* slogan on them and a web address. Maggie denies putting them on there, but who else would have done it? Thankfully, she, or whoever she had do it, stuck them to the title pages and not one of the pages with story text. We might have to remove that front page if we can't get the stickers off, but at least the books can still be read."

Buchannan's scowl deepened. "We should talk." Then, to me. "Go home. I'll make sure this gets taken care of."

I nodded, but my mind wasn't on home.

If Maggie had put stickers on the books in the library without anyone noticing, could she have done the same thing at Death by Coffee?

Jimmy and Buchannan went inside, already talking about what could be done to make Maggie pay for damages. I had a feeling that since it sounded like no one actually saw her do it—and knowing the budget crunch, it was unlikely they had security cameras inside—Maggie was going to skate by without much more than a stern warning to not do it again.

What scared me was, What would a woman like Maggie Reed do if she realized she wouldn't face repercussions for her actions?

13

"Are you sure you're okay?" Vicki asked, trailing after me with a concerned look on her face. "How many pain pills did you take?"

"I'm fine." I grabbed a book from the shelf, flipped through it, and shoved it back where it belonged. "She might have put stickers in the books."

"You said." Vicki glanced back to Mason, who was downstairs manning the counter at Death by Coffee. He shrugged and took one of our regulars, Todd Melville's order. Todd, who was wearing a mask, sneezed twice, eyes flickering toward the bookstore where Vicki's black-and-white cat, Trouble, lounged on top one of the shorter shelves.

Admittedly, I was feeling a tiny bit woozy as I went through the books. Despite Vicki's concerns I'd overdone it, I hadn't actually taken any pain meds before coming in. I also had yet to eat anything substantial since my slice of pie. I checked another book, and then leaned my forehead against the shelf when a wave of dizziness washed over me.

"Come on, let's sit down."

I didn't resist as Vicki led me away from the shelves, to the couch. I sank into it and leaned my head back.

"I think I'm going crazy."

"Possibly. But we still love you anyway."

I glanced at Vicki out of the corner of my eye. She winked, making me smile.

"Why does everything have to happen now?" I asked, leaning back again. "Sidney's murder. This whole Maggie situation. Thanksgiving. This." I raised my wrist, and then winced when it screamed at me to stop moving it. "I'm letting all the insanity get to me and don't know how to make it stop."

"I'm not sure you can," Vicki said, and then added, "Don't forget your date tonight."

I raised my head. "How'd you know about that? Wait. Never mind. Rita was here." My head hit the back of the couch with a soft thump. I didn't think Rita had overheard Paul and me talking, but someone must have caught wind about the date and passed the word on.

"You really should go home and get some sleep," Vicki said, putting a hand on my bicep since my wrist was currently a no-touch zone. "You don't look so good."

"I don't *feel* all that great." My stomach was in knots and my head was starting to throb. Maybe it was time I stopped avoiding Darrin's pain meds. "What if Paul can't figure out who killed Sidney? If he was killed for his beliefs, what if Maggie is next?" She might have destroyed a book and said some mean things to me, but she was still a person. I didn't want to see anything happen to her.

Vicki squeezed my arm. "Don't worry yourself over that. I'm sure Paul will do everything he can. If Maggie shows up here and tries to put stickers in books, I'll deal with it. And if someone comes after her . . ." She shrugged. "There's nothing either of us can do about that but hope she can get away and identify them to the police."

She was right, but it was hard to let it go. If Maggie was right and Kevin Tewksbury had killed Sidney, it wasn't like I could show up at his place and demand he admit it. He'd just deny it, and likely add me to his target list. This was a job for Paul, Buchannan, and the rest of the Pine Hills police force, not an injured coffee shop owner.

"All right." I heaved myself to my feet, only swaying briefly before catching my balance. "I'll go home, wait for Paul, and try to focus on the good things in life."

"That's the spirit." Vicki rose with me and stayed close as we headed down the stairs. I was happy for her nearness, because I wasn't so sure I was steady enough to walk down them without her support.

This is what I've been missing. Maybe I'd find a way to spend a few hours just talking things through with her *before* Thanksgiving. Lord knows I could use a mental break.

"Everything good?" Mason asked from the counter. Todd was gone, having taken his coffee and fled from the cat, who he was allergic to.

"No stickers," I said. "But keep an eye out, okay? Maggie or one of her pals might show up."

Mason shot a questioning look to Vicki.

"I'll explain later," she said, guiding me to, and out, the door. "I want you to take it slow. If you start feeling off, stop driving and call me. I'll come get you."

"I'll be okay," I said.

"And if you're not?"

"All right, all right, I'll call you to come get me." And then, with a smile, "Mom."

Vicki laughed and nudged me with her elbow as I climbed into my Escape. She watched as I pulled onto the road, hands on her hips, and a healthy dose of skepticism on her face.

The drive home was long and slow. I felt like I could fall into bed and sleep until Thanksgiving. Not even the colorful leaves covering the ground and half the road could lift my spirits. I desperately needed a break from the stress.

Vanna Goff was standing in the driveway at the house next door, hands on her hips, staring toward my place like she was considering setting it on fire when I arrived. I parked, but didn't have the energy to deal with her today. I waved, hoping she would take the friendly gesture as a peace offering, but all she did was turn and walk into Eleanor's old house.

"Oh well," I muttered, sliding the key into the lock. I all but dragged myself through the door and to the couch where I immediately fell asleep.

I dreamed of giant turkeys chasing me through the street, human-sized basters in hand. Pies with faces screamed at me as I ran, while leaves with sharp edges swirled around me, cutting my clothes into tatters. As I ran, I began to realize I was in a giant, world-sized oven, and that someone was about to turn it on.

I jerked awake, bathed in sweat and with Misfit staring

at me from across the room. My wrist was throbbing and my mouth felt as if I'd been sucking on cotton. At least I wasn't woozy anymore.

I rose and went into the kitchen for water. I drank the entire glass without taking a breath. I filled it again and grabbed the pain pills from my purse. I was about to pop the lid, when I reconsidered. Those were some strange dreams, and I didn't know how the pills would affect me on an empty stomach. And I definitely didn't want to make myself sick before my date with Paul.

I dropped the bottle back into my purse, then headed for the shower.

An hour later, showered, dressed, and with a little extra moisturizer and lotion, I felt more like myself. I made some toast and ate it without butter, just so I'd have something in my stomach. I took two ibuprofens to take the edge off, and sank down at the counter with my laptop. I still had some time before I was due at Paul's place. I planned on using it.

I didn't have the web address on the stickers Maggie had stuck to the library books, but I did have their slogan. I typed in *Freedom from Filth* into my browser, and prepared myself to be appalled.

I wasn't disappointed.

Other than a song I'd never heard of before then, there was only one link. I clicked on it and was met by a bald eagle and the American flag with the slogan splashed across it. Crossed rifles were below that with *We will fight for what we believe* beneath them.

"Oh, boy," I said, scrolling down.

The main page was little more than a diatribe that matched a lot of what I'd heard in Sidney's podcasts. The grammar was okay, I guess. Whoever wrote it managed to spell everything correctly, but kept using the wrong form of *their*. I couldn't say I was surprised.

I skimmed through the page, groaning at how vile it all sounded. I didn't understand how anyone could blame books or the media or even music and movies for corrupting innocent minds. They acted like all killers learned their trade through various media, not that there was something wrong with those people, or, in many cases, how killers acted out of sheer, sudden emotion.

There were a pair of links at the bottom of the page. One led to a donations page. Needless to say, I didn't click it. The other was to subscribe to their newsletter. Once again, I avoided clicking it.

Instead, I scrolled back to the top. The menu had five other options. One led to Sidney's podcasts. I wondered why he never promoted this website on his page, considering the similarities, and then decided it was likely because the two entities were separate. Could Sidney not have known about this page? Or did one of them inspire the other?

There was no *about me* or members page, so I couldn't see who controlled the site. There *was* a page called *grievances*. I clicked that, and was met with a wall of text, all about Pine Hills. I saw names of places I knew, including Death by Coffee and Jules Phan's Phantastic Candies. Even the diner, J&E's Banyon Tree, was included.

It appeared as if no one was safe from Freedom from Filth's wrath.

There were no names of members on this page either. Obviously, Maggie Reed and her band of protestors were involved, and by extension, so was Sidney Tewksbury. After that, I was clueless.

The wall of text was too much to read in its entirety, so I went back to the menu, but there was little that would help me figure out who ran the site. Even the *contact us* link was a generic email that left no hint as to who it would lead to.

I frowned. Maggie didn't seem to be the kind of person who would hide from publicity. She showed up at the library, face uncovered, protesting the books. Why not let people know who they were dealing with on the web so that they could contact her and join in on her protests?

I went back to the home page and scoured it again, hoping to spot something I'd missed in my first perusal of the site.

There were the *their* mistakes, but the paragraphs were written by someone who was obviously educated. The sentences were crisp, didn't meander, and used words I wouldn't connect to someone uneducated. I'm not saying that Maggie wasn't smart—I knew nothing about her, really—but why would someone make an obvious mistake like confusing *their* with *they're* but spell other, bigger words correctly? Even the punctuation was correct.

I spent the next half hour reading and rereading every page on the site. After only five minutes of that half hour, I began to suspect the mistakes were on purpose. By the time I finished reading, I was positive they were.

Either Maggie wanted people to believe she wasn't as smart as she really was, or she didn't make the page at all.

But if that was the case, who did?

I rose from the stool and cracked my back. What all did I know?

The website was promoted through the stickers stuck to library books. No one saw who placed the stickers and Maggie denied doing it. The stickers, as well as the site, used the *Freedom from Filth* slogan. The site linked to Sidney's podcasts, but he never once promoted the Freedom from Filth website, which was done as anonymously as possible. The flyers placed at my store, the ones Maggie didn't deny placing, didn't have the slogan nor the web address anywhere on them.

Conclusion: This wasn't her website.

It was entirely possible she had something to do with it, but someone else was running the group's web presence. The same could be said for the flyers. They weren't professional. Anyone could have thrown together the design and printed them off at home. If the jobs were delegated—the website, Sidney's podcasts, the stickers, the flyers—there was always a chance that one hand didn't know what the others were doing.

But still, the mistakes on the website made me think otherwise. In fact, the use of the wrong *their* was something that might bother a teacher. You know, like an English teacher.

"Kevin." His name slipped from my lips unbidden. Why would he create a site that promoted hatred when he claimed that he and his brother were at odds over that very thing? Had it all been lie, a way to cause as big of a ruckus as possible as to draw attention to their mutual dislike of anything they deemed inappropriate?

I didn't think about what I did next. I snatched up my phone, found Kevin Tewksbury's number, and dialed. He answered on the second ring.

"Do you run a site called *Freedom from Filth*?" I asked before he could say anything more than "Hello?"

"I, uh . . . Who is this?"

I decided revealing my identity might not be the best course of action right then. I only hoped he didn't have caller ID. I changed my voice to be a smidge deeper, and a little more gravelly. "Answer the question, Mr. Tewksbury."

"I think you have the wrong number."

"No, I'm sure I don't." I cleared my throat, which was already feeling raw from the voice change. "I found the site." And then, on a whim, "I tracked it to you."

"Who is this?" This time, it came out angry. "I don't appreciate you calling me out of the blue and throwing accusations my way. That page belonged to my brother."

Doubts crept in. I supposed it was possible Sidney had created the site, but if it was his page, why didn't his podcast page link back to it?

"Were you a part of your brother's group?" I asked.

"What? No. I'm going to hang up now. Don't call me again."

"Wait!" But it was already too late.

I held my phone in my hand, not quite sure if I'd learned anything. Kevin wasn't happy about my call, but then again, why would he be? I'd accused him of belonging to what amounted to a hate group, one his brother—who he, as well as others, claimed to be at odds with—belonged to.

A new thought crept in, one that made me nervous about my visit to the site.

What if the website was a way to track members of the group in order to hunt them down and kill them?

It made an odd sort of sense. A disgruntled person goes online, looking for a way to vent their anger against people who weren't actually responsible for their problems, but made convenient scapegoats. They'd seen the stickers in the book, decided to look it up.

And then what? To donate, personal information would need to be provided. To sign up to the newsletter meant giving up an email address, which could be tracked. Once the website owner had your name, they could easily find out where you lived, where you worked, and then . . . murder?

It was possible, but I was having a hard time imagining it. Only Sidney had died as far as I was aware, and it had been done publicly, through poison, which wasn't exactly an easy method of killing someone. I mean, I didn't want Maggie outside Death by Coffee with her pals and their signs, driving customers away, but I wouldn't make up some elaborate plan to kill her for it.

But if it *was* family related . . .

Glancing at the clock, I realized it was time for me to go if I wanted to make my date with Paul on time. I bookmarked the link on my laptop, then checked my phone to make sure my Chrome had it saved as well, and then shut everything down. I didn't plan on bringing any of this up to Paul while we were having dinner, but if the murder investigation were to come up in the course of conversation, I wanted to have it at the ready.

14

My Escape idled as I sat in Paul Dalton's driveway, staring at the front door as if it might eat me. The house was squat and charming in an outdoorsy sort of way. The property was backed by a smattering of trees that didn't quite number enough to rightfully be called a forest or woods, but enough to give the illusion of privacy. I could see a pair of doghouses surrounded by a tall chain-link fence from where I sat, but of the dogs, there was no sign.

"Okay, Krissy, you can do this." I took a deep breath and shut off the engine.

I didn't know why I was so nervous. I'd gone on dates with Paul before, had spent hours with him, talking over coffee or sandwiches, so why should this be any different? He'd been to my house. We've both visited each other at work. We've even been trapped in the same closet together.

Yet, here I was, practically shaking in my fancy bargain-bin shoes.

Clutching my purse to my chest like it might protect me from making a fool out of myself, I climbed out of my vehicle and headed for the front door. I could smell woodsmoke in the air, and faint voices and laughs could be heard somewhere beyond the trees. One of his neighbors was apparently having a cookout. My stomach, which was already twisted in knots, growled at me to feed it already.

I stepped up on the front stoop and raised my fist to knock. Before I could, a flurry of nails on wood and a pair of deep woofs came from the other side of the door. A few seconds later, the door opened and there Paul was, dressed casually, but carefully so. His shirt was pristine, void of wrinkles, and showed just enough of the musculature beneath, I felt myself flush.

Behind Paul, a pair of beautiful huskies were giving me the stink eye. They probably could smell my cat, which likely put me on their untrustworthy list.

"Krissy! Come on in." Paul tried to back up, but was nearly tripped by the dogs, who tried to surge forward at the same instant. "Kefka. Ziggy. Back."

The two dogs listened about as well as I did whenever he told me to stop investigating a murder. They rushed forward the moment they had a clean shot at me and shoved their cold noses into my hand.

"Good doggies," I said, petting them and hoping I was making a good impression. "I'm just visiting."

Paul reined in the huskies with a sigh. "I'll put them up for now. Sorry about that."

"No, it's all right." I scratched each dog behind the ears. "I like animals of all kinds."

"They probably smell your cat on you," he said. The dogs flat-out refused to be led away. Every time he tried to guide them away from me and down the hall, they'd jerk free and their noses would find my hand again.

"Misfit is going to love getting a nose full of me when I get home," I said, and then yelped when one of the dogs decided to round me and ram her nose into my backside.

It took ten minutes and me having to walk down the hall, into a small study that looked as if someone had picked it up and shaken it, before Paul managed to extract the dogs from me. He rounded them up with promises that they'd be getting steak afterward, which didn't make much of a difference if the whimpering said anything. He closed the door and gave me a dopey grin that put his dimples on display.

"I really am sorry about that. They're not used to strangers coming around. They know me, Mom, and Susie, but everyone else is a stranger."

"Susie?" I asked, trying to keep the curiosity out of my voice.

"She's my neighbor. When I'm at work, she watches the dogs for me. I'm not sure what I'd do without her."

I didn't pry because, quite frankly, it was none of my business, but I did wonder. Was Susie young? Old? Did she spend hours next to Paul, talking about the dogs? How long had they known one another? Did she want to be more than a mere dog sitter?

Stop it, Krissy. There was no reason to get jealous. It surprised me I had never heard the name before, which made the devil hitching a ride on my shoulder question why.

Paul took a deep breath and let it out with a sheepish grin. He brushed down his once-pristine shirt, which was now coated in dog fur, and then led me away from the study to an eat-in kitchen. The steaks were already on.

I followed after him slowly, taking in the sights. It was strange seeing Paul at home, in a place that looked nothing like what I'd expected. He was on the job nearly all the time, so a part of me assumed his house would look like an extension of his work: papers on the table, a fax machine, maybe a jail cell or two. Instead, it looked like a getaway, a cabin in the woods.

And by the comfortable way he moved, it was likely exactly what he needed so he didn't go crazy from the pressures of his job.

Paul moved to the stove to tend to dinner. "They'll be finished soon," he said. "I hope you're hungry. I might have gone a little overboard."

"I'm starved," I said, not quite sure what to do with myself. Should I sit? Should I offer to help? I'd dated before, but somehow this was different. Will and I had gone on dates, as I had with Robert, but being here with Paul was an entirely different experience, one that had me feeling like an awkward teenager all over again.

"There's potato salad in the fridge. And tomato salad. And pasta salad." He frowned. "The only thing I don't have is salad salad, I guess."

"That's okay." I opened the fridge, figuring I could at least prepare the table and was surprised to find the side dishes to be homemade, not store-bought. "You really shouldn't have gone to so much trouble."

"It was no trouble." Paul flipped the steaks. "I wasn't

sure what you'd prefer, so I made a little bit of everything. If you don't want something, don't force yourself
to eat it. I'll pack it in my lunch or grab it for dinner over
the coming days. I don't get home-cooked meals all that
often, so it'll be a treat."

Now, *that,* I could see: Paul coming home from a late
night keeping Pine Hills safe, carryout from J&E's Banyon Tree in hand. The dogs would beg and he'd oblige
them. He'd lounge on the couch and watch TV until his
eyes grew too heavy, wishing he'd had time to make
something for himself, but knowing he wouldn't get to
sleep until late if he did.

I wondered what it would be like to be able to cook for
him so he wouldn't have to eat out or bring cold food
home, but squashed the thought before it showed on my
face.

I carried the salads to the table and took a seat while
Paul finished the cooking. I took the time to enjoy the
moment and take in the scenery as I peeled back the cling
wrap. I could watch Paul cook all day—especially since
he was facing away from me and the sights were, shall
we say, not unpleasant—but I found myself looking out
the glass back door. A trio of bird feeders were set up at
the edge of the trees, but there were currently no birds
there now.

I could do this, I realized. If Paul's and my relationship
ever progressed and he asked me to move in, I thought I
could do it without a hint of regret. Misfit would love sitting at the back door, watching the birds and other
wildlife. He might not enjoy the two huskies, but after a
few boxed noses and some serious sulking, I bet he'd get
used to them.

More fantasies began filling my head in rapid succession. Paul, a freshly appointed detective, would come home, bringing his work with him. Together, we would sit at the table, and go over the clues and solve the crimes. There'd be no more warnings, no more frustrated sighs as he told me to lay off his investigations. We'd be a team. The town would be crime-free in months.

It would be bliss.

I jerked in surprise as Paul slid a plate in front of me. "I'm sorry it wasn't done before you got here. I tried to time it, but Ziggy was being a pest, like usual." He said it lovingly. It honestly sounded like me talking about Misfit. I loved my cat, but he could be a handful when he wanted to be.

"It's fine," I said. "I don't mind waiting."

He took the chair opposite me and we began heaping the various salads onto our plates. It was kind of strange how quickly we'd jumped to eating, without all the socializing that was usually done beforehand, but I wasn't complaining. I *was* hungry.

"Shoot," Paul said, knife poised over his steak. "I didn't ask you how you eat it. I hope medium rare is okay?"

"It's perfect."

He gave me a skeptical look, as if he wasn't sure if he should believe me. I cut into my steak and took a big bite to prove to him that I was happy with it, no matter how he cooked it. After a few moments of him watching me chew, he lowered his eyes to his own food.

We spent the next twenty minutes eating and talking about nothing. I asked him about his dogs and he inquired after Misfit and my dad. It felt like a normal, everyday kind of conversation. We were oddly comfortable with one another, despite never having a home-cooked meal together.

Like he promised, Paul cut small portions of steak and set them aside for his dogs. Once we finished eating—and I admit, I ate far more than I probably should have—he dumped the scraps into a bowl, added something from a can he kept in the fridge, and then released the hounds. This time, they paid me little mind as they rushed the bowls to scarf down the steak and whatever else he'd added to it.

"Let's go to the living room," he said, leading the way.

A grandfather clock in the corner ticked the seconds as we both sat on the couch. I leaned back, hands on my stomach.

"I think I might pop."

Paul laughed. "I'm glad you liked it."

"Liked it?" I gave him an incredulous look. "It was fantastic. The best I've ever had." And no, I wasn't exaggerating.

He reddened. "Thank Redd's Meats in Levington. I always get my meat there. The cuts are the best I've ever found, and they do more than steak. You should check it out."

"I'll do that." I made a mental note to do my meat shopping there from now on.

A beat, and then, "I heard about what happened at the library."

Buchannan must have told him. "I was trying to drop off a book and Maggie was already there harassing the Carltons with some of her friends. She destroyed my book!"

"That's what he said." Paul shook his head as if he couldn't believe someone would go so far as to destroy a perfectly good book—and it *was* a good one. "Some people have little respect for other people's property." He paused, then added, "Speaking of which, I have confirmation that Maggie Reed did indeed place those flyers on your windows. If that glue doesn't come off, I'm pretty sure you could get her to pay for any repairs you might need."

"Thanks," I said. "She didn't deny it when I mentioned it to her at the library."

"She was pretty upset when I talked to her." Paul scooted away from me on the couch. I thought that perhaps I'd said or done something wrong, but then two giant fur balls leapt onto the couch between us. After some more wet noses and smacks in the face by wagging tails, both dogs settled down on the couch for their post-dinner naps.

"You talked to Maggie?" I asked.

"I did. She demanded I bring others in for questioning. In fact, she named about a dozen people, you included."

"For what?" I paused. "Did you arrest Maggie for harassment?"

"No, but I did talk to her. She was assaulted."

"What?" My voice was a bit too loud, and both dogs jerked their heads up to look at me. "Sorry," I told them and then, at a lower pitch, "Assaulted? When? What happened?"

"Apparently, after Buchannan told her to leave the library, Maggie went straight to the school and started causing a ruckus there. She didn't break any laws, and there wasn't anyone there but the teachers since the kids are out on break, but she didn't endear herself to the few people who were there."

"How did she get in?" I asked, thinking about the

hoops I had to jump through to enter the building. Then again, it hadn't been too hard for me to talk my way past Naomi either.

"The front secretary claims she never saw Maggie enter," Paul said. "And no one else admitted to letting her in. Most said they heard her talking in the hall and closed their doors to her, as if this was something that happened often."

I thought of Sidney and what I was told about his constant badgering of the teachers by said teachers. Had Maggie done the same thing to them? If so, why didn't they mention her when I'd brought Sidney up?

"No one escorted her out?" I asked. Both the principal and guidance counselor didn't much care for me hanging around the property, but I supposed that was when there were still some students hanging around. I guess the same rules didn't apply when it was only teachers at an in-service.

"Not precisely. But she was nearly *knocked* out."

"Someone hit her?" I couldn't keep the shock from my face. I mean, I'd wanted to lash out at her, but had restrained myself.

He nodded. "Apparently, Maggie pressed the wrong buttons on the wrong person and ended up with a whole lot more than she could handle."

I mentally ran down the list of teachers I'd talked to who might have attacked Maggie. "Mr. Alvarez?" I wondered out loud.

"No. He didn't make his dislike of Ms. Reed a secret, though."

"Then who?"

I didn't expect Paul to answer, but he did. "She was attacked by a woman named Tori Carmichael. She's an English teacher at the school, I believe."

My mouth fell open. "Ms. Carmichael attacked her? But . . . She's tiny!"

Paul laughed. "She is. She's also a black belt in more than one discipline. Ms. Reed didn't stand a chance."

"Wow." I sat back, stroking Ziggy. Or was it Kefka? I couldn't tell the difference yet. "I knew she didn't like Sidney, and I suppose by extension, Maggie, but I never thought she'd attack one of them."

Paul's face grew somber. "It doesn't look good on her. Maggie is now claiming that Tori Carmichael killed Sidney Tewksbury over some sort of feud. She dragged another teacher into it as well."

"Kevin Tewksbury?" I asked, already knowing the answer. "When I ran into her at the library, she made sure to bring his name up when she was accusing me, and the rest of the world, of having a hand in Sidney's death."

"She does seem to be an angry woman." Paul sighed. "Either way, Ms. Carmichael is in some serious trouble at the moment. She attacked Ms. Reed on school property. There weren't any students present, as far as I'm aware, but parents will complain nonetheless. The school will be forced to do something, no matter how justified the assault may have seemed."

"Tori's going to get fired?" I asked.

Paul shrugged. "I can't say. But I wouldn't be surprised if she did."

I took a moment to absorb that. I didn't know much of anything about Tori Carmichael, but she didn't seem like a bad person. Then again, she *did* attack Maggie. Was it so hard to believe that she might have taken it a step too far when it came to Sidney?

I opened my mouth to bring up the website and my suspicions that it wasn't legitimately part of Maggie Reed's group of censorship champions, when Paul stood, stopping me short.

"As intriguing as all of this might be, let's not worry ourselves over assault and murder tonight," he said, holding out a hand to me.

I took the proffered hand and let him help me to my feet. "Where are we going?" I asked.

"I have a firepit. It's cold out, but I think we can find ways to keep ourselves warm."

Any and all thoughts about Maggie Reed, websites, and Sidney Tewksbury were gone, just like that.

Paul led me by the hand, out the back door, to the promised firepit. Comfortable-looking chairs were set up around it, and all the makings of s'mores were placed on a table nearby, telling me this wasn't an impromptu suggestion. He lit the fire and we spent the next couple of hours doing nothing but eating fattening foods and talking about whatever popped into our heads.

Everything but murder, anyway.

"I'd better go," I said sometime later. I had no idea what time it was, only that my wrist was really aching and the neighborhood was completely silent. All I could hear was the crackle of the dying fire and the insects in the trees.

"It *is* getting late," Paul said, looking to the sky.

"It is." I rose and was surprised by a yawn. "I need to get some sleep."

"Sleep." There was an odd lilt to his voice as he doused the fire and stood. "You know, you don't have to go quite yet." The only light streamed from the dining room behind us, yet I swear I saw Paul's eye glimmer in the dark.

"Oh?" I asked, heart suddenly thudding in my ears. "If I'm not going to sleep, then what am I going to do?"

Paul didn't answer. He merely led the way inside.

And without hesitation, or a thought of home, I followed.

15

Early-morning light stung my tired eyes as I crept toward the door. The house was silent, as were the houses next door. My Escape ticked as the engine cooled, which normally wouldn't have been noticeable, but I was trying to be sneaky here. To my semi-frazzled self, every noise sounded like it was amplified a thousand times over.

The key slid into the lock, which clicked as I turned it, and the doorknob. The door eased open with the faintest of squeaks.

The meow that followed was the sound of pure torture.

Giving up all pretenses that I could sneak into my own home, I straightened with a sigh. "Oh, all right, I'm coming."

Misfit was sitting in the kitchen, a panicked look on his fuzzy face. His bowl was empty and pushed all the way into the dining room. It had been licked clean at least twice over.

"You're not starving, you know?" I'd fed him before I'd left last night. He answered with a grumpy meow, and walked over to his dish.

I poured dry into the dish for the dramatic kitty, gave him a couple of strokes for good measure, and then I all but skipped my way to the shower.

Last night was seared into my brain. The walk of shame and a demanding feline couldn't dislodge the euphoria I was feeling. I didn't think a bomb could knock it free, though I didn't want to think too hard on that considering Sidney's podcast threat.

I cleaned up quickly and got dressed for work. I was in good enough a mood, I hardly felt the throb of my wrist, though I did take some Tylenol for the inevitable flare-up.

The doors to Death by Coffee were open by the time I arrived. Lena and Beth were busy finishing the last steps of morning setup. They each waved to me and then went right back to work as I deposited my things in the back room.

"You're looking chipper," Lena said when I returned.

"I feel chipper." I spun around the counter like a clumsy ballerina. "I'm going to head upstairs and take some inventory. You two going to be okay down here?"

"We've got this," Lena said.

Beth nodded, then shot a glance at Lena, who winked.

Since Vicki had yet to stop in, Trouble wasn't haunting the shelves, which I figured gave me the perfect opportunity to dive deep into the books. I still wanted to buy new, taller shelves, and now, I also wanted to adjust our stock. While the books were mostly organized by genre, some of it blended together in a way that made it hard to find exactly what you were looking for, which, in turn, made it difficult to determine how many books in any given genre we actually had.

Sure, the computer helped, but I've always been a hands-on type of person.

Notepad in hand, I spent the next two hours going up and down the shelves, taking a rough estimate of what we had on offer and how it all came together. I was forced to stop once to help out downstairs when the morning rush called for it, and four times more to check out a customer at the book counter, but otherwise, I was able to focus solely on inventory.

By the time I was done, I had a good idea of what I wanted to do. Our sci-fi and fantasy section was a bit spare, and I was pretty sure nearly all the Westerns we had when we opened were still there. I jotted down some notes and then stepped back to give the shelves one more good look. I was starting to see how we could reorganize without having to lose the couch and chairs. In fact, I thought there might be a way to add a few smaller chairs throughout the upstairs for readers who wanted to read somewhere not so front and center.

That done, I scribbled out a note to Vicki, since I would inevitably forget to tell her what I wanted to propose before I left, and added the notes about the books, and alterations to the remodel plan I'd made months ago, to it. I even added a question about possibly adding a local books section. While most of Pine Hills's residents didn't have anything published by big publishers, I'm sure a few had self-published a book here or there. It would be good for morale to sell their hard work, though I'd have to figure out how to do it so they got paid without breaking my own budget.

I was feeling really good as I turned to the stairs. Perhaps I'd give the books one more perusal in an hour or two, just in case another idea popped into my head. I'd just hit the top step when the door opened and Deb Foster walked in.

Her presence shouldn't have affected me, but it did. My heart did a small leap as my eyes shot over her shoulder, fully expecting to see Will follow her in.

He didn't.

Deb scanned the store, and then her eyes fell on me at the top of the stairs. She was smiling, but there was a tension to it as she made directly for me.

"Krissy," she said. "Would it be all right if we talked?"

I swallowed. "Sure."

Uncertain whether to go downstairs or let her come to me, I hesitated. Deb made the decision and ascended the three steps, and then headed for the couch. I followed after her, mentally calculating why she would come here to talk to me without Will. Whatever it was she wanted to discuss, I was afraid it wasn't going to be something I wanted to hear.

Deb took a seat in one of the chairs, perching on it like she might bolt if I reacted badly to whatever she had to say. I sat down across from her, feeling much the same way, but I did manage to lean back with an air of relaxation I didn't feel.

"What's on your mind, Deb?" I asked. And then, as casually as I could, "Where's Will?"

"He's out shopping with his mom and sister." Deb smiled fondly. "They're making him buy a swimsuit for a vacation we're planning. Did you know he didn't have one, that he actually *borrowed* it from Carl whenever they went swimming?" Carl was another doctor and one of Will's friends, like Darrin.

"I didn't." Which was probably why we'd never quite connected in a way that truly mattered.

"He acted like it was some big secret." Deb laughed and then sobered. "But I'm not here to talk about his swimsuit or lack thereof."

I wasn't sure how to respond to that, so I merely rested my hands in my lap and waited to be slapped with an accusation or a threat or something of that nature. I mean, why else would my ex-boyfriend's current girlfriend come to see me?

"Will still cares about you," she said. "I don't hold it against him. In fact, I'm happy he's not one of those guys who uses and loses women like they're replaceable. That he still cares and worries how you feel, proves to me he's someone I should hold onto."

"I agree," I said. It was the only thing I could think of to say.

"I want you to know I'm okay with it if you two are friends. I don't want there to be any hard feelings between the two of you. Between us." She reached out and touched my hand with her fingertips. "I've heard good things about you, and while I understand if you don't want to be friends with me, I wouldn't mind getting to know you better. You're an important part of Will's past, his life."

I was forced to blink rapidly to keep from bawling like a baby. "I'd like that," I said and I meant it. Will and I might have broken up, and yeah, it might not have been the most graceful of exits on his part, but I held no ill will toward him or Deb.

Deb smiled and wiped at her own eye. "I'm glad." She

stood and I joined her by reflex. "I'll let you get back to work."

Before she could go, I stopped her. "Hey, Deb?"

"Yeah?"

"I'm having a Thanksgiving dinner at my place. I know Will probably has plans with his family, but if you two find time, I'd love it if you could stop by. I'm inviting all my friends."

The smile that spread across her face warmed my heart and made me realize I was doing the right thing, no matter how awkward it might feel. "I'll bring it up to him. I hope we can make it."

"Me too."

Deb left with a friendly wave. I watched her go with a sense of rightness. Things were going to work out for all of us, I was sure of it.

The rest of the workday was thankfully uneventful. Vicki showed with Trouble and Mason in tow. I handed her my notes for the bookstore, and then waited while she perused them.

"Interesting," she said after a moment.

"Interesting good? Or interesting bad?"

She smiled. "Good." She looked toward the bookshelves. "You're right; it's time for a change, and I think this might work."

"You sure?" I asked, suddenly not so certain my math worked. "With taller shelves, our shorter customers will struggle to reach the books placed higher up."

"We'll find a way," Vicki said, handing the notes to Mason. "But for now, take care of yourself."

I raised my arm in salute—though not very high—and then I took my leave. My arm ached, but I thought it was getting better. I hoped I could lose the sling by the end of the day, if not tomorrow, because cooking a big Thanksgiving dinner was going to be difficult with only one arm. If I had to mentally force it to get better, I would.

As I climbed into my vehicle, I considered going home, but something Paul had said last night crept into my mind. Curiosity has always been a nemesis of mine, one that almost always got the better of me, as it did now. I put the Escape in gear and without much more than a quick Google to make sure I knew where I was going, I was on the way.

Tori Carmichael lived close enough to the school, she could walk to work on warm, sunny days. Her house was bigger than I expected and resided on a sprawling property that vanished over a small hill. A small fountain stood in the middle of her driveway, which was more of a roundabout in front of her house than an actual drive. The house itself was clean and well-maintained.

She can afford this on a teacher's salary?

When I'd talked to her at the school, I hadn't noticed a wedding ring, but I supposed she might not wear it at work. And it was always possible she was once married, but her husband had died, or they'd divorced and she'd fleeced him for everything he owned. Or, perhaps, her parents were rich and had given her the place as a graduation present.

I parked beside the fountain and climbed out, suddenly wary. If Ms. Carmichael was never married, and if her family hadn't left her the house or a bunch of money, I was worried there might be other, not-so wholesome reasons as to why she was living in a big house like this.

Murder for hire? It was a ludicrous thought, but after Sidney's death and her attack on Maggie, I couldn't dismiss it out of hand.

I stepped up to the front door and pressed the bell, which was one of those fancy light-up ones that had a camera built in, much like I'd seen at Kevin Tewksbury's house. Maybe it was time I invested in one. I scanned the eaves and nearby windows, searching for more cameras, or maybe a hidden turret of some kind, when the door opened and Tori Carmichael appeared. She looked me up and down before she frowned.

"What are you doing here?"

"Hi, I'm sorry to drop in unannounced. I'm Krissy Hancock, we met at the school."

"I remember."

"I was hoping we could talk."

"About?" No change in expression. No change in tone. She was annoyed, and was going to stay that way.

"You fought with Maggie Reed."

"So?"

"At the school."

She blinked once. "I repeat: So?"

This wasn't going the way I'd hoped, but couldn't say it was unexpected. "It seems strange to me a teacher would get into a fistfight with another woman at the school where students might see."

"Look, Ms. Hancock, I don't know what you're trying to accomplish here. Maggie Reed came in, ran her mouth, and I shut it for her. There were no kids around to see it, so that wasn't an issue. It's unfortunate it happened in the school, but if given the chance, I'd do it again."

"She was Sidney Tewksbury's friend."

Finally, a reaction. Tori's eyes narrowed and her jaw clenched briefly at mention of Sidney's name. "And?" Hard.

"And, don't you think it looks kinda bad that he dies

and then you attack one of his friends? I'm not saying I blame you. Maggie got on a lot of people's nerves. But the police . . ."

"They can think what they want. I refuse to let that woman come in and ruin my inner peace with her accusations."

"What sort of accusations?" I asked.

"That it was *my* fault Sidney was murdered." I could almost see the rage boiling off of her. "She all but accused me of poisoning him myself."

Did you? was on the tip of my tongue, but I bit it back. "Why would she think that?" I asked instead.

"How should I know? The woman is nuts, more so than Sidney ever was." She raised a finger and jammed it under my nose. "If it wasn't for my respect for Kevin, I would have knocked Sidney down a few pegs myself. That man deserved what happened to him, just as much as Maggie. I would never kill either of them, but honestly, I can't say I'm unhappy that someone did what I couldn't do."

I stared at her, shocked by her honesty. It's not every day someone admits to wanting another person to die. Especially when that other person actually *did* end up getting murdered.

Tori took a deep breath and dropped her hand. "I don't know what you hoped to gain by coming here," she said. "Maggie succeeded in taking everything from me, and she's still walking around, running her mouth, so I hope that's proof enough I'm not responsible for anyone's death, let alone Sidney Tewksbury's."

"I never said you were."

"You were thinking it." Quite suddenly, the fight went out of her and she leaned against the doorframe. "I've been suspended, and it's almost a sure thing I'm going to get fired. It's unfortunate and honestly, I wish none of it would have happened. She just made me so angry, and when she dragged Kevin's name into, I sort of lost it."

My ears picked up. "What did she say about Kevin?"

Tori's laugh was bitter. "That she had proof that he killed his own brother. She claimed I influenced him, though she wasn't quite specific on how I might have done that." She closed her eyes briefly, and something passed over her face that brought a whole new host of questions to mind.

Like, how well did she know Kevin? Were they more than just coworkers? If so, was it a onetime event? Or did they see each other often? And if so, how close did they get when they were together?

Those were all good, solid questions, but I settled on, "Did she tell you what proof she had?"

Tori shook her head, straightened. "I find it hard to believe she has anything more than unfounded suspicions. I never influenced him, and if I had, I would have—" She bit down on her lower lip, cutting her own thought short.

"Would have what?" I asked, a growing sense of certainty that her answer was important.

Tori didn't look like she wanted to answer. Some of the hardness came back into her expression, but it quickly dissipated, and she sagged back down. Her fight with Maggie must have taken a lot out of her.

"You have to understand; Kevin was tired," she said, sounding tired herself. "He spoke often of his brother, how he wished someone would come along and remove him from his life. He says he lost everything because of Sidney, and I believe him. If you ever saw the two of them together, you'd understand."

I thought back to my impression of Kevin Tewksbury. He didn't seem like a man grieving the loss of a close relative, which tracked with what Tori was telling me, but Kevin didn't seem vengeful either.

"Did he do something to Sidney?" I asked. I wasn't sure if I was asking if Kevin had killed his own brother, or if I meant something else.

"No, but Sidney's presence made Kevin . . ." She trailed off, shook her head. "Look . . . Check out Your Secret Man. It's a website. You'll find everything you need to know there."

16

Misfit sat under the table, watching me with an incredulous expression on his fuzzy face. My hands were on my hips as I surveyed my work. The living room looked empty. The TV and couch were still there, but I'd moved everything else out, putting it in my spare bedroom, which was now little more than a storage room.

"I think this will work." I glanced back at Misfit. He didn't appear convinced. "I'll move everything back after Thanksgiving. I need room for another table."

With a huff, my orange cat rose, swished his tail twice, and then sauntered into the bedroom where he'd pout until dinnertime.

"He'll get over it," I muttered, turning back to the living room.

A light rain pattered the windows outside, and a gloom had fallen over Pine Hills. I was doing everything in my power to keep busy and not think too much about Sidney Tewksbury's murder, but I was running out of things to do. My laptop was sitting on the counter, begging me to open it and do a little digging. I mean, what could it hurt?

"No, Krissy," I reprimanded myself. "You're going to be good and let Paul handle it."

But if I found something important, I could give it to Paul. It might help him solve the case, and then Chief Dalton would have no excuse not to give him the detective job.

I took a step toward my laptop before jerking my phone from my pocket and dialing. It rang twice before a raspy voice answered.

"Hey, Buttercup, how's it going?"

"Hi, Dad." I sank down onto the couch and spread my legs out. With no coffee table, there was more than enough space to slouch. I found I rather liked it, though I wouldn't have anywhere to put my coffee or snacks when I was lounging in front of the TV.

"Uh-oh." His chair squeaked as he lowered himself into it, telling me he was in his study, likely writing his latest mystery. "You'd better tell me."

"It's nothing. If you're busy . . ."

"No, I could use a break. What's on your mind?"

I took a deep breath, and then I told him.

It spilled out of me in waves. I told him about the Thanksgiving festival, the storm, and Sidney's death. I told him about Maggie and Kevin. About my concerns about Darrin, about anyone and everyone who even remotely connected to the case. As I spoke, I became more and more relaxed. It wasn't quite the same as actually investigating, but it did make me feel better to talk about it to someone.

"I see," he said, a thoughtful lilt to his voice. "Do you believe this Maggie woman?"

"I'm not sure. She seems pretty convinced that Kevin Tewksbury killed his brother. Tori—the other teacher— seems to agree."

"And her other accusations?"

"I think she's trying to rile everyone up for her own personal vendetta against us. She blames books for causing Sidney's death, and since I sell those books in my store, I'm guilty by association. The same goes for the library and the librarians. And it's the same when it comes to the school and the teachers. We're peripherally connected, and that makes us accessories to the murder."

"Does she have any proof that Kevin killed his brother?" Dad asked. "Or, better yet, do you have proof that any of these people are involved at all?"

"No, I wish I did. And Maggie's only proof seems to be rooted in her prejudices, not something that would ever stand up in court."

"I see." I could imagine Dad tapping his finger on his desk thoughtfully as he considered the information. "You said something about a website? Have you looked into it?"

Assuming he was referring to what Tori had told me, and not the Freedom from Filth site, I answered with a, "No. I'm kind of scared to. I don't want to get involved any more than I already am. I want Paul to get his detective's badge."

"And you're afraid you could screw it up if you poke around too much."

"Yeah." I deflated. "I should call Paul and tell him everything I've discovered and let him deal with it. He won't be happy I talked to Tori, but since I've been relatively good on this one, he can't be *too* mad."

There was a long pause where I thought Dad was considering my rationale and would drop some sort of wisdom on me that would make my path forward clear.

I was wrong.

"Things are going good between the two of you, I take it?"

It took my brain a couple of seconds to realize what he was asking. "I don't know what you mean."

Dad chuckled. "I can hear it in your voice. Before, whenever you talked about Officer Dalton, I could tell you were smitten. And when I was in town and saw the two of you together, it was as obvious as the sun on a clear day."

"I'm not *smitten*." I shifted uncomfortably. Talking about my relationships with my dad always made me feel like an awkward teenager. "We're adults doing adult things."

The pause that followed was one of the most awful moments in my life. The instant the words were out of my mouth, I knew I'd made a huge mistake.

"That's not what I meant," I said, stumbling over my words. "I mean, we—I—argh!"

Dad laughed a full-throated laugh. "It's all right. I understand."

Which was precisely the problem: I didn't *want* him to understand.

"How's Laura?" I asked, desperate to change the topic. "I haven't talked to her in ages." Laura Dresden was Dad's girlfriend, and as far as I could tell, his perfect match.

"She's good. She's in the other room if you'd like me to pass you over?"

"No, that's okay." Now that some of the embarrassment was receding, the worries were starting to climb back into my head. And here I was, talking to my dad, the one person I'd always been able to go to when things got tough. *Have they become too difficult?* I wondered, even as I said, "I was thinking . . ."

"Uh-oh. This doesn't sound good either."

"I don't know. It's not bad, but . . ." I took a deep breath. "You know how I was planning to have Thanksgiving dinner here with friends?"

"Mm-hmm."

"Well, with everything that's happened, I'm beginning to wonder if I'm making the right choice." I looked around my empty living room and tried to imagine Paul and Will and Vicki and everyone else I'd invited filling the space. "Maybe I should just cancel it and come home instead."

"You *are* home."

I almost said, "You know what I mean," but realized there was more to that statement than first blush. California had once been my home. I was born there, grew up there with loving parents, and even after Mom died, I still had Dad to look up to. It was where I went to college, where I met Vicki and Robert. In my heart, I'll always think of it as home.

But then I moved to Pine Hills and everything changed. The people here, despite my many faults, took me in and treated me like family the moment I'd arrived. Now, there was Rita and Vicki and Paul and so many others. Wasn't it time I started thinking of Pine Hills as home?

I sighed and leaned my head back.

"Listen, Buttercup," Dad said. "Things are hard, I get that. And you're worried you might be screwing things up."

"More than you can ever know."

"But that doesn't mean you should give up. Would I like to see you? Of course. But I can wait until Christmas or New Year's or whenever you decide to come this way again. I might miss having you around, but I'm thrilled that you're happy. I can hear it in your voice, see it whenever I'm around you. Have Thanksgiving dinner with your friends. It'll do you more good than you realize."

I eyed the open area in the living room. This time, when I imagined my friends packing the space, I imagined them laughing, sharing stories and drink. The thought of giving them all a day to just laugh, even if it was at my expense, would be worth it.

"You're right," I said, sitting up. "I can do this."

"Of course, I am," Dad said, the smirk obvious in his voice. "Aren't I always?"

As usual, he was.

We said our goodbyes and I rose from my slouch with a renewed vigor. Readying the house for Thanksgiving was going to be a lot of work, but I was confident it was going to be worth it.

But first . . .

I sat down at the counter and opened my laptop. If I wanted to focus on Thanksgiving, Sidney Tewksbury's murder needed to be solved. And while I didn't plan on doing all the investigating myself, I saw no reason as to why I couldn't do a little online digging. If I found something, I could pass it on to Paul. If not, then all I did was waste a little time.

My fingers hovered over the keys. The site Tori had given me, Your Secret Man, wasn't something I wanted in my browser history, but if I wanted to look into her claims that there was more to Kevin Tewksbury than just a gigantic, yet oddly mousy teacher, I would need to do it.

"Let's hope this doesn't get me put on a list somewhere," I muttered as I typed it in to a search. The website was the first on the list. I clicked it with some trepidation.

Shirtless men filled my vision, making me cognizant of the windows behind me. It was raining and Vanna wasn't next door, yet I felt exposed sitting there with so many half-naked men on my screen. I rose and spun my laptop around to face the kitchen. There was a window there that faced Jules's house, but the angle was wrong, so there was no way he could see in without putting his face to the glass.

Still feeling self-conscious, I began my search.

"*Hot men in your area,*" I read out loud, wincing at how loud my voice sounded. I read the rest silently in my head.

Not interested in a long-term relationship? Looking for a discreet meet for one hot night of passion? Look no further. Simply input in your area code and your preferences, and we'll match you with the man of your dreams. All interactions are discreet and will never be made public. You have our word.

As if I'd accept the word of an anonymous online entity. I sat back and frowned at the screen. There was no way to search for someone by name—not that I expected Sidney to use his real name here. And a quick look around the site told me I wasn't going to find a picture either.

What if Tori was lying?

It was a distinct possibility, but what reason would she

have to lie? To throw me off her trail? I mean, if she killed Sidney and feared I was getting too close, she might send me on this wild-goose chase in order to distract me. And boy, if I wasn't already infatuated with Paul Dalton, this site could be *very* distracting.

"Guess there's only one way to find out."

Feeling as if I was betraying Paul's trust, I typed in my area code and hit *enter*.

There are 829 matches within your area.

"What?" The exclamation came out as a shout. I winced and glanced toward my windows to make sure no one was spying on me or coming to check on me. I needed to narrow this down.

I found a pull-down menu where I could narrow my search to within ten miles. That chopped the list down to twenty-two men, which still felt like a lot. Apparently, there were a lot of lonely people in Pine Hills, and not all of them were looking for long-term relationships.

The next section included menus to choose what I was looking for. I sat back, pulling a mental image of Sidney from memory. I did my best to answer each question in a way that I thought would make me match up with him. It wasn't easy. Did I choose between sultry smile or tight tushy? Neither fit my image of Sidney; I didn't want it to.

I filled out the form and waited for it to narrow my results down, feeling guilty all the while. What would Paul say if he found out about this? And what if I discovered something important to his case using the site? How in the world would I ever explain why I was trolling around a dating site without making him a little suspicious?

There are 3 men in your area that match your criteria.

Below that was a list of profiles. Once more, there were no names or pictures, but at least now there was information I could use to make the best choice—one that I hoped would lead me to whatever information on Sidney that Tori was pointing me toward.

The first profile mentioned the guy was a world-caliber athlete, whatever that meant. Sidney hadn't appeared all that athletic, so I moved on to the next profile, which was more promising. This one said the guy was an intellectual and he could spend the night *showing* me what he's learned in his life. I shuddered, not wanting to imagine what *that* could mean.

The final profile was a miss since it mentioned a big-city man looking for a small-town woman. Pine Hills was most definitely not a big city, which meant candidate two was my best choice.

"Forgive me, Paul," I said as I clicked.

A congratulations screen popped up with—I kid you not—a schedule of availability. I noted that man number two had an opening for tonight at nine.

I frowned at the message. There was no way for me to know if this was actually Sidney Tewksbury's profile without actually meeting him, and well, he was dead. You'd think the site would have taken his profile down once news of his murder got out, but I supposed it was possible they'd leave it up until whatever time he'd paid for expired—I didn't believe for a second that the desperate men on the site used it for free.

What if someone knew about this and they killed him for it?

If Sidney and Maggie were dating and he was using the site to get a little something on the side, could she have killed him for it? I found it possible, considering how aggressive she'd been when we'd met. Or had he matched with someone who expected more than a one-night stand and proceeded to stalk him afterward? If that was the case, how would Tori have known about it? Then again, why would she have known about the site at all unless she used it herself?

And what if this wasn't Sidney's profile, but someone else connected to him? Someone who might have wanted to murder him, perhaps?

I needed to play this through, even if it turned out to be a waste of time.

Before I could change my mind, I chose the nine o'clock opening. I was met with a menu asking if I'd rather meet anonymously, or at my home. There was absolutely no way I was going to invite a stranger here, even if said stranger was dead, so I clicked to meet anonymously. Then a box popped up, asking for my email so the details could be sent to me, with promises that my information wouldn't be sold or used in any other way.

I started to fill in my normal email, but stopped myself before hitting *enter*. I erased what I'd typed and then opened a new tab. I made a new Gmail account, checked to make sure it worked, and then used that one instead.

See? I do learn.

As soon as I hit *enter*, my email pinged. I checked it to find the promised details.

My date with Sidney Tewksbury was scheduled for tonight at nine at a hotel simply named, Hotel. It was followed by an address and a room number. Below that was a link to donations if the date were to go smoothly.

I had a feeling there wouldn't be much of a date, not unless Sidney's ghost was still out there.

Not sure what I'd accomplished, I closed my laptop and grabbed my keys. Since I'd gone so far as to schedule the date, I figured I might as well go see if anyone showed up. Perhaps instead of Sidney's lonely ghost, I'd come across some sort of information about who or why he was using the site.

And if not, all I would lose was a few hours. It'd be a small price to pay if my little escapade turned out to yield the identity of a killer.

17

Since I had some time before I needed to be at Hotel for my date, I found myself at Death by Coffee, sipping a black coffee with a chocolate chip cookie floating in it. My hands weren't quite shaking, but they weren't steady either.

What am I doing? What if someone actually *did* show up at the hotel? What if I'd guessed wrong and a stranger who had nothing to do with Sidney Tewksbury showed, expecting me to sleep with him?

What if it turned out to be someone I knew?

Business at the bookstore café was winding down, so I had the dining area to myself. A pair of older ladies were sitting on the couch upstairs, talking about a book they'd read. Their voices were a smidge too loud, as if both of them were hard of hearing, but I was okay with that. I'd much rather focus my mind on a fictional love affair than the fake, real-life one I was about to embark upon.

The door opened and my chest clenched. Before my mind could come up with some crazy idea that Sidney's spirit was going to waltz through the door, demanding to know why I'd summoned him, Rita's voice rang out.

"I can't believe you've never been here! One of the owners is a friend of mine. She named the store after her father's books—have you ever read James Hancock? He's the best! Why, I—Krissy!"

Rita yanked on the arm of the man with her, nearly dragging him off his feet as she headed my way.

"Hi, Rita," I said, setting my coffee next the spoon reserved for scooping out the remains of the cookie when I finished with it. My eyes shifted from her, to the man she was clutching.

He was short and a little plump around the middle, but not outright fat. I'd put his age somewhere in his fifties, maybe a well-maintained low sixties. Next to Rita, he seemed excessively calm, almost sedate. His smile was friendly, if not a little embarrassed.

"Johan, this is my friend Krissy Hancock, the one I was telling you about." Without asking, she dropped into the chair next to me and motioned for Johan to take the chair opposite. "We were just talking about you, dear."

"I heard." I couldn't stop shooting glances at Johan. In all the time I'd known her, Rita had never dated, so seeing her with someone was an oddity I couldn't help but marvel at. And he seemed so . . . normal.

"Well, I figured it was high time Johan saw your place himself. I've talked about it many times, haven't I, Johan?" Before he could so much as open his mouth to reply, she carried on. "I'm glad you're here, honestly. Did you hear about what happened at the school? It's such a shame. Those poor kids having to watch their teacher attack another woman, all because of something as silly as jealousy. Can you imagine?"

"School wasn't in session, so there weren't any—wait. Did you say *jealousy*?"

Rita nodded and leaned forward. "Way I heard it, the victim confronted the teacher—what was her name?"

"Tori Carmichael."

Rita snapped her fingers and pointed at me. "That's it. Apparently, the victim—"

"Maggie Reed," I provided, mostly because I didn't like thinking of Maggie as a victim. The woman really got under my skin.

"Well, she showed up at the school and accused Ms. Carmichael of trying to steal her man, and then failing that, killed him. It's such a pity to think they got into it over a man who wasn't worth their time."

"Is it official that Sidney and Maggie were an item?" I asked. I assumed so, based on the way everyone talked about them, but I didn't think anyone had actually confirmed it.

"It's what I heard," Rita said, which wasn't much of an answer.

"I thought Tori was more interested in Sidney's brother?" It came out as a question, though it was more of a thought to myself. The way she'd spoken of Kevin made me think there was something between the two. *Could that be why she sent me to the website?* She met Sidney there and somehow, Kevin found out and killed his brother because of it?

"I don't know anything about that," Rita said. "All I

know is, the fight should have been televised. Georgina heard that they darn near tore the entire school down in their scuffle. It was as if the tension had been building for months and they were releasing their animosity all at once. If I hadn't been so distracted"—she reached a hand across the table and rested it on Johan's own—"I might have seen it coming."

"It would have been interesting to watch." Johan's voice surprised me. There was an underlying tone to that simple statement that had my skin crawling, like he would have loved to watch two women bloody each other.

Rita playfully swatted him on the arm as if she hadn't noticed. "Well, it's done and over with now."

I studied Johan, who was still smiling, though now that I was really looking, I didn't think the smile quite reached his eyes.

"It's very nice to meet you, Krissy," he said, obviously noting my stare. There was no accent to his voice, as I might have expected with his first name.

"I'm glad we've finally met," I said, not entirely sure I was actually happy about it. I wasn't getting good vibes from Johan, but that might have more to do with my mood than any malice on his part. "How long have you and Rita known each other?"

He glanced over at Rita and the smile brightened, as if he truly did care for her. "Two weeks, three days, and . . ." he checked his watch, "four hours."

"It happened so fast," Rita said. "We met and it was like those stories you read where sparks fly the moment eyes meet. I couldn't help but go over and talk to him. He was shy at first, but you know me! I wouldn't take no for an answer."

"Not that I'd ever say no to her."

They made googly eyes at one another.

I watched the exchange, my worries growing. Rita was obviously head over heels with Johan, but could I say the same for him? I knew people kept tabs on how long they'd dated, and perhaps how long they'd known one another, pre-dating, but to have it down to the hour? It seemed excessive in my book, almost *ob*sessive, in fact.

"Well, I'm glad for you," I said, breaking into their eye lock. It was starting to make me uncomfortable. "The both of you."

Rita jumped as if someone had goosed her, and then checked her own watch. "Oh, Lordy Lou, look at the time! We'd best hurry and get our coffees before you close. Here we were, gabbing away, and not a coffee in sight!"

"You're a friend," I said. "We won't kick you out if you stay a little past closing."

"No, no, dear, we really shouldn't keep you." She stood and Johan obediently followed. "I just wanted to stop in here for a quick visit before, well . . ." She grinned and leaned in closer to me, though her whisper wasn't all-too quiet. "I'll just keep that to myself."

A snap decision. "If you two aren't doing anything on Thanksgiving, I'm having a big dinner with all of my friends. You're welcome to join us."

Rita smiled in a way that told me she already knew about the dinner and had been waiting for an invitation. "We'll be there, won't we, Johan?"

His smile was just this side of creepy as he nodded. His eyes didn't leave mine until Rita guided him away from my table, to the counter to order their coffees. Even then, I could feel his attention on me, as if he had the proverbial eyes in the back of his head and he was using them to make sure I didn't interfere in whatever he had planned for Rita.

Jeff paused in the process of closing the counter down to take their order. The old ladies upstairs rose, and still talking about their book, left Death by Coffee. Rita and Johan were soon to follow, with Rita waving jovially, and Johan giving that friendly smile that was beginning to look more and more sinister the more I saw it.

I hurriedly finished off my coffee, scooped out the cookie, and ate it with a contented sigh. Once done, I gathered my things and rose. I still had a little time to kill, but didn't want to do it here where Vicki might decide to come out from the back and ask me what to her might seem like innocent questions like, "Where are you going?" or "Do you plan on doing anything exciting this evening?"

I headed for the door with a wave to Jeff, thinking that I was going to escape without having to talk my way out of an uncomfortable situation, when the bell jangled and my worst nightmare walked through the door.

"Paul!" I said, jerking to a stop. My first instinct was to flee in the opposite direction, but there was no escape that way. I was caught, though I wasn't really sure what I'd been caught doing. "What are you doing here?"

He took off his hat and smiled. "I saw your car when I was driving by and thought I'd stop in." He glanced at the counter. "Were you working?"

"No, just visiting," I said with a shaky laugh. "I was about to leave."

Paul nodded as if that was exactly what he'd expected.

Jeff slid around the counter, gave me an apologetic head bob and smile, and then he flipped the *Open* sign to *Closed*.

Both Paul and I waited until Jeff headed back around the counter to pull the register to take back to Vicki for counting before we continued our conversation.

"You worked late, I see," I said, not sure what else to say. Normally, I'd have loved to bump into Paul on my way out. I could invite him to my place, where we could watch a movie or sit and talk about our days over cups of coffee and maybe a coffee cake or that pumpkin pie I'd baked.

But now? Sweat was popping out on my brow and I had such a sudden urge to pee that I was practically dancing back and forth.

"I had some paperwork to get done, but for once, it was actually a pretty calm and quiet day."

"No more issues with Maggie Reed?"

"None that I'm aware of." He cleared his throat and spun the brim of his hat around in his hands. "I was wondering—"

"I can't!" I blurted, and then mentally smacked myself upside the head. So much for playing this cool and calm. "I mean, what were you saying?"

The questioning expression on Paul's face had me wishing I could sink straight through the floor. This was a guy who was looking to become a detective. He had to see right through my pathetic attempt to cover my embarrassment.

And what am I embarrassed about? A date with a dead guy?

"Are you okay?" Paul asked. "You're not looking too good."

"Fine. I'm fine. Why wouldn't I be fine?"

His eyebrows rose. Even I could tell I wasn't fine, but how was I going to explain to him that I was recently on a website looking up men? I mean, I wasn't actually looking for a date, and it had to do with his case, but it was just too embarrassing. And I'd promised not to get involved, which only added to the embarrassment.

"It's been a busy day is all," I said, faking a yawn. "And Rita stopped by with the guy she's dating. There's something odd about him."

"Something odd?" Paul asked. "What do you mean?"

"He's . . ." A dozen terms shot through my head, none of them kind. I settled on the tried-and-true, "Creepy."

"Creepy?" He sounded skeptical.

"I don't know. Something about him seemed off. His name is Johan." I paused, mentally calculating whether or not to ask what I was thinking, and then went for it, since it might keep Paul from asking what I was up to for the rest of the night. "Do you think you could look him up?"

"Look him up?"

I shrugged, feeling stupid. "Check into him. See if he's got a criminal record or something."

"Krissy, I can't do that."

"It doesn't have to be official," I said. "Just, like, run his name or something. I'm worried about Rita. I don't want her to get hurt."

Paul sighed and rubbed at his face. I knew I was asking a lot out of him, and honestly, if I wasn't trying so hard to keep him from asking me what I was doing that night, I might not have asked him to do it at all.

"All right," he said. "I'll see what I can do."

"Thank you!"

"But don't expect much. I'm not going to do anything illegal just because you don't like Rita's new boyfriend."

"That's okay. If you look, even a little, it'll ease my mind."

"You said his name was Johan?" he asked. "Do you have a last name?"

"No last name. Sorry." Besides, how many Johans could there be in Pine Hills? It wasn't a common name in these parts.

"I might not find anything," Paul said. "And, as I said, I'm not going to do anything illegal. Just a quick look, something you can probably do on your own."

"That's all right. Whatever you can do will help."

There was a moment where we just stared. Then, because nothing is ever easy, Paul asked, "So, do you have plans for tonight?"

I scrambled to come up with something to say that wouldn't hurt his feelings by making him think I was rejecting him. "There's work here I was thinking of doing. Not physical work, but, like, planning. You know what I mean? Shelves. Books." I sagged. "Shelving books."

Paul just stared at me. I was floundering, and we both knew it. I would have been better off if I'd just ignored him on the way to my car. Talking had only dug me a deeper hole, one that wouldn't have been there in the first place if I could have kept it together.

"I'm sorry," I said. "I didn't get much sleep last night."

"Neither did I." There was a hint of a smile, but it was buried beneath the concern. "Is there . . . Did I do something wrong?"

"No!" I reached for his hands, but instead of grabbing them, all I managed to do was knock his hat from his grip. We very nearly knocked foreheads when we both bent to pick it up. I stepped back as not to make any bigger of a fool of myself. "No," I repeated. "It's just . . ." How to explain without explaining. There was absolutely no way I was going to tell Paul was I was planning. Not only was it embarrassing, but it was dangerous. He'd insist on me canceling, or possibly invite himself along.

While both options weren't entirely a bad idea, just the thought of telling him about the website and me scheduling the meet, made me sick to my stomach. I didn't want him to think of me in that way, even if I was doing it in the name of research.

And the guy I'm supposed to meet is dead, so it's not like I expect anything to happen.

Paul lowered his head and dusted off his hat. I could see the wheels turning in his head, the questions he wanted to ask. His jaw worked briefly, and then he slid his hat back onto his head.

"Well, I suppose I'd better get home," he said. "You stay safe now, Krissy, all right?"

Like the idiot I am, I merely nodded and watched as he turned and walked back out the door. He didn't glance back, didn't hesitate. He walked the short distance to his car, climbed inside, and drove off.

The back room door opened. I didn't look to see if it was Jeff, Vicki, or someone else. I bolted for the door, torn between chasing after Paul to explain why I was acting like such a dope, even if it made him think less of me, and finding a bridge to drive off of. I got into my Escape, and very nearly gave in and chased after Paul.

But if I did that, I'd miss my date. Tori gave me the address for a reason, and the only way I was going to get to the bottom as to why, would be to see it through, even if it meant a lonely night sitting in my car.

And, hey, if something did come of it, and I slipped the information to Paul, even anonymously, he'd likely get the detective's badge and our little awkward encounter at Death by Coffee would be forgotten.

Or, so I hoped.

I pressed my forehead into the steering wheel and took deep, calming breaths. Everything would be okay. Once this was over, I could explain. We'd laugh over a cup of coffee about it, and then retire to my room. We could go on like nothing had ever happened.

But before that could happen, I needed to see this through. I started up my vehicle, put it in *drive*, and then I was on my way.

18

My eyes flickered to the digital display. I was sitting in my Escape outside the hotel where I was to meet my date. I chewed on my thumbnail as I watched the door to room 117, which hadn't opened since I'd arrived twenty minutes earlier. The hotel didn't have a real name; it was simply called Hotel. It consisted of burnt-out lights, cheap exterior, and from my own knowledge of the place, cheap interior as well.

I wasn't entirely surprised that Sidney—or whomever I was due to meet, if anyone—had set his meetings to take place here. It was out of the way, with a nearby bar in case the woman needed extra fortitude to go through with the rendezvous. It wouldn't surprise me to learn that hotel management received some sort of stipend for allowing their business to house the meetups.

A car drove past the parking lot, causing me to sink

down deeper into my seat. I was thrilled when I'd bought the orange Escape because it was a different color than what I usually saw around town, and was big enough—and bright enough—I could see it in a full parking lot.

Now, I wasn't so sure I'd made the right decision. It's hard to be inconspicuous in a conspicuous vehicle.

I watched the car roll by and breathed a sigh of relief when it didn't turn in. My nerves were jumping all over the place, and I was seriously regretting setting this whole thing up.

I could always drive away. No one had to know I was here. And it wasn't like I paid for this little get-together, nor did I have to leave anything more than an email address—one I'd made up on the spot, so I couldn't easily be tracked. I could forget this ever happened and never mention it to anyone. Ever.

I was reaching for the *start* button when another car pulled into the lot. Headlights washed over me briefly and then died away as the car's engine shut off. There were a few moments where no one moved, and I wondered if the driver had seen, and recognized, me.

I watched the car, wondering if it was a traveler looking for a place to rest, or if it was whomever I'd booked for a romantic evening. One thing was for sure: It couldn't possibly be Sidney.

What if I guessed wrong? Anyone could step out of that car. I kept coming back to the same questions: What if it was someone I knew? What if it was an employee of mine?

The car door opened and a Tewksbury stepped out.

Just not Sidney.

He'd tried to hide his identity, but I knew it was Kevin the moment I saw him unfold his seven-plus feet out of the car. His head was covered with a baseball cap pulled low over his eyes. He had a hoodie thrown on over that, further concealing his features. But, with that size, there was no mistaking him.

I scrunched down in my seat until I was looking through the steering wheel at him. He glanced around the lot, eyes briefly passing over my Escape, before he turned and headed to the office. He was inside for less than a minute before he returned, shoulders hunched, heading straight for room 117.

It looked like Tori hadn't been lying that the website connected to the Tewksburys, but I'd assumed it was the wrong one. Was it possible that Kevin's secret activities led to his brother's death?

He fumbled with the key briefly before managing to insert it into the lock of room 117. Even from this distance and with only seeing his back, I could tell he was nervous. He pushed the door open, stepped inside the room, scoured the parking lot one last time, and then he closed the door.

"Whew, okay." I blew out a nervous breath. I checked my cell phone to make sure it was fully charged and turned on before slipping it into my pocket. My purse, I tucked under the seat, out of easy view. The Escape didn't have keys like my old Focus, and for the first time since I'd gotten it, I regretted it. Keys could work as a weapon in a pinch. Tonight, I was going to be relying solely on my wits.

Certain I had everything I needed, I got out of my vehicle and pressed the keypad on the door to lock it. I had a fob, but had a tendency to press the wrong button and set off the alarm instead, so I rarely used it. I patted my pocket to make sure it was still there, figuring if nothing else, the car's alarm might serve as a distraction if Kevin were to take exception to my presence.

The walk to room 117 was as nerve-racking as the wait in my Escape. Every sound caused me to jump, thinking someone I knew would pop around the corner, already aware of where I was headed. If someone saw me and told Rita about it, she'd have it all over town—and in Paul's ear—in minutes.

I stepped up to the door, took a deep breath, and then knocked. I turned my back to the door, just in case Kevin tried to peek out before he opened it. I didn't want him to know it was me until it was too late.

The door opened a crack. "Are you her?" he asked in a whisper.

Lowering the tone of my voice to disguise it, I husked out a "Yeah."

"Come on in." Kevin stepped deeper into the room.

I pushed the door open the rest of the way and stepped inside. Room 117 wasn't much different than any other room I'd been in inside the hotel. It looked clean enough, I supposed, but it was run-down in a way that made it feel dirty. The light by the bed flickered and buzzed, making me wonder if it was a fire hazard, and a constant hum was coming from the bathroom. I kept my head down as I entered, which meant I got a good look at the stained, patterned carpet. There was no way I'd ever want to touch it with my bare skin. The stains didn't look healthy.

"Make yourself comfortable," Kevin said as I closed the door. "There's water by the bed if you're thirsty."

There was absolutely no way I was going to drink anything he offered me. I didn't think Kevin would need to drug the water, nor did I believe he was the type of man to do so, but I wasn't going to take any chances. I mean, this guy could very well have murdered his own brother. I didn't *think* he did, but what I thought mattered little when it came to reality.

I stopped in front of the bed and simply stared at it. There was a faint impression in the mattress where Kevin had sat to wait for me. One corner of the covers had been turned, exposing the white sheet beneath. Something about that made my heart start thumping in my ears, even though I had no intention of so much as nudging the bed with my knee, let alone lying down on it.

"We can do this however you want," Kevin said, moving across the room. He remained out of my line of sight, but was keeping his distance, as if he was afraid he might scare me if he got too close. "This your first time? Using the site, I mean."

I nodded.

"There's no rush, and you don't have to do anything you don't want to." His voice was soothing and kind, not like a man who would kill anyone. Then again, if all killers were screaming lunatics, it would be a whole lot easier to catch them. "If you'd like to talk, we can do that."

It's now or never, I decided. I turned to face him. "I think I'd like to talk."

Kevin froze with his mouth hanging open like I'd caught him in the middle of a large yawn. Panic flashed through his eyes as they jerked toward the door. For a second, I thought he might actually make a run for it. If he did, there was nothing I could to do stop him; he was too big.

"Please," I said, holding up my empty hands. "I just want to talk. Sit." I motioned to the bed. "I'll stand." I backed up toward the door. If he lunged for me, I wasn't sure I'd get it open before he had me, but I could at least try.

Kevin carefully lowered himself down onto the edge of the bed. He watched me the entire time, like he thought *I* might be the one to run. *Or that I might be a killer.* "What do you want?"

"Like I said: To talk."

"We could have done that at my home. We *did* do that there. It's Krissy, right?"

I didn't confirm or deny my name. I'd kind of hoped he'd forgotten it. "Do you do this often?" I asked instead. "Meet people here?"

"Do you?"

"I'm not judging," I said, once more showing him my empty hands. "I just want to understand."

Kevin snorted. "There's nothing to understand. Look at me. Do you think it's easy for someone like me to get dates? I'm too tall for many, too out of shape for others. Too old. Too bald." He sighed as he touched his scalp. "Is that what you wanted to hear?"

Guilt seeped through me, but I held strong. Kevin was lonely and, apparently, had low self-esteem. I wasn't making things any better by dragging him out here for an interrogation. *Not that I'd expected him to be the one to show.*

"No," I said, gently as I could manage. "I want to know what happened to Sidney."

Confusion distorted his features. "Sidney? What does he have to do with me coming here?"

"That's what I'm trying to find out. In fact, I thought when I booked this meet, it tied back to Sidney somehow. Not you."

Kevin opened his mouth, but suddenly looked away without saying anything.

"What is it?" I asked.

"Nothing." He rose. "You should go." He glanced at me out of the corner of his eye. "Unless you want to . . . ?"

"No. I'm not going anywhere"—*or doing anything*—"not until you tell me what you know."

"I don't know anything!" Kevin said, dropping heavily onto the bed. Something underneath crunched, like he'd broken the frame or the box springs. He didn't seem to notice. "I came here because I have no one else and this allows me to get close to someone without commitment. Sidney had nothing to do with that."

"He didn't know about your . . ." I struggled to come up with a word to describe whatever this was, and failed, so I let it hang.

Once more, Kevin opened his mouth as if to say something, but he closed it before he could.

"He did, didn't he?"

Kevin's shoulders sagged. "He found out."

"I take it he didn't approve?"

He laughed. "No, he most definitely did not." Kevin rubbed at his face with his big hands. I noted two of his fingers were tipped in ink. A broken pen during grading? "It's complicated."

"Sidney seemed pretty conservative in his views," I said. "I can see why he wouldn't approve of you sleeping around with strangers you found online."

Kevin winced as if I'd slapped him. "It's not that. I mean, in some ways, yeah, he didn't approve, but there was more to it than that."

I waited for him to go on, but he seemed content to leave it at that. I wasn't. "What was it, then?"

Loud voices came from outside the door. Both Kevin and I tensed, as if we both feared that whoever was out there was going to waltz right in and catch us together. The voices passed by the door, and then faded as the men continued down to a room farther down the line.

"Kevin," I said, voice gentle. "Tell me what you know. If there's a chance it might have led to your brother's death, I can help."

"It's hard to be a teacher, you know?" he said instead of answering me straightaway. "You have to behave a certain way, even on your own time. Want to go out for drinks? Well, you'd better keep it to one lest you get a bit tipsy and a parent sees you having a good time and complains to the board. Want to see a scary movie? Again, be careful or a student might see you during the inevitable shower scene and think you're enjoying it a tad too much."

Kevin started to rise, then dropped back down as if he didn't have the energy to move. "As a teacher, your life isn't your own. I couldn't go on dates like a normal person because if someone saw me, it would be all over the school by the next day. Then a parent would call in and complain, even though it's none of their business what I do with *my* free time."

"It sounds rough."

"It is." He sighed. "Do you know how hard it is to find someone when you can't go out without your every move being scrutinized? And then to have Sidney following me around, hounding me to 'clean up my act' as he put it; it was too much. I signed up for the site because it's anonymous and I could let myself go for an hour or two."

"But what if a parent showed up?" I asked, genuinely curious. Pine Hills wasn't a big city where you could go months without seeing someone you knew. The same people came in and out of Death by Coffee every day. I might not know all of their names, but I recognized a lot of the faces.

"The nature of the meeting is enough to keep most people quiet," he said. "You'd be surprised how many married women show up for this sort of thing. If they outed me to the school, then they'd reveal their own infidelity. It's not a perfect solution to a complicated problem, but it allows me to get out for a little while. And, yeah, I enjoy the company, even if all we do is talk."

"Do a lot of women just want to talk?" I asked.

"More than you'd think." Kevin allowed himself a smile. "Sometimes, that's all any of us need; someone to listen, to talk to. It was my getaway, the one safe place where I could be me."

"But then Sidney found out. How?"

The smile on Kevin's face twisted to a near-scowl. "About a month before Sidney died, I had a get-together scheduled for here. I followed the same pattern as always, kept everything secret and my identity hidden, but this time, when I arrived, I found Maggie Reed waiting for me."

I blinked. "Maggie Reed came here? She used the site?"

"Apparently. I don't know if she'd somehow hacked the system or if someone told her about my profile, but she was here when I arrived. When I first saw her, I thought she was surprised, but if she was, she covered it quickly. She . . ." He thought about it before answering. "She threatened me."

I remained silent for a couple of minutes as I tried to mentally put the pieces together. Maggie was seeing Sidney. Kevin goes on anonymous one-night stands with women, and Maggie turns up at one of them. Now, she's connected to both of the Tewksbury brothers. Awkwardly connected.

But there was another person involved, one who didn't seem to fit.

"How is Tori Carmichael connected to all of this?"

"Tori? She's not."

"She told me about the site. I thought she meant that Sidney used it, but I see that's not the case. She was referring to you." I paused, wondering if telling Kevin that Tori was the one who outed him would make him go after her. Or, if nothing else, if it might ruin their friendship. "She's worried about you," I added to soften the blow.

"We . . ." Kevin frowned and shook his head. "I don't know what we are. Friends? Colleagues? She knows what it's like to be a teacher. She's suffered the same way I have, possibly even more so since women are held to a different standard. And, yes, we've spent some time together to kill the loneliness, but she's never used the site as far as I'm aware."

"She knew about it."

Kevin's sigh was resigned. "Maggie. She must have told her."

"Why would she do that?"

"Because she's a—" He bit off whatever he was about to say. It took him a moment to realign his thoughts. "Maggie told Sidney about meeting me here, but she changed the story, making it seem like I'd sought her out and invited her. She claimed she'd come just to gather proof." He shook his head. "As if I wanted to have anything to do with her."

"Did he believe her?"

"Of course, he did. Sidney wanted to think the worst of me, and she gave him an excuse to do just that. He'd do anything for her, believe anything she said. If Maggie strode out into the middle of the street and started shooting up the place, Sidney would say it was justified." He paused. "He would have, if he were still alive."

It made me wonder about Maggie's motives. She went around town trying to censor everything she could, yet she shows up here to meet what she thought would be an anonymous man she didn't know? It didn't fit. She must have known what to look for on the site and picked him out specifically, just like I had.

I looked at Kevin and tried to picture him as a killer. He was oppressed in ways most people never experience, but he was still a free man, capable of making his own decisions. If Sidney tried to force him to stop seeing women on the side, could he have snapped?

It made sense as long as you didn't consider the fact that poison was used as the murder weapon. And that it had happened publicly.

Could the poison have been meant for Maggie? Kevin knew she'd tell Sidney about meeting him here, and she could have told the school, which likely would have gotten him fired. It would make sense for him to go after Maggie, not Sidney.

"Please, go," Kevin said, cutting into my internal debate. "I need time to think."

I wanted to press him, but decided it best to give him the time he needed. If he was debating on whether or not to strangle me with those massive paws of his, I'd much rather he decided to do it after I'd left so that he would never get the chance.

"I'm sorry," I said. I didn't know what I was apologizing for, but Kevin seemed to accept it nonetheless.

Kevin remained seated as I slipped out the door and hurried back to my Escape. Did I learn anything important on my little escapade? I wasn't sure. Sidney was dead—that couldn't be denied—but could his brother have done it because Sidney had found out about the website? Or was Sidney's death an accident?

If Kevin was the killer and if Maggie had been his intended target, then she was likely still in danger.

19

The phone rang for what felt like an eternity before it went to voicemail. I considered leaving a message, but I wanted to talk to Paul face-to-face, so I clicked off, keeping my eyes on the road. I'd barely slept after my visit with Kevin in the hotel room, and after struggling with myself through my morning routine, I'd finally given in and called Paul, but to no avail.

Sunlight gleamed off the moisture left over from an early-morning rain. There was hardly a cloud in the sky, but the temperature had plummeted. I was wearing my coat instead of my jacket, and had a feeling that Death by Coffee would be jumping thanks to the colder weather. If nothing else, it would keep my mind off how my last conversation with Paul had ended.

I parked a short distance from the store, wanting to leave the better parking spots for guests who might not want to walk the distance for their morning warm-up. I climbed out of my Escape and stretched, careful not to move my right arm too much, lest it start aching again. I was feeling minutely better, and hoped that I could lose the sling completely in another day or two.

It wasn't until I finished stretching and started down the sidewalk that I saw what was happening outside the store.

"Hey!" I called, quickening my pace. "Hey, stop!"

The hunched figure didn't bolt. Even with a heavy jacket with a hood covering her features, I already knew who it was.

Maggie Reed turned to face me with a sneer. Her bottom lip was slightly swollen and a healing cut split it into two. She had a black eye and a scrape across her right cheek. I couldn't say I felt sorry for her.

"What do you think you're doing?" I demanded, even though I knew exactly what she was doing. The flyers weren't completely stuck to the windows yet. The slight breeze caused them to flutter, but whatever superglue she was using had already dried enough to hold them in place.

"I'm warning the public about you."

"About me?" I came to a stop, slightly winded from the short jog. I really needed to get more exercise. "I'm not the one going around harassing people."

"Harassing?" She laughed. "I'm doing my civic duty here. I have every right to protest the filth you're providing. The sidewalk is a public space, so you can't claim I'm trespassing."

"No, but you don't have the right to deface my property," I said. "And what about *my* freedoms? Or don't you care about anyone but yourself?"

I took a deep breath to calm myself before I started shouting. My nerves were already taut and finding Maggie outside Death by Coffee nearly snapped them. No wonder Tori slugged her one.

"Look," I said, "I'm not trying to upset you by carrying books my customers will enjoy. I'm also not showing up at your place of business or home and accusing you of anything. All I'm asking for is a little respect here."

"Respect?" She snorted and then winced, since it must have hurt. "It's because of you the police showed up at the library. You're the reason that teacher attacked me. And it's because of you and your books that Sidney was killed. If you learned to respect my beliefs, then you'd change so nothing like that ever happened again."

It took all my self-restraint not to take a swing at her. The motion would likely hurt me more than it would her, but it would be satisfying nonetheless. "I had nothing to do with Buchannan showing up; that was all you. And I wasn't even *at* the school when you got into the fight. How is any of this my fault?"

Maggie took an aggressive step toward me. I refused to back down, which brought her up short. A surprised look passed over her face briefly before it vanished and was replaced by her usual sneer.

"You're trying to turn everyone against me," she said. "Sidney was right about you and your kind. Your mind is corrupted by the media and you spread your ignorance to others around you. And look what happened? Sid died and you continue to pander your filth. I *will* put a stop to it."

"Yeah?" I asked, puffing up my chest. My wrist throbbed in anticipation of striking out. Sprain or not, I'd had just about enough of her. "Tell me, how does your use of a website promoting one-night stands with anonymous men fit in with your ideology?"

The shock that splashed across Maggie's face should have been gratifying, but I just wanted this to be over.

"Please, stop trying to preach at me," I said. "You're not as innocent as you try to make yourself out to be. Did Sidney find out about your attempted dalliance? Did you kill him for it?"

"How *dare* you?" Maggie said. "Sidney and I—" She snapped her mouth closed, jaw working, but she never got to say whatever hateful thing that was zipping through her head.

"Is there anything I can assist you two ladies with?"

Paul's voice cut straight through my anger. I took a step back from Maggie and made an effort to look far more composed than I felt.

"There's no problem here, Officer," Maggie said, never taking her eyes from me. "I was just leaving."

Paul was in full uniform and was holding himself like . . . well, like a cop. He stood at the edge of the sidewalk, thumbs tucked into his belt like a sheriff in a Western. He watched as Maggie walked over to an old Jeep and climbed inside. She shot each of us an ugly glare before speeding off.

"Thanks, I—hey, wait!"

Paul stopped halfway back to his cruiser. "I've got some work to do, so I can't stick around."

He didn't *sound* angry with me, but there was an edge to his voice I didn't like.

"I'm sorry about last night," I said, not caring that Pine Hills was starting to wake up and there were other people appearing on the sidewalk. Soon, guests would be expecting their coffees and I had yet to go inside to get the pots percolating, but they could wait. "I didn't mean to upset you."

Paul smiled, yet it was somehow sad. "I know. I'll talk to you later, all right?"

I dropped my head. I didn't have any fight left in me. "Yeah. Okay."

Paul opened his car door, but didn't climb inside right away. "I almost forgot to tell you. I found out who hit your vehicle."

My head snapped up. "Who?"

"Guy's name is Irving Barrow. His insurance company should be calling you sometime today or tomorrow."

"Irving Barrow?" I repeated, unable to believe it. "The guidance counselor at the school?"

"The same." Paul's face grew serious. "I expect you to explain to me why you were at the school in the first place. But not now. I'm not kidding when I say I have stuff to do. I'll talk to you later." He climbed into his car. "And Krissy?"

"Yeah?"

"Don't go looking for this guy, all right? Let the insurance company handle it."

The word *but* was on my lips, but I swallowed it back. "Okay."

Paul didn't look convinced, but he didn't press. He closed the door, started his car, and drove off without so much as a goodbye wave.

Work for the next few hours was a blur.

I tried to focus, but my mind kept drifting back to my talk with Kevin in the hotel room, as well as Paul's revelation that Irving Barrow had hit my Escape. And then there was Maggie and her flyers and accusations. It was all weighing me down, and no matter how much I wanted to put it all behind me, I couldn't.

Sidney's death had ruined my mom's apple cider. It had torn the Tewksbury family apart, had likely cost Tori Carmichael her job. Maggie was now acting out far more aggressively than she once had. And Darrin was acting strange, and was possibly withholding evidence from me.

"You all right?" Lena asked once we slowed and I had a chance to breathe. "You seem distracted."

"I'm okay." I rubbed at my back, which was hurting almost as much as my wrist. "It's been a pretty crazy couple of days."

"Tell me about it." She glanced up into the bookstore where Mason was measuring the shelves, the walls, and pretty much everything he could. "How long before the remodel happens?"

"Actually, I don't know," I said. I almost went upstairs to ask Mason, but decided I didn't have the energy for it. I changed the subject instead. "Hey, do you remember a teacher named Kevin Tewksbury?"

"Mr. Tewksbury? Yeah, why?" It took her a moment, but then her eyes widened. "Wait! Wasn't the dead guy's last name Tewksbury? They're related?"

"Brothers."

"Wow." She leaned back against the counter and swiped her purple hair back from her eyes. "It never occurred to me."

"What did you think of Kevin? Mr. Tewksbury?"

"He was all right," Lena said. "He sometimes droned on, and tended to play favorites every now again."

"Favorites?" I asked.

"Smart kids always got the attention. Girls most of all."

"Do you think he was . . ." Even though I knew he dated Beth after she was fresh out of high school, I couldn't finish the thought. It was just too icky to think about.

"Nah. Mr. Tewksbury wasn't like that. He might have given them bonus points or whatever, but he didn't seem like a creep to me." She frowned. "Why? Did something happen?"

"No," I said, not wanting to ruin her opinion of the man by calling out his nighttime activities. If he was eventually convicted of his brother's murder, then he'd have ruined it himself. "I was just wondering." Though I did want to talk to Beth about him again, but privately.

Lena didn't look convinced, but she let it go. "I hope they find the person who killed that man. I keep wondering if I might have seen something."

"Have you come up with anything?" I asked. "Like, do you remember seeing him with someone when he bought his drink? Or perhaps afterward?"

"I wish I did. Jeff might know more since he was the one who served him. If I'd known he was going to up and get killed, I would have paid more attention."

"That's all right." At this point, I was sick of thinking about Sidney and his death, so I changed the subject yet again. "How was your thing with Zay the other day?"

Lena grinned and then slowly drifted toward the back. "Thing? What thing? I have absolutely no idea what thing you're talking about."

"I'll find out!" I called after her as she vanished into the back room, likely to work on some of the dishes and restock the cookies since the display was looking a little bare.

As I got to work scrubbing down tables and getting the place ready for the next rush, I turned my mind to my Thanksgiving dinner. It was stressful to think about, but it didn't involve someone dying, and right then, that's exactly what I needed.

My guest list was already looking rather full, but I found myself considering asking if Lena might want to show up with Zay. Not only would it tell me something about their relationship, it felt like the right thing to do. Of course, if I kept at it, I'd end up with the entirety of Pine Hills crammed into my house.

Mason finished up with his measurements and went back into the office to crunch some numbers. He was better at that sort of thing than me, so I was happy he was taking the initiative. If left up to me, it would never get done. I got good ideas every now and again, but I often struggled to follow through with acting on them.

I didn't have the same problem with my bad ideas. That was something else to think about later.

Jeff and Beth both arrived a short time later, but before I could ask either of them about what they might know of the Tewksburys, we picked up again and I spent the next hour and a half solely focused on making sure I was filling orders correctly. And by the time it was all done, my entire body ached, and all I wanted to do was go home and have a nice, long soak in the bath.

I grabbed my things and, with a round of goodbyes, I headed for the door. It was a testament to how stressful the day had been that I didn't think of Paul at all, right up until the moment I ran into him on the way out.

And I do mean *into* him.

"Oh!" I said, stars bursting in my vision at the pain in my wrist. It took me a moment to speak without screaming. "I'm sorry; I didn't see you coming in." I really needed to pay better attention to where I was going.

"No, it's my fault," Paul said. He picked up his hat, which had fallen from his head at our collision. "I wasn't watching where I was going." He paused, took in my disheveled state and gathered purse and coat. "You're done for the day?"

"I am," I said, some of the trepidation about the state of our relationship returning. "You?"

"Still on duty," he said with a faint smile. "Thought I'd stop in for a coffee and a little chat if you had the time."

As much as I wanted the bath and perhaps a nap, I wanted to be right with Paul even more. "I'd like that."

Before we could head inside, however, fate intervened, and his phone rang.

"One sec," he said, glancing at the screen. "I've got to take this."

I nodded and stood just outside the door as he wandered off a few paces to talk to whomever had called. He didn't say much, though his smile did slip, and then finally faded completely away. He glanced at me twice during the brief conversation and from his expression, he knew I wasn't going to like whatever it was that was being said.

After less than a minute, he clicked off and shoved the hat back onto his head. He returned to where I was waiting and before he could speak, I did.

"You've got to go."

"Something's come up," he said.

"And it can't wait." It was a statement of fact, but he answered anyway.

"No, it can't." He looked torn, like he was seriously considering shirking his duty and staying here instead of taking care of whatever it was that was dragging him away.

"Go," I told him with a playful shove on the shoulder. "I can wait. Besides—" I lifted my sprained wrist—"I could use some rest after the day I've had."

He still didn't look convinced, but he nodded. "All right. Will you be home later?"

"All night."

"Mind if I stop by?"

A dopey grin spread across my face. "Not at all."

"All right. I'll be there at six, seven at the latest."

"I'll be waiting."

Paul hesitated as if he had something else he wanted to say, and then he turned and walked to his cruiser, which was parked in the same spot where he'd parked it earlier when he'd chased Maggie off.

This time, when he pulled away, he did so with a wave.

20

The bottle rattled as I shook it back and forth. The pills inside appeared to be normal, though I had yet to actually hold one in my hand to know for sure. Even though it had been hours since I'd left work, I was still aching from head to toe, with my wrist being the worst culprit. Paul was due within the next hour and I didn't want to be dealing with my pain while talking to him.

Darrin is a good man. The thought kept repeating in my head. He wouldn't poison me. And even if he did decide to get rid of me, he wouldn't do it in such an obvious way.

It took some work, but I managed to pop the cap off without twisting my wrist too much. Maybe my sprain *was* getting better. I shook two pills into my palm and, without thinking too hard about it, I chased them down with a full glass of water.

So far, so good.

My stomach was churning from both hunger and worry, but I didn't think I could eat anything until after I'd talked to Paul. I wanted to say all the right things this time, to heal any damage I'd caused by blowing him off in such a questionable way. I paced my kitchen, muttering to myself. Misfit watched me from the hall, tail swishing in time with my steps.

My phone rang, causing me to start, and Misfit to bolt for the bedroom. I snatched my cell from the counter and thinking it might be Paul calling, swiped *accept*.

"Hello? Paul?"

"No. It's Irv Barrow."

It took my brain a moment to process that information. "Irv?"

"That's what I said."

I sank down onto a stool, nerves hopping. "Sorry. I wasn't expecting your call. I was told I'd be hearing from your insurance company."

"I didn't contact them."

"What? Why not? Officer Dalton said you hit my car."

"That's what he says."

"Are you saying he's wrong?"

Irv sighed. "I'm calling because I want to bring this situation to a close. Can you meet me at four tomorrow? My home?"

"I, uh . . ." My mind raced as I tried to figure out what he was trying to accomplish. The man had hit my car. The insurance would pay for it, but would ding him on his rates. It was possible he wanted to pay in cash to avoid that ding, though why he'd want to deal with it at his home was beyond me.

No, it's not. I barely knew him, but was already aware that Irv Barrow liked to be in control. And what better way to control the situation than to take care of it on your own territory.

"Ms. Hancock, please," Irv said when I didn't respond. "There's no need for this to get ugly. We can discuss details when you get here." He rattled off his address. "Four sharp. I have things to do, so be on time."

"Sure. All right. I'll be there."

"Good." He clicked off.

I sat back with a frown, nearly tipping over backward since my stool didn't have a back. Now that I was thinking about it, maybe going to see Irv in person wasn't such a good idea. If he'd hit my car on purpose, what made me think he wouldn't hit *me* in the same way?

"He's a school guidance counselor, Krissy," I reprimanded myself. He might not be friendly, and might have sided with an ultraconservative murder victim who'd made a nuisance of himself around town, but that didn't mean he was going to physically harm me. I couldn't say the same about a possible verbal assault, but I could handle that.

I typed in an alert to remind myself of the meeting and then set my phone face down on the counter. After some debate, I went ahead and put on some coffee, figuring that when Paul got here, it would be nice to have with pumpkin pie.

Twenty minutes later, the coffee was long done, the pie waiting, and Paul had yet to arrive.

And I was feeling about a thousand times worse.

"Come on, Paul, where are you?" I glanced out the window through squinted eyes. The world shifted slightly, wobbled, and then came back into focus. I shook my head, paced away, and the floor seemed to dip. I steadied myself on the counter and lowered my head. Maybe waiting to eat hadn't been such a good idea.

I'm not sure how long I just stood there breathing. I felt not just dizzy, but sick to my stomach. At least my pains were a distant memory, though if I moved the wrong way, my wrist still flared up. The pills were doing their job and—

The pills!

A sudden fear gripped me as I snatched them from where I'd left them. I tried to read the label, but my vision wasn't cooperating. It was either that, or my language processor was on the fritz. *What had he given me?*

There was a knock at the door, which caused me to jump. With the pill bottle clutched in my hand, I hurried over as quickly as I dared in my loopy state and jerked it open. I was about to thrust the bottle at Paul when my brain finally registered that it wasn't Paul who was standing on my front stoop.

"Robert?" I asked, not entirely convinced I wasn't seeing things.

"Hey, Kris." He slouched his way through the door without an invitation. "Sorry about dropping in on you again, but I wasn't sure where else to go."

"What happened?" I closed the door and pocketed the pill bottle before leaning against the wall so I wouldn't fall.

"It's Trisha." His sigh was dramatic. "I'm trying to be patient, but I'm starting to wonder if she might be seeing someone else."

"You think she's cheating?"

He shrugged and plopped down onto the stool at the counter like he owned it. "I don't know. She's been secretive the last couple of days, and whenever I bring up the proposal, she changes the subject."

"That doesn't mean she's cheating, Robert." And he should know, considering his history.

"Yeah, I guess so." He looked up at me with puppy-dog eyes. "Could you talk to her for me?"

I just stared at him.

"I know it's a big ask," he said. "But I figure you might be able to get a straight answer out of her. If she isn't interested anymore, then, well, we could both move on with our lives. There's no sense in us dragging this out if we don't have a future together."

"I barely know her," I said, and that was the truth. I didn't even know her last name. "I don't think it's my place to talk on your behalf, considering we once dated."

"Yeah, I know, but I can't take it anymore. Please. Do this for me and I promise to stay out of your hair for good."

I didn't believe that in the slightest, but I found I felt for him. Maybe it was how the drugs were making me loopy, or perhaps it was because I wanted him out of there before Paul arrived, but my not-so-hard-line stance wobbled and then fell away before I could beg off.

"All right," I said. "I'll talk to her."

"Great!" Robert popped up from his stool, his entire demeanor changed. He was grinning from ear to ear, and had a bounce in his step that told me I'd fallen for yet another patented Robert Dunhill production. "When?"

"I don't know. I'll figure it out and let you know. For now, I'm expecting someone—"

"It's gotta be soon," Robert said, cutting me off as if I hadn't been speaking. "Like Thanksgiving soon. There's something I want to ask her, but it can't wait until afterward."

"Fine," I said, just wanting him out of there. "Thanksgiving works. I'm having a get-together here. You can bring her and I can talk to her then."

Robert beamed. "Fantastic. I'll get it set up. We were just going to have a quiet meal together since neither of our families live in town, and we didn't want to travel. A party with friends sounds great."

I was already regretting the invite, but what's done is done. I was definitely blaming Darrin's pills on that one.

"Okay, good," I said. "Now, if you'll—"

A knock at the door cut me short. With a groan, I answered, already prepping an explanation for Paul.

"Hey, Krissy. I'm sorry to stop by unannounced like this."

"Will?" He stood outside my door, alone, with shoulders hunched as if against a blow that didn't come.

"I just need a minute of your time, if that's all right. It's about Deb." His gaze flickered over my shoulder. "Unless you're busy, that is."

"No, come in. I don't have long, so it'll have to be quick."

Will entered and I held the door open, expecting Robert to leave, but he just stood there, watching Will with a wary eye. I made a frustrated sound, but since he wasn't leaving, I simply closed the door. The faster Will said what he had to say, the faster the both of them could get out of there so I could have the place alone with Paul.

"We can't come to Thanksgiving," Will said as soon as

I turned to face him. "I know Deb said we could make it, but I just don't think it's appropriate."

"I'm going," Robert said, puffing his chest out like it was some big accomplishment.

"Half the town is coming," I said, shooting him a glare before turning to Will. "Why wouldn't it be appropriate?" I asked him. "We are no longer dating and we've both made peace with that, right? I invited her because you are my friend, and I'd like it if she was too."

"You don't think it'll be weird?"

"No, why would it be?"

"Deb has insisted we go. She's got my mom on her side too."

Good ol' Maire. One of these days, I was going to have to buy her a gift for everything she'd done for me. "Then come. Even if you can only stay for dinner, it'll be nice to have everyone together at the same time. Vicki and Mason will be here. Rita too. And so will Paul, and Jules, and Lance."

"And me," Robert added.

"Everyone," I finished. "There's room for you in my life too."

Will nodded slowly. "If you're sure we won't be in-truding . . . ?"

"You won't be." I took a step back, intending to go for the door to usher both Will and Robert through it, but vertigo struck me just as I went to move. I staggered as the floor seemed to turn briefly vertical and the walls moved horizontal.

Will shot forward and steadied me before I could fall. Even after I'd regained my balance, he kept his hand on my arm.

"I'm fine," I said, squeezing my eyes closed to make the spinning stop. "Just a little woozy."

"What happened?" he asked, guiding me over to my couch. I didn't so much sit as fall into it. "Is it your wrist?" He began gently examining my sprain.

"No. Well, kind of. I haven't eaten today, so that probably doesn't help."

"No, it doesn't," he said, some of the doctor coming into his voice.

"And I took the pills Darrin prescribed me." I tried to reach into my pocket to remove them, but with the way I was sitting, I couldn't easily get to them, especially since my pocket appeared to be dancing along my leg.

Will watched me flounder a moment before he plucked the bottle from my pocket for me. He examined the label and then set them aside. "You are to take these with food."

"I know. I wasn't hungry."

"Then you shouldn't have taken them at all. Did you follow the prescribed dosage?"

"Sure. Just two." Though, now that I thought about it, I wondered if I'd read it wrong. I tried to rise, but Will kept me sitting. "I'm fine. I'll eat something and I'm sure I'll feel better afterward. It's been a long couple of days."

Will didn't look convinced.

Robert, on the other hand, seemed to have grown disinterested. He shrugged and walked away, toward the door. I hoped that meant he was finally leaving.

"Do you think Darrin would try to poison me?" I asked, turning my attention back to Will. "He had a history with the guy who was murdered. And I was asking questions of him and about him, and well, since he knows poisons—"

"Don't even think it," Will said. "Darrin would never do something like that." He glanced back at the pill bottle. "He wouldn't prescribe something dangerous to you and think he could get away with it, even if I believed, for a second, he might want to."

"Get away with what?"

Both Will and I looked up to find that Robert had returned.

He wasn't alone.

"Paul!" I struggled to my feet with some assistance from Will. "You're here."

"What's going on?" he asked, gaze flickering from me, to Will, and then to Robert, before finally settling on me. "Krissy, are you all right?"

"Peachy," I said, though I felt anything but. "I can explain about these two." I waved a hand toward Will and Robert, which nearly sent me off-balance again. "They're coming to Thanksgiving."

"Which is still a few days away," Paul said, speaking slowly, as if to an obstinate child. He then turned to Will. "Who is trying to get away with what?"

"She thinks Darrin—Dr. Crenshaw—might have poisoned her," Will said. "I think she's having a reaction to her pain meds. They're making her dizzy, and it's causing her to imagine things."

"I'm not imagining anything!" I said. "Darrin knew Sidney."

"They were friends?" Paul asked.

"No, he was his doctor." I frowned. "Darrin was Sidney's doctor, not the other way around."

Will gave Paul a pointed look.

"Let's all sit down so we can talk about it," Paul said, motioning toward the couch. I thought it was a fine idea because I wasn't so sure I could remain upright for much longer.

Will helped me back to the couch and we all arranged ourselves around the room, with Paul joining me on the couch. He rested a hand on my shoulder and I leaned into it. If we were alone, I might have dozed off, but since Robert and Will were there, I made an effort to appear alert.

"Okay, explain," Paul said.

Not sure where to start, I just started talking, bouncing around the timeline and saying whatever came to mind. I told Paul, and by extension, both Will and Robert, about my concerns about Darrin's connection to Sidney, about Tori and Maggie and Kevin. I brought up the podcast and the website and the books. Finally, I told Paul about my visit with Kevin.

"I'm so sorry," I said. "I didn't mean to upset you, but I didn't know how to tell you about it. I just wanted to see if anyone would show up, and was surprised when it was Kevin."

"It's all right," Paul said, though I could tell it bothered him. "You're okay now."

"She should eat something," Will said. "And soon."

"I'll make sure she does." He rose and turned his attention to both Will and Robert. "If there's nothing else . . ."

I remained seated, face buried in my hands as Paul showed the other two out. They all spoke quietly at the door for a good couple of minutes before Paul returned to my side.

"Let's get you something to eat."

He guided me from the couch to the counter, where I plopped back down and resumed my embarrassed face-in-hands posture.

"I should have told you," I said, voice muffled by my palms. "I feel so stupid."

"It's all right. You did what you thought was right."

"I did. And I knew you wouldn't approve."

"Of you going to meet with a stranger, who turned out to be a man who might have killed his brother, at a location that was out of the way, without telling anyone that you were going? Why wouldn't I approve?"

I dropped my hands to find Paul smiling at me. "It wasn't very smart, was it?"

"Not at all." He pushed a peanut butter sandwich my way. "You need to do some grocery shopping. This is all I could manage to throw together quickly."

"There's pie," I said, even as took a bite of the sandwich. I knew it was my imagination, but after only one bite, I felt a thousand times better. "So, what do you think?" I asked once I swallowed.

"About?"

"About Darrin? Maggie and Kevin?"

"I'm not sure what to think," he said. "I don't believe Dr. Crenshaw has anything to do with the murder, but I can't rule it out entirely."

"And the others?"

Paul rested a hand on my own. "How about we not talk about murder tonight?"

The next bite of my sandwich didn't go down quite as easily as the last. "What do you want to talk about?"

"Anything, just as long as it doesn't have to do with the investigation. We can make a night of it."

"An all-nighter?" I asked, mischief coming into my voice.

"Someone has to keep an eye on you to make sure you don't have any further reactions to your pain meds. Besides," he said, "there's pie. What more could a man ask for?"

21

"I looked into that guy you asked me about."

"Hmm?" Even though I was staring right at him, I jerked in surprise when Paul spoke. "Who?"

"Johan Morrison. Rita's new guy."

I sat up straighter. We were sitting at my table, coffee and bagels between us. I'd have been content staring at Paul's face, wondering how in the world I'd ever gotten so lucky, for hours more, but talking worked too.

"What did you find?"

"Not a lot, to be honest." Paul sipped at his coffee before plucking a chunk of bagel from the whole, rather than biting it off. He popped it into his mouth.

"That's a good thing, right?"

"Not always. Now, as I already told you, I can't go digging into the guy like I could if he was suspected of a crime."

"I know."

"And I can't interrogate him. Nor am I going to go to Rita to ask her what all she knows about him, so you really need to take this with a grain of salt."

"Okay." Now, I was worried. I'd figured my negative impression of Johan was my imagination, or my over-protectiveness of those close to me. Paul was making me think my concerns weren't just valid, but warranted.

Paul picked at his bagel some more before he continued. "Based on my admittedly limited research, I found nothing."

I blinked at him. "He has no record?"

"As in, he doesn't exist."

"What does that mean?"

Paul leaned forward and held up a hand, checking off points with his fingers. "He didn't pop up on a cursory search of his name online. He has no social media profiles. I found nothing on where he lives, or when he came to town. He's a mystery."

"Rita never said how they met," I said. "Just that it happened fast."

"Could he be after something?" Paul asked. "Her money, perhaps?"

"Maybe." I wasn't sure how much money Rita really had, but she didn't need to work for a living and she didn't appear to be struggling. Could she be sitting on a huge stash of cash and Johan had somehow found out about it? "What can we do?"

"Do?" Paul asked, shaking his head. "Nothing."

"But what if he's here to hurt Rita?"

"Remember, I can only go so deep, Krissy," Paul said. "There might be information tucked away somewhere explaining exactly why he seems so mysterious, but I can't get to it. It could be as simple as me not knowing where to look."

"Like he's in witness protection or something? New name, new place?"

"Could be." Paul shrugged. "There's really no way to know, not unless he gets himself involved in a crime. Even then, I might not get very far. We're just a small force with a small budget. It's not like on TV where I can magic up the answer with a few keystrokes."

I chewed over that while Paul continued to chew on his chunks of bagel. I wanted to rush to Rita's and warn her against Johan, but what if I was blowing everything out of proportion? She deserved the chance to be happy, and I didn't want to ruin that in a misguided attempt at saving the day.

"My advice would be to keep an eye on them and see if anything else strikes you as odd," Paul said, wiping his hands on a napkin and then tossing it onto his now-empty plate. "Don't go prying into their lives and don't try to discover anything on your own. Rita knows how to take care of herself."

A "but" was on my lips, but I swallowed it back. Paul was right. "Okay," I said. I'll—"

The buzz of Paul's phone caused me to jump so badly, I smacked my knees against the bottom of the table. Both our coffee mugs jerked, sloshing coffee out onto the tabletop.

As Paul removed his phone to answer it, I rose to grab some paper towels to clean up.

"Dalton," he said. He sounded like a real hard-nosed TV detective, the kind that only ever went by their last name. *Kinda like how I think of Buchannan.* The thought didn't sit well with me, because I really wanted Paul to get the detective's job.

I sopped up the coffee, straining my ears to try to hear what was being said on the other end of the line, but it was too muffled and whoever it was spoke too quickly. Paul's expression darkened as he listened.

"All right, I'm on the way." He clicked off and rose. "I've got to go."

"What happened?" I asked.

Paul gathered the few things he'd brought in with him before finally answering.

"It's the library," he said. "It's been vandalized."

I couldn't talk Paul into taking me with him, but he couldn't stop me from driving there myself. He didn't tell me anything more than that the library had been vandalized somehow. But I knew what had happened. Or, more accurately, *who* had happened.

Maggie Reed.

Who else could it have been? Sure, kids vandalized things all the time, but in Pine Hills, that rarely happened. And while it was possible the vandalism consisted of Maggie plastering the entire front of the library with flyers, I doubted they'd have called Paul for that. No, this was going to be a big deal.

Paul was driving his personal car, though he did have a spare uniform in the trunk that he'd changed into before we'd left. He didn't speed as I followed him, which drove me bonkers, considering I wanted to get there as quickly as possible to assess the damage and make sure the Carltons were okay. And nothing said Maggie would stop at the library. I wanted to know what I might need to expect to happen at Death by Coffee if she wasn't stopped.

It felt like it took forever, but we eventually arrived. The library was still standing and no smoke poured from the windows, but it was impossible to see inside to know if the bookshelves had been upended. Red paint had been sprayed across the front of the building and over all the windows. It took me a moment to realize there was a pattern to it, but for the life of me, I couldn't make heads or tails of it.

Paul parked next to a cruiser that was still ticking, telling me that whoever had driven the car had just arrived. What did it mean that they called not just Paul, but another cop?

This isn't good.

I pulled in next to Paul and got out of my Escape, intent on following him inside. Paul gave me an exasperated look, but didn't complain as he headed for the doors. It wasn't like this was a murder scene that needed to be cordoned off and he knew I wouldn't walk around, touching anything, so there was no reason for him to stop me.

Still, I walked a couple of steps behind him, letting him take the lead. If I played this right, I could always act like I'd arrived by chance. As far as I knew, no one else knew Paul and I had spent a couple of nights together. I didn't know how the other cops would react when they found out.

The library doors had a smaller version of what was painted on the rest of the place sprayed across it. It kind of looked like a knife stuck through a watermelon, but that didn't make much sense to me. Whoever the artist was, they didn't do a very good job.

Jimmy and Cindy Carlton were standing in the lobby

and they weren't alone. Jimmy was gesturing wildly and yelling. The two cops standing before them—John Buchannan and Becca Garrison—nodded along with him with dour expressions on their faces. When Paul and I entered, only Cindy glanced our way. She looked relieved, though I don't know if that was because more help had arrived, or if she was just happy to see a friendly face.

"Something needs to be done!" Jimmy yelled, biceps flexing. His shirt looked as if it might pop its seams. "Do you realize how much it's going to cost to fix that?" He flung an arm toward the door. "We don't have the resources for this."

"I understand, Mr. Carlton—" Buchannan began.

"Do you?" Jimmy shouted over him. "You saw what she did to that book when she was here last. Arrest her. Better yet, let me talk to her. We'll see if she ever tries something like this again." He took a step toward the door, as if he was going to march right out of the library and do just that.

Buchannan stopped him by taking a step between him and the exit. "I don't think that would be a good idea."

"What do we have?" Paul asked, joining the group. I lingered to the back, out of both Buchannan and Garrison's sight lines.

It was Officer Garrison who answered. "You saw the paint when you came in." Paul nodded. "There's also damage to the foundation."

"Looks like someone took a sledgehammer to it," Buchannan said.

"And some lines are cut. The place still has power, but the phones are dead, as is the cooling and heating system."

"We can't function like this," Jimmy said. I could practically see the steam coming from his skull.

"Do we know who did it?" Paul asked.

Before either of the other cops could answer, Jimmy shouted over them. "Who do you think did it? Maggie Reed, that's who."

"Do you have evidence of this?" Paul asked. "I'm not saying I don't believe you, but we can't accuse her of vandalizing the property without having some sort of proof."

Jimmy gnashed his teeth and fumed, but didn't respond. He left that to Cindy.

"Nothing definitive," she said. She sounded scared, and I had a feeling it had more to do with her husband's rage than what else Maggie might do. "But she and her friends have been harassing us for a long time now. Who else would deface a library, of all places?"

"Do you know what that symbol that was painted on the front means?" Garrison asked. "Have you seen it before?"

"No, neither of us have."

"It's a warning," Jimmy said. "A knife to the skull, is what it is."

I glanced at the door, but couldn't see the paint from this side of it. I supposed the watermelon could have been a skull, but only if you turned your head and squinted at it sideways.

"All right," Paul said. "Let's take a few deep breaths here and get this taken care of." When no one opposed the suggestion, he went on. "John, Becca, check outside, see if you can find any more damage, or any other signs as to who might have done this. They might have made a mistake and left something behind." Jimmy opened his mouth, but it was Paul's turn to talk over him. "You and I are going to sit down and talk about this calmly. We'll get to the bottom of this, but we can't run on pure speculation."

"I'll check the neighboring buildings and see if anyone saw anything," Buchannan said. He turned and came to an abrupt stop when he saw me. "What are you doing here?"

I had no good answer for that, so I gave him a chagrined smile and shrugged.

Buchannan shot a look at Paul, who had his back turned to us, so he didn't see it, and then he made for the door. "Stay out of trouble," Buchannan told me as he passed.

Officer Garrison made less of a spectacle about leaving. I got a slight nod of acknowledgment, and then she too was gone.

Paul was leading Jimmy away, deeper into the library, presumably to have that calm discussion, leaving Cindy and me alone in the lobby. When they were gone, we looked at one another, as if expecting the other to say something profound.

"Uh, hi," I said.

Cindy managed a weak smile before she started wringing her hands. She kept shooting glances in the direction Paul had taken her husband. As the seconds turned into minutes, her agitation only grew, and it soon became obvious something other than the vandalism was bothering her.

"Did you see something?" I asked, keeping my voice down so no one would overhear—not that anyone else was around, but still.

Cindy's shoulders jerked as if I'd smacked her on the back. "No. It's just . . . I . . . This has all gotten out of hand."

Something made me think she wasn't only talking about the library. "What has?"

I didn't know Cindy as well as I'd like, but I thought I'd known her well enough. She'd always seemed kind and levelheaded in my interactions with her. She cared about the library, about the community, and yeah, she might have a wild streak buried in her somewhere, but if it came out, I imagined it only ever did when she was alone with her husband.

Cindy leaned into the library proper, glanced around, and then took me by the arm to lead me across the lobby, toward where the floor was torn up and the water damage from the storm was the worst.

"I might have made a mistake," she said at a whisper.

"What kind of mistake?"

She wrung her hands and gnawed on her lower lip a moment before answering. "It wasn't my idea," she said. "Jimmy was so upset with that woman, and I didn't know how to make it any better. I wasn't happy with her either, but I'm not one for violence."

"Jimmy is?" My mind immediately flashed on Sidney facedown in the tub of apple cider and the conversations I'd had with the young librarian about Jimmy's fight with Sidney.

"Well, no," she said. "But she was rubbing at his last nerve, and I was worried."

I nodded as if I completely understood. "What happened?"

"It was a few days after the . . . the . . ." She lowered her voice to a breath, one that I barely heard. "The murder." She shuddered. "A man came to see me. Jimmy wasn't here at the time, so it was just the two of us. He came to me and apologized for Sidney dying at my dunking station."

"He what?" My voice rose briefly, before I brought it back down to a whisper. "Did this man admit to killing him?"

"No, nothing like that," Cindy said. "He claimed he was Sidney's brother, but I'm not sure if that's true or not. His name's Kevin."

Kevin Tewksbury. Again.

Cindy went on. "He acted like Sidney died where he did to spite us, which, as you know, is how we'd already felt anyway. We got to talking—a shared dislike, I guess—and the next thing I knew, we were talking plots."

"Plots?" I asked. "As in murder plots?"

Cindy looked taken aback. "No! Neither of us were looking to kill anyone," she said with a shudder. "But I did want to get rid of that Maggie woman and stop her from ruining the library any more than she already had. If anyone was poisoning the minds of our readers, it was her and her hateful rhetoric."

"So, you and Kevin plotted against her?"

"I suppose you could say that." Cindy closed her eyes and pinched the bridge of her nose as if a headache was coming on. "Kevin had the idea about putting the stickers in the books and blaming it on Maggie. He said he'd been working on a website and that we could promote it that way. He didn't tell me anything more about it, and honestly, I didn't want to know. I just wanted that woman to go away."

"*You* put the stickers in the books?" I asked, shocked. "It damaged them!"

"I was careful," she said. "No text was ruined, just a few copyright and title pages. Kevin assured me that when people saw the website, whatever they found there would come back down on Maggie and it would somehow make her go away." She lowered her head. "I was so stupid."

I couldn't say I disagreed, but my excitement was growing. If Kevin Tewksbury had plotted against Maggie, could he also have targeted his brother before that?

"Did he say if he killed Sidney?" I asked. "Or if he knew who did?"

Cindy shook her head. "He seemed as mystified by it as I was. But now, the more I look back on it, I find that Kevin's behavior was unnatural. He'd just buried his brother and here he was, already plotting against his brother's friends." She met my eye. "If you were to ask me, either Kevin Tewksbury killed Sidney at the festival, or he knows who did."

22

I'd have liked to have told Paul what Cindy had told me, but by the time he was finished with Jimmy, Buchannan and Garrison had returned, and people began showing up at the library. Some were there to gawp at the vandalism, while others—not many, mind you—were looking to check out or return books. Not wanting to be swallowed up in the chaos, I ducked out and headed for home.

Thanksgiving was two days away and I still had a ton of work to do. The guest list kept getting bigger and bigger, while my house was looking smaller and smaller by the minute. I needed some time to focus solely on that, lest I become overwhelmed on the big day and end up hiding in my bedroom until Christmas.

Of course, me being me, the moment I was through the door, I found myself sitting in front of my laptop, bringing up multiple tabs: Sidney Tewksbury's podcasts, the Freedom from Filth site, and anything else I thought would help me to tie it all together. Admittedly, it wasn't much.

Now that I was looking at it again, it was pretty obvious the Freedom from Filth site was Kevin's. The mistakes were the kind that would annoy an English teacher, the kind of errors that someone like Kevin would think unintelligent people might make. It was too structured, too on point to have come from Maggie's mind.

But why make it at all?

I still couldn't figure out how Kevin thought signal-boosting hatred would hurt Maggie's cause. People who thought like her would come to the site and find exactly what they were looking for. Was that the point?

Maggie, by all accounts, was close to Sidney before his death. Were they dating? I wasn't clear on that. Either way, she ended up using a dating site—or whatever you'd call the thing—and found herself alone with Sidney's brother, Kevin. I only had Kevin's word that the encounter ended badly. What if they went through with the meet and, afterward, they plotted Sidney's demise?

I didn't want to play the podcasts again, but I scrolled through them, checking the dates and attempting to remember what was said when. There were times when Sidney seemed almost apologetic for his anger. Other times, he was ranting mad. Was that because he'd found out about Kevin and Maggie, and not that she was in the room, egging him on?

It was hard to tell, not without some sort of video evidence. If she was ever with him, she never spoke.

I leaned back in my chair and stared at the screen. I

was missing something. If Sidney was mad at Maggie and Kevin, you'd think he would have called them out on his podcast. Not only that, he would have been the one committing murder; not the other way around. If Maggie and Kevin were the ones intent on offing Sidney, why do it in a public place, especially if they were keeping their relationship a secret?

Was that why Kevin created the website? Was he in love with Maggie, and it became a symbol to prove how much he cared?

I had no idea and rereading the site wasn't helping. I clicked over to other tabs, these ones about Darrin Crenshaw, but found little that tied him to Sidney, Maggie, or Kevin. He'd once been Sidney's doctor, but that wasn't something that would be plastered all over the internet.

I rose and paced away from my laptop. Sitting there staring at websites wasn't helping. In fact, it was only making me more confused. I got that Sidney rubbed a lot of people the wrong way: Dr. Crenshaw, Jimmy Carlton, Kevin Tewksbury, Tori Carmichael, to name a few. And then there were all the people he'd verbally attacked over the years, which included Vicki and Jules. The list of names seemed endless.

"It has to be one of them," I muttered. Not Vicki or Jules, but the people who'd had more than a couple passing encounters with Sidney.

He died in the dunking tank. The one run by the librarians. Coincidence?

Frustration caused me to mutter something quite unladylike, and unrepeatable, under my breath. I grabbed my jacket, and leaving my laptop sitting on the table, I walked out the door.

I probably should have stayed home and focused solely on pies. I could have eaten the one I'd already made, while I baked a couple more for Thanksgiving.

But right then, I wanted chocolate. And there was one place in town where I knew I could get as much of it as I wanted.

"Hi, Jules," I said as the door to Phantastic Candies closed behind me. "I need your richest, unhealthiest chocolate."

"Uh-oh." He rounded the counter and plucked a chocolate bar from one of the myriad of colorful shelves that made up the candy store. Chutes filled with candies of all sorts ran along the back wall, and tubs and shelves of sweets filled the other spaces. Often, kids would be scurrying around the place, buying all the sugar-filled treats they could wish for, but today, the shop was empty.

Jules handed the candy bar over and leaned against the counter. He was dressed in a lime-green getup that included a green top hat and clogs. He dressed up for the kids, but I always enjoyed his outfits.

He gave me time to unwrap my chocolate and take a few large bites before asking, "What happened?"

I wiped chocolate from my lips and licked my fingers clean. Already, I was feeling better. "Nothing really *happened*," I said. "Well, the library *did* get vandalized, but that's not why I'm here."

"I heard about that." He shook his head sadly. "You know how fast news travels in Pine Hills. The moment the police were on their way, the rumor patrol was out in force." He smiled. "Speaking of . . . Rita stopped by with that new man of hers, Johan. She was so intent on telling me all about the library, she barely acknowledged him while they were here."

That sounded like Rita. "What did you think of Johan?"

Jules made a so-so motion with his hand. "He seems quiet and nice enough, I guess, but something about him rubbed me the wrong way."

"Me too!"

"I'm sure it was my imagination. I'm not used to seeing Rita with anyone. She's got enough personality for three or four people, which leaves little room for anyone else. But if she's happy, I'm happy."

I almost told him about Paul's brief investigation into Johan, but decided to keep that to myself for now. One, it made me look like an even bigger snoop than I really was; and two, if Johan turned out to be innocent of nothing more than falling for Rita, I didn't want to make Jules apprehensive of him.

If we continued to talk about Rita and her new flame, I wouldn't be able to resist, so I changed the subject.

"I can't stop thinking about the murder," I said, taking another bite of my chocolate. It was just what I'd asked for; rich and creamy. "It's bad enough a man died, but now, Maggie Reed is escalating her attacks. I'm pretty sure she's the one who vandalized the library, or at least, she had someone do it for her. And now, I keep finding reasons to suspect Sidney's brother, Kevin, of his murder."

The door opened and a pair of teenagers walked in. One of them shot Jules a finger gun and a "Yo, Mr. Phan," before the two kids snatched up a couple bags of sour worms and checked out. Jules fell right into character, joking and laughing with the teens, right up until they walked out the door.

When he turned back to me, his face was serious. "I don't know that much about Kevin Tewksbury," Jules said. "He's a teacher, right?"

"He is." I debated on whether or not to spill his secret and once again, decided to keep it to myself. I wouldn't make a very good gossip. "From what I've seen, he didn't like his brother all that much. They fought about books."

"That's a shame, especially this time of the year. Thanksgiving is all about family and friends and setting aside differences."

"Not everyone can manage to do that."

"I know." Jules looked sad, as if thinking about something from his own life. I wondered if it had to do with Lance and his trips, or if it was something else. I didn't want to pry, so I brought up another name, one I hoped to clear sooner rather than later.

"What can you tell me about Darrin Crenshaw?"

Jules's surprise at the question was palpable. "Why do you ask? Does he have something to do with the murder? I know he was there at the festival and that he checked on Sidney when he collapsed"—he shuddered—"but I thought that was as far as it went."

"He was also Sidney's personal doctor."

"Really?" Jules said. "I never knew."

"Apparently, they'd had a falling-out a month or two before Sidney died. Darrin won't talk about it because of the doctor-patient confidentiality thing, but there seems to be some meat to whatever they fought about."

"But murder?" Jules shook his head. "I can't believe a doctor would go so far, especially one as well-liked as Dr. Crenshaw."

"Me either," I said with a heavy sigh. "But he was there when Sidney died. He knew the victim. He also studied poisons, which was the cause of death. Will vouches for him and honestly, so do I, so I'm having a hard time thinking badly of Darrin. But . . ."

"You can't dismiss him out of hand."

I buried my face in my hands, elbows propped on the counter for support. "What am I supposed to do?"

Jules laid a hand on my shoulder and squeezed. "Don't stress yourself out about it too much," he said. "It'll all work out. These things always do."

"I guess." I straightened, already in need of another chocolate, but I forced myself to stick to just the one. I didn't need a bellyache on top of everything else. "Thanks for listening to me whine, Jules. I really needed it."

"Anytime." He bowed with a flourish.

I paid for my chocolate and then left the candy store, feeling marginally better. I was no closer to figuring out who killed Sidney Tewksbury, and people I liked were still on the suspect list, but at least I'd gotten some of it off my chest.

I checked the time as I climbed back into my Escape, and seeing I still had a few hours before my meeting with Irving Barrow, I made the short drive to Death by Coffee. Chocolate hadn't helped. Maybe coffee would.

Beth and Jeff were behind the counter, with Vicki and Mason together upstairs in the books. Trouble trailed behind the couple as they worked. Every now and again, Vicki would bend down to scratch him behind the ears, before she'd point something out to Mason, who'd scribble into a notebook he was carrying.

I considered going up to talk to her, but decided not to intrude. Not only was she busy, but she was with Mason, and I'd feel like I was interrupting their personal time, even though they were working on a project I'd come up with.

Instead, I turned toward the counter to find Lena standing on the customer side, dressed in a black jacket and torn jeans.

She wasn't alone.

"Hey, Lena," I said, joining them. "Zay."

Lena took an abrupt step to the side, away from Zay, when I spoke. "Hey, Ms. Hancock. I didn't expect you in today."

Zay gave me a lazy wave before shoving his heavily ringed hands into his pockets with a jangle of bracelets. His hair was the color of grape Kool-Aid and, like Lena, he had more piercings than I could count. I noted his jacket looked an awful lot like Lena's, almost as if they'd coordinated. *Or he'd bought hers for her.*

"I'm just visiting," I said, fighting to keep the stupid grin off my face. "What are you two up to?"

Lena shot Zay a warning look before answering. "Just hanging out. We should probably get going."

I almost let them go without saying anything more, but something about seeing them together, at the awkward way Lena tried to pretend there wasn't anything between them, warmed me from the inside out. My house was already going to be bursting at the seams, but at this point, I didn't care. I wanted *all* of my friends together and darn it, I was going to make it work.

"If you two don't have plans for Thanksgiving, I'm having a big turkey dinner at my place," I said. "Everyone's invited." I looked past Zay and Lena so I could see Beth and Jeff. "That includes the both of you and any dates you might want to bring along."

"Cool," Zay said.

"Maybe." Lena looked embarrassed. "I'll let you know, Ms. H." She coughed and took Zay by the arm. "We've gotta run."

Before I could comment, Lena hurried Zay out the door. The grin I'd been fighting sprang free then, and my heart felt ten times lighter. I found Lena's reticence to admit they were an item—or so close to being one that it amounted to the same thing—cute.

"Ms. H?" Jeff asked. "Should I call you that?"

"Krissy is fine," I said. "Or Ms. Hancock, if you insist. Just not *ma'am*."

Jeff flushed and then took my order.

I carried my fresh coffee to a seat by the window, and sat down to relax. Maybe I was focusing my attention on the wrong thing. Why look at Darrin as a possible murder suspect when I could instead turn my attention to Lena and Zay's budding relationship? Why look into Maggie and her tangled relationships with the Tewksburys when I had Rita and Johan to consider?

And why in the world was I not focusing the rest of my attention on Paul?

I sipped at my coffee and watched the world go by. I tried to keep my mind on the good things in life, I really did, but the longer I sat there, the more the bad stuff started to slip in. Sidney's death. Maggie aggressively protesting books. Kevin and his secret life. Darrin and his affinity for poison. Cindy and Jimmy and their secrets. Tori and her attack on Maggie.

Somehow, it all tied together in a meaningful narrative that would lead me to the killer.

There was no way I could ignore that.

I finished off my coffee and left Death by Coffee, determined to start checking names off my ever-growing list. If I couldn't solve the case, I could at least prove someone's innocence for my own peace of mind. And if I was going to do that, the best place to start would be with someone I knew personally.

The drive to the doctor's office felt like it took forever thanks to my nerves hopping all over the place. I parked in the lot, thankful I'd shoved the prescription bottle back into my purse after my not-so graceful reaction to them. I was curious to see how Darrin would react when I told him how they'd affected me. Would he appear guilty? Nervous?

Or like any good doctor, would he grow concerned about my well-being?

I double-checked my purse to make sure I hadn't lost the pill bottle somewhere, and once I was certain it was tucked safely away, I opened the door and stepped out onto the lot. A brisk breeze blew my hair into my face, briefly blinding me as the door to the clinic opened. Using my good arm, I brushed my hair out of my face.

When I saw who was exiting the clinic, I jerked to an abrupt stop.

"Kevin?" I asked, the name popping out of my mouth on reflex.

The big man froze, as if he hadn't noticed me until I'd spoken. He didn't look sick or hurt.

But he *did* look guilty as hell.

"I think we need to talk," I said, nodding toward the clinic. No doctors were within sight, but Bea was watching us with a disapproving glare over the top of her bifocals.

Kevin nodded, and without complaint, he turned around and headed back inside the clinic.

With a deep breath to steady my nerves, I straightened my back and followed him inside.

23

"This is highly irregular," Darrin Crenshaw said, pacing the small exam room. "I have patients I need to attend to."

I was seated in a chair in the corner, while Kevin sat with his head down on an exam table. When I'd dragged him back into the clinic, Bea had gone for Darrin right away. Instead of asking me to leave or throwing me out, he'd guided both Kevin and me to the exam room in which we now sat.

"As long as everyone is truthful with me, this shouldn't take long," I said, crossing one leg over the other.

"There's nothing more to say," came Kevin's lament.

I doubted that very much. I wasn't going to let either of them get out of this that easily. "Please, Darrin," I said. "Take a seat."

He scowled at me briefly before dropping into the stool beside the computer. "I'm only entertaining this because of Will. I trust him, and since you two were once an item, I suppose I should trust you."

"That's big of you."

He flashed me a smile that was all annoyance. "Yeah, well, I'm starting to wonder if I should change my stance, considering you two *did* break up, and he fled the state afterward."

I caught the implied accusation, but I ignored it. I aimed my next question at Kevin. "Care to explain why you are here?"

"Is that really any of your concern?" Darrin cut in before Kevin could speak. And was that a warning look I saw him give the other man?

"No, it might not be, but I do think it might do you both some good to start talking. I find it strange to find two men, both connected to a murder victim, spending time together?"

"This *is* a doctor's office." Darrin's voice came out flat.

Kevin kept his head down, but I caught the snort he'd tried to hide.

"Okay, if that's the case, then there's something wrong with Kevin, right? Are you sick? Injured?"

Kevin glanced up, but didn't answer.

"Krissy—" Darrin began, but I held up a hand to stop him.

"Don't," I said. "I came here to talk to you, to clear you of any suspicion in Sidney's death." Shock registered on Darrin's face, but I didn't stop to give him assurances. "And what do I find when I get here? The brother of the deceased leaving your office without an obvious ailment.

You have to realize how that must look. What do you think the police would think if they saw it?"

Darrin opened his mouth to retort, but closed it with a frown. He shared a look with Kevin, who finally spoke.

"I needed to know."

I crossed my arms to wait for him to go on. After a few moments of mental tug-of-war, he did.

"I told you before; Sidney was disturbed," he said, speaking slowly and carefully, as if afraid he might let something slip. "He refused to see a psychiatrist, but I knew Dr. Crenshaw was his doctor. I didn't know what medications he'd prescribed, what he might have diag-nosed Sidney with. I was afraid I missed something about my brother, something big that would explain why he was killed. I . . . I needed to know if he was the man I once knew, or if he was lost to me in ways I couldn't under-stand."

"He was troubled," Darrin said, voice barely above a whisper.

"Troubled how?"

"Sidney was a misguided, mentally unstable individ-ual who was acting out in an effort to garner the attention he so desperately craved."

It came out so clinical, so lifeless, it caught me off guard. Darrin sounded like he was reciting a line out of a textbook he was forced to read for a class, not that he was talking about someone who he'd once treated.

"Did you learn anything by coming here?" I asked Kevin.

"That I was right." Kevin sighed. "Sidney wouldn't have hurt anyone, nor would he blow up your store, no matter what he said. He didn't have it in him. His death was unnecessary."

"And you agree?" I asked Darrin.

"To the best of my knowledge, what Kevin says is true. I'm not a psychiatrist, mind you, but I did what I could to help Sidney understand why he felt the way he did." He lowered his eyes to his hands, which were folded in his lap. "My help, apparently, wasn't enough."

"Sidney would never take medication," Kevin said. "Even if it would help him."

Speaking of medication . . .

"I took those pain pills you gave me," I said to Darrin. "They made me sick."

Darrin sat up, brow furrowed. "You had a reaction?"

I nodded. "I got dizzy and didn't feel too great afterward. If it wasn't for Will being there, I might have called an ambulance." Okay, that was a bit of an exaggeration, but I wanted to gauge Darrin's reaction.

He frowned as he turned to the computer. He typed quietly for a moment before saying, "The dosage was strong, yes, but you shouldn't have experienced symptoms that badly." He glanced at me. "Did you take them with food?"

"Not exactly." It was my turn to become sheepish. "Even without it, I'm surprised I'd have such a strong reaction to them."

"You and me both," Darrin said, closing my file. "Are you sure there wasn't a mistake and you picked up the wrong prescription?"

I gave him a flat look and mentally prepared myself for what I had to say next. Playing good cop wouldn't get me the reaction I wanted, so I had to play nasty. "I seriously doubt the pharmacy would make such a drastic mistake. I'm more apt to believe you overprescribed my meds."

Darrin's face reddened in anger. "What? Are you going to accuse me of trying to poison you now?"

"No. But I do find it curious that Sidney died by poison, in a location in which you were present, after having concerns that his own stepmother might have tried to poison him. I'm not the only one who finds it strange. And then, when I got dizzy after taking the meds *you* prescribed, you can't blame me for wondering."

Darrin's chiseled jaw flexed, before he sagged. "I suppose I can't blame you for wondering. If our roles were reversed, I'd probably wonder the same thing. But I never killed Sidney Tewksbury, and I most definitely didn't try to poison you."

"That's good to hear."

"Now, if you truly did have a reaction to the medication, I suggest you discontinue their use. I can prescribe something else. Or I can have Paige do it for you, if you'd prefer."

"No, I'm all right." I sagged. I didn't enjoy accusing people I liked of having ill will toward me, let alone murder.

"I never poisoned Sidney," Darrin repeated. "I might have studied poisons, but I did so to *help* people, not hurt them. You have to know that."

"He had no reason to hurt my brother," Kevin said, startling me. I'd almost forgotten he was still there.

"What about the argument I'd heard about?" I asked Darrin. "Sidney dropped you as his doctor, did he not?"

"He did, but that's no reason to want him dead," Darrin said. "I was angry, yeah, but not angry enough to hurt him. I was worried, and since he refused to take my advice, things got a little heated. I only wanted what was best for him."

I found I believed him. Maybe it was his connection to Will, or perhaps it was the sincerity in his voice, but I didn't think Dr. Crenshaw capable of killing anyone, especially a man like Sidney who was in desperate need of help.

"When you talked to him, did he ever say anything about someone wanting to hurt him?" I asked.

"No, if he had, I would have recommended he go to the police," Darrin said. "Though, if anyone had reason to kill him it would be—" he cut off abruptly.

I uncrossed my legs and sat forward. "It would be . . . ?"

Darrin looked like he'd swallowed a lemon. He grimaced as he spoke. "I hate accusing anyone of wrongdoing, especially since I don't have any proof."

"You don't need proof," I said. "We're just talking. If it's something the police need to hear, I can always tell them for you. Your name doesn't have to come into it at all."

Darrin rubbed at his chin and ran his fingers through his hair. His eyes were focused elsewhere as he fidgeted.

"Please, Darrin. Someone killed Sidney, and you might know who did it without realizing you know."

"I doubt that." Before I could object, he continued with, "But if it does turn out to be relevant, I couldn't live with myself if I kept it to myself." He took a deep breath. "About three, four months back, Cindy Carlton came to see me. She's a patient of mine, so I thought nothing of it. She'd called, claiming she'd hurt her back, but when I examined her, I couldn't find anything wrong with her."

"Okay?" I asked, not quite sure where this was going, but didn't want to press him too hard. Darrin could get into a lot of trouble if anyone found out he was talking about his patients to a civilian.

"She wanted something for the pain she claimed she was having. There was something in her voice, a tremble, like she was scared, that cued me in that she wasn't telling me the entire truth. When I pressed her, she told me not to worry about it and left."

"Was she hurt?"

"I don't think so," he said. "I saw Jimmy at the grocery a few days later and he was limping. When I asked him about it, he said he'd been in an altercation and that he'd wrenched his knee. I thought nothing of it—people get into stupid fights all the time—but then I remembered that when I'd seen Sidney last, he'd had a bruise on his cheek. Knowing the friction between Sidney and the Carltons, it was easy enough to put two and two together."

"Sidney told me he'd fallen," Kevin said. "He'd shown up at my home and he was, I don't know . . . somber? I'm not sure that's the right word for it. He didn't attack me or my books. It was kind of nice. When he left, I'd hoped that would be the end of his harassment, but he started right back in the next day."

"You think Jimmy Carlton punched Sidney and then later, killed him?" I asked, to be sure. I'd been told about an argument between Jimmy and Sidney, but didn't think they'd ever come to blows.

"It makes sense," Darrin said. "I don't know of anyone else who was that aggressive toward Sidney. There were verbal complaints floating around town, I know, but nothing physical until then."

I didn't like where this was going. I turned my attention to Kevin. "You created the Freedom from Filth website. Why?"

Kevin jerked in surprise. "How did you know—" He

gave a bitter laugh. "Cindy told you, didn't she?" At my nod, he sighed. "It was retaliation, I suppose. My motives, I mean. I knew Maggie Reed used the phrase, and I wanted to hurt her without actually *hurting* her, if you know what I mean?"

I did and said as much.

"I made the site so I could compile names and then, I don't know, turn them in or something. These were the people who Sidney associated with. They egged him on when they should have tried to make him understand the damage he was doing to the community. I wanted to ruin them, just like Maggie tried to ruin me."

I didn't need to ask what he was talking about, especially in front of Darrin. "Do you think she killed your brother?"

"It would make things a whole lot easier if she did," Kevin said. "She loved him, and he loved her. They had their issues, but what couple doesn't?"

"If not Maggie, then who?" I asked. "Did you discover anything from the site?"

Kevin shook his head. "I wish I could say yes, but I can't. It was a bigger undertaking than I expected, and I'm not as computer-savvy as I needed to be. Sure, I got a few names from people signing up for the newsletter, but none of them meant anything to me." He paused. "Well, almost none."

"You recognized one of the names?" I asked.

Kevin didn't look happy about it, but he nodded. "I did." And then he hit me with it. "Tori Carmichael signed up."

"What?" I couldn't help it; I shouted it. "The teacher? She doesn't even like Sidney or Maggie or . . ." I trailed off, shocked. I couldn't fathom why a woman like Tori, someone who'd complained about the harassment she'd received at the hands of Sidney Tewksbury, would join the same group who'd been harassing her in the first place.

"I was as surprised as you," Kevin said. "It wasn't easy to ask her about it without admitting I created the website, so I tied it to Maggie, hoping Tori wouldn't dig too deep. When I brought it up to her, she claimed she signed up so she could be kept abreast of the situation around town. I took that to mean she wanted to see what people like Maggie were thinking, not that she was interested in becoming like them."

"Do you still believe that?"

Kevin raised his hands and dropped them. "I don't know what to believe anymore. I really do like Tori, and I don't want to believe she could have had anything to do with Sidney's death, but the more I think about it, the more I question her motives."

I left a short time later. I hadn't cleared Darrin or Kevin from my list of suspects, but I was feeling a whole lot better about them—and the pills in my purse. Cindy and Jimmy, on the other hand . . .

I hated to think it, but the librarians weren't coming out of this looking all that great. I understood that they wanted to protect the integrity of the library; that they, like me, didn't believe in censoring books, just because a few people might not like what was inside them. But how did Jimmy getting into an altercation with Sidney lead to a man's death? The same went for Cindy. Why become involved with Kevin's plot against Maggie to the point of damaging books?

I hopped back into my Escape and made for the library, intent on asking those very same questions. I needed to get to the bottom of this before someone else got hurt.

Sidney Tewksbury was already dead. Could Maggie Reed be next? As much as she got on my nerves, I didn't want her to die.

I pulled into the empty library parking lot and realized the trip was pointless. There were no cars, no indication anyone was here at all. The tarp on the roof fluttered in the breeze, but it was the only movement in or around the building. I got out of my Escape and tested the doors, just in case, but they were locked.

"Well, crap," I said, cupping my hands over my eyes and peering into the dark library. No one was there. The graffiti still covered the doors and walls, but Cindy and Jimmy were gone. A part of me wondered if they'd ever return.

I had a little over an hour until I was supposed to meet with Irving Barrow about my car, but figured it couldn't hurt to show up early. Besides, the sooner I could put the damage he'd done to my taillight and bumper behind me, the easier it would be for me to focus on other, more important things.

And if I was lucky, I might learn a thing or two more about Sidney Tewksbury and why he was murdered.

24

Irving Barrow lived in a large home buried behind a virtual forest of pines. The long driveway was paved and didn't have a single crack in it. There was a glint of light in the trees as I passed, but whatever had caught the sun was too small or too well-hidden for me to see as I drove by.

I parked out front, not sure where else to park. A large four-car garage sat off the driveway, but the doors were closed, and I couldn't see in to know if there were many vehicles inside.

"He has all of this on a guidance counselor's salary?" I wondered out loud. A politician? Sure. A sports figure, or maybe a television personality? Yeah. Someone who works in public education? No way, not unless something fishy was going on with the bookkeeping at Pine Hills High.

Considering Tori Carmichael's house, it's very likely.

I climbed out of my Escape, feeling rather small and insignificant in the shadow of the manor. I knew a lot of wealthy people lived in Pine Hills, but I rarely had opportunity to interact with them outside of murder investigations. And, honestly, based on the personalities of a lot of the rich people I knew, I'd rather keep it that way.

A gargoyle-faced knocker met me at the door. Using two fingers, I knocked three times in quick succession.

It took only a couple of seconds before the door opened and Irv Barrow stood facing me, a scowl on his face. He stared at me just long enough to make me uncomfortable before he said, "You're early."

"Sorry about that," I said. "I was free and figured I could stop by so we could get this over with."

He grunted and then said, "Come on in, I suppose. Close the door behind you." He turned and walked off.

"Butler must be on vacation," I muttered, before doing as he said.

Vases and small statues stood on stands just inside the doorway. A long rug ran down the short hall, to the intersection where Irv waited. Beneath that, the floors were done in a dark hardwood that shone with a recent polish. There were paintings on the walls, some I thought I recognized, and I wondered if they were the real thing, or very good replicas of famous works.

"I know the artist," he said, as if reading my mind. "He does a fantastic job re-creating the best artwork in the world. Costs nearly as much to hire him as it does to buy the real thing, but they're not quite as rare."

"It's lovely," I said, and I meant it. I felt underdressed as I walked down the hall toward Irv, who'd turned and entered a room to the left. I followed after him and soon found myself in a small library filled with leather-bound books and soft leather chairs. The books appeared well-read, but something about them made me think they were there more for show than they were useful.

Irv motioned to one of the chairs before taking a seat of his own. He didn't offer me a drink, nor did he look inclined to. He rested an ankle on his knee, placed both his hands atop that, and then stared me down until I was comfortably seated.

"Well?" he asked, as if *I* was the one who'd set up the meeting.

"Well what? I'm here to talk about my taillight and bumper."

"Your parking job caused the damage. If you had pulled into the space properly, it wouldn't have happened."

"I was as far forward as I could go. There's no way you should have hit me."

Irv sniffed and looked away. The motion caused the leather to groan. "I suppose I should have stopped to take a picture so I could show it to the police. Unfortunately for me, I didn't, and now I'm on the hook for the damages that *you* caused." He huffed. "Not that I expect it would have mattered since you're in tight with the police. I'm sure things would have been altered to support your argument."

"What's that supposed to mean?" I asked, annoyed he'd even *think* that Paul would manufacture evidence, especially when all that was damaged was my taillight and bumper.

"Nothing," Irv said. "I have no choice but to pay for the damages. I'll pay cash so we can keep this little problem between us. Does that suffice?"

"Yeah. Sure." And then, because I was curious, "How can you live like this?" At Irv's raised eyebrow, I continued, "You work at the school. I can't imagine they pay you enough to buy a house this big."

"They don't," he said, and then noting my glance at his naked ring finger, he raised and wiggled it. "I'm not married. Wife left me for a former student of mine, if you can believe it. It's been a while, and she had no money of her own, so it's not like I fleeced her for anything, though I could have if she'd had anything for me to take. I simply know how to handle my money."

"Tori Carmichael has a pretty big place too," I said. "Did you share your money-saving ideas with her? Or don't you get along? She fled pretty quickly when we met at the school."

"I don't see how any of this is any business of yours." Irv rose and crossed the room to a fireplace. He removed a check from atop the mantel and held it out to me. It was already filled out. "That should cover the costs."

I glanced at the amount, and then shoved the check into my pocket before he could change his mind and take it back. He'd said he'd pay cash, but a check worked just as well. I could probably replace both taillights, the bumper, and my wheels on the amount he'd offered. "If not, I'll let you know."

"If it comes to more than that, you're being ripped off," Irv said. "Now, if that's all, you know the way out."

I wasn't ready to go; not yet. I had questions and while Irv didn't seem all that forthcoming, I wanted to ask them, just in case he'd let something slip. He *was* the guidance counselor at the school, which meant he might know a few things about the teachers, such as Tori Carmichael and Kevin Tewksbury, thanks to student complaints.

I made a point to settle deeper into my chair when I asked, as casually as you'd like, "Did you know that Tori signed up for a newsletter from an ultraconservative website that promoted the censorship of books?"

If Irv was surprised by the question, he didn't show it. "No, I did not."

"You're interested in the same sort of thing, right?"

"Once again, that's none of your business."

"It's just that Sidney Tewksbury was into that sort of stuff too. He came to the school a lot before his death, a place where his brother, Kevin, works."

"That's common knowledge, Ms. Hancock."

"It is. But Tori didn't seem like the type to get involved with people like Sidney. She complained about him, in fact. So, why would a teacher who claims she's against censoring the books she wants to teach, sign up for a newsletter at a website that demands she do just that?"

"You'd have to ask her."

"I'm asking you."

A clock in the corner ticked the seconds by loud enough for me to hear as Irv and I stared at one another, neither wanting to back down. I thought it was telling that he hadn't demanded I leave. Did that mean he was interested in what I had to say? Or was he trying to figure out what else I might know?

Finally, Irv returned to his chair and eased down into it. "What is this website?" he asked.

"Freedom from Filth." There was a moment where I almost told him that Kevin Tewksbury had created it, but caught myself before I did. If the wrong person received that information, it could get Kevin hurt. "The site links to Sidney's podcasts. Do you know of them?"

Irv ignored my question. "What does this have to do with me?"

"I was just wondering what you might know," I said. And, because I wanted him to talk to me, not get annoyed enough to throw me out, "You're the guidance counselor at the school, which means you know a lot about the people there; not just the students."

He sat back with a smug, "I do."

"Does Tori Carmichael seem like the kind of person who would be interested in Freedom from Filth?"

His ankle returned to his knee as he stroked his chin in thought. "She always struck me as an odd duck," he said. "Tori made a fuss whenever Sidney or Maggie showed, but something about her reaction never sat right with me. It was as if she reveled in it."

"You mean she *wanted* Maggie and Sidney to harass her about her books?"

"It would make a good show, would it not?" Irv smiled. "I wasn't a fan of the disruption, especially during school hours, but I can't say I disagreed with the protests. If Sidney's methods were more subtle, more, shall we say, professional, I imagine we could have removed many more damaging titles from the school before they marred the views of the children forced to read them."

I bit back a retort, though it was a near-thing. I had to take a calming breath before I asked, "Do you think Tori was friends with them? Maggie and Sidney, I mean."

"Friends?" He laughed. "No, I don't think so. If you were to ask me, I'd say Tori Carmichael signed up for the newsletter for research purposes. That way, the next time she saw either of them, she would know what to say so she could get close to them."

Which sounded a lot like what Kevin had told me.

"Close?" I asked. "For what purpose?"

He shrugged and rose. "I'm sure you can fill in the blanks, Ms. Hancock. Now, please, if you would." He motioned toward the exit.

I stood, still not quite satisfied with the answers, but it was all I was going to get. "Thank you, Mr. Barrow." I patted my pocket where I'd stowed the check. "I'm glad we could work this out."

His smile was strained as he gave me a single, short nod.

As I left the room, I glanced down the hall, toward another door that was left slightly ajar. Plastic lay on the floor and there was a faint scent of paint I hadn't noticed before. Irv was wearing nice clothing, so he wasn't the one doing the painting. I wondered if he'd hired someone, or if he had a friend helping him out.

"Doing some redecorating?" I asked, jerking a thumb toward the door.

"Something like that," Irv said. "Please inform your cop friend that we've taken care of everything." He urged me toward the front door by walking so close, I really had no choice. "I do not wish to hear from either of you again." He reached around me to open the door.

"I'll let him know." I stepped outside and before I could so much as say "thank you," Irv had already closed the door.

I grumbled all the way back to my Escape, but at least I was happy with the results of my visit. My taillight and bumper were going to get fixed and it wasn't going to come out of my pocket. I could call the insurance company and tell them they wouldn't have to worry about it either. My questions weren't answered to my satisfaction, and I still didn't know who'd killed Sidney Tewksbury, but I was starting to think I might be on the right track.

I turned my Escape around and headed back down the driveway. I looked for the glint of light I'd seen heading in, but if it was still there, it didn't make itself known.

I was on my way downtown, thinking I might stop by Death by Coffee for some mental fuel, when I realized I wasn't too far from where Tori Carmichael lived. A quick internal debate, and then I took a right when I should have kept going straight. Two minutes later, I was sitting out in front of Tori's house, wondering what in the world I was doing.

Tori must have been wondering the same thing because she came outside, hand on her hip, and approached the driver's-side window. I rolled it down to greet her.

"Hi, Tori."

"What are you doing here, Ms. . . . ." She frowned as if she couldn't remember my name.

"Hancock, but call me Krissy."

"All right, Krissy, why are you here, sitting in my driveway?"

There was no good answer for that other than, "I'm nosy," but I wasn't about to tell her that. Instead, I got directly to the point. "Why did you sign up for a newsletter from Freedom from Filth?"

A slight widening of the eyes was the only physical reaction she showed. "I have no idea what you're talking about."

"You never received emails from them?"

"If I did, they went straight into the trash. What makes

you think I'd sign up for something like that? It sounds like something that woman, Maggie, would dream up."

"That's what the owner of the site wanted you to believe," I said. "Have you interacted with the group before?"

"No, and I don't plan to." Her brow furrowed. "You said *owner of the site*. Are you telling me it has nothing to do with the Freedom from Filth group?"

"It doesn't. It was a scam."

"I see." Tori tapped a foot and stared off into the distance. "I guess that explains why I never received anything from them."

"So, you did sign up for it?"

Tori sighed. "Yes, I did. But not for the reason you might think. I received an anonymous email with a link to the site. I almost trashed it without looking, but decided to see what it was all about. I quickly realized the website was going to be used for propaganda, and thought that it might serve as an interesting example of how words can sway people's morals. I signed up for the newsletter, hoping I'd find something I could use in class, but never received anything after that first email."

"Do you know who sent the email?" I asked.

She snorted. "By definition, *anonymous* means it was sent in a way that prevented me from knowing that very thing."

Tori's tone made me feel all kinds of stupid, but I pressed on. "Don't you think it would have been dangerous to use something from the Freedom from Filth people in class?" I asked.

"I would have been careful. If nothing in the newsletter served my purposes without being too damaging, I would have blocked the sender and forgotten all about it."

I sat back and wondered how much of what she was telling me was true. If Tori and Maggie had found common ground somewhere along the line, they might have staged their altercation to draw attention to Maggie's cause. I was having a hard time believing Tori would have *wanted* the Freedom from Filth people sending her anything, even if she'd intended it for a class.

"Look," Tori said, clearly tired of the conversation. "I don't know how you found out about it, but the site and newsletter were merely a means to an end for me. I'm almost relieved it isn't legitimate, because that means I won't be hearing from someone like Maggie again. I want life to go back to normal, though I know it's not going to happen. The school is done with me, and I can't say I blame them. And for as much as I want to blame Maggie for all my troubles, I can't. I brought some of it on myself."

A glance at her house made me wonder if my theories were correct and she and Irv were scamming the system somehow. I'm not sure how they'd managed to steal from the school, considering how underfunded most schools were these days, but it *was* possible.

I could have pressed her for more information, though what? I wasn't sure. Instead, I thanked her for her time and said my goodbyes. As Tori stepped back from my vehicle, I turned it around and with an apologetic wave, I left.

It wasn't hard to figure out who had sent the link to Tori. Kevin Tewksbury was in charge of the thing, and was likely the culprit. The only question I had was why? Was he seeking some sort of revenge against her? Was he curious to see where she stood? Or was he trying to get her into trouble somehow? Tori knew about Your Secret

Man and Kevin's connection to it. What else did she know about him that might make him want to go after her?

Kevin had been less than honest every time I'd talked to him. I was beginning to wonder if I should believe anything he said. I just couldn't figure out his motives. Did he want to find his brother's killer?

Or was Kevin Tewksbury attempting to put the blame on someone else because he'd done the deed himself?

25

"Krissy! I'm glad you're here. Come check this out."

I followed Mason's voice up the stairs, into the books at Death by Coffee. He was standing at the back wall, hands on his hips, with a wide smile on his face.

"What am I looking at?" I asked. The bookshelf he was staring at looked like it always had.

"Not that," he said. "This." He pointed to the left of the shelf where a page was hanging.

I glanced at him in curiosity before leaning in close. The page depicted a lifelike image of the upstairs portion of Death by Coffee, but . . . not. The bookshelves were taller, the space more organized. The way it was laid out, there was still room for the couches, and there had to be at least twice the number of books on the shelves as before.

"Wow," I said. "How did you manage this?"

"Found a computer program," he said, sounding as proud as if he'd created the program himself. "It allowed me to punch in the dimensions of our space here, and then of the objects I wanted to place in it. I could link directly to a product, and the program would plug it right into the room. From there, I could move the object wherever I wanted to place it. It's pretty neat."

"Sounds it." And complicated. I'm glad Mason decided to handle it himself because I would have been overwhelmed. "This looks great."

"Doesn't it? I have yet to run it by Vicki, but I think she'll approve. And if you look here"—he pointed to a spot in the corner, back behind the counter—"Trouble can have a cat bed, a food and water dish, and be out of the way of customers."

Sure enough, a tiny food and water dish sat beside a circular cat bed.

I loved what he'd come up with, but doubts were already starting to seep in. "How much is this going to cost?" I asked, dreading the answer.

"Not as much as you'd think." Mason beamed as he pulled another paper—this one folded into a little square—out of his back pocket. "I took your numbers, and then did a little digging to see if I could discover cheaper options that still worked with the aesthetic we are going for. I found the same shelves you wanted at half the cost, thanks to a friend of mine. While it'll bite into our profits a little, it's not bad at all."

I glanced over the numbers, which were thankfully laid out in a way I could understand. Mason was right; we could do the whole remodel at nearly half the cost I'd come up with. "Labor?"

"What we can't do ourselves, I know a couple of guys who'd be willing to chip in if we provide them with free coffee whenever they stop in."

As long as they didn't live in the store and drink us out of business, I was thrilled. "Let's do it," I said and then added, "As long as Vicki approves."

"She will." Mason folded the page back up and shoved it into his pocket. "I'm feeling rather proud of myself right now."

"I can tell."

He laughed. "Yeah, well, it's nice to have something positive to focus on." The laughter dried up. "I almost forgot to tell you: Beth was looking for you earlier."

I immediately thought of Mason's dad, Raymond Lawyer. He'd promised to stop harassing Beth for leaving his insurance company to come work with me, but I couldn't make myself believe it. Raymond had been a thorn in my side since I'd moved to Pine Hills, and I doubted he would ever stop causing trouble. It was in his nature to be contrary.

Mason must have read my thoughts on my face because he shook his head. "Don't get the wrong idea. Dad's been good. This is something else."

"Okay, thanks. I'll talk to her." I left Mason, who'd resumed proudly staring at his work, and headed downstairs to find Beth.

The dining room was mostly empty, with only a couple of tables occupied. Two men at separate tables were dressed smartly, laptops in front of them, earbuds in their ears. One was typing furiously, while the other was watching a video of, all things, cats falling off of objects. Every now and again, he'd chuckle. A pair of elderly women who I'd never seen before sat close to the door, chatting amicably amongst themselves.

Beth was just leaving their table as I descended the stairs. She saw me and veered my way. I led her a few steps closer to the counter before I asked, "What's up? Mason said you were looking for me?"

"Yeah, I was." She glanced back at the customers and the clean tables, before turning back to me. "It's about that day. You know; at the festival?"

"Yeah." I tried to keep the eagerness out of my voice, but failed. "Did you remember something?"

"Kind of. I'm not sure it means anything, but thought I'd tell you and you can—I don't know—tell Officer Dalton or something. I don't want to waste his time, and thought that if I ran this by you, you could decide whether or not it's important."

"Good thinking," I said. I doubted Paul would be angry if she gave him information that didn't pan out, but it *would* take him away from the case while he was dealing with it. "What did you remember?"

Beth apparently didn't like having the door at her back, because she walked around me so that she could face it. When she spoke, she kept her voice low, as if we were sharing a secret.

"I've been thinking about the festival," she began, "trying to run through the day to see if I could remember anything that might help the police. Something kept nagging at me, and it took me longer to figure out what that something was than it should have."

"That's understandable. It was a pretty stressful situation."

"Tell me about it." She managed a smile that vanished

almost as soon as it appeared. "Anyway, I'd taken a break to run to the restroom. The closest place I could go were those outhouses—"

"Porta-potties," I said. The park had restrooms, but not nearly enough of them for the entire festival. Someone—I'm not sure who—managed to snag a dozen portable toilets for the event.

"Yeah, those." Beth made a disgusted face. "I didn't want to use them, but I didn't want to wait in line for too long either. There was hardly anyone there, so I was in and out pretty quickly."

I didn't know what to say to that, so I simply nodded for her to go on.

"While I was inside," she went on, "someone started hammering on the doors of the other potties. It startled me, and angered quite a few other people because I could hear them complaining. I'd just finished up and had opened the door when the guy doing the hammering reached me. It was Sidney Tewksbury."

I wasn't sure how Sidney using the bathroom would help the police, but I asked, "What did he do?" anyway.

"Nothing, as far as I know," she said. "He pushed past me and slammed the door as if I'd made him wait on purpose. I didn't even recognize him at first. He was just some impatient guy who couldn't wait five minutes for a stall to open up."

"Not surprised," I said. "Sidney didn't seem like the waiting type."

"Tell me about it." She took a deep breath and finally seemed to relax. "Anyway, he did his business, and I left. It wasn't until today that I remembered something else that happened then, something so small, I'm not sure it means anything."

"Anything could help," I said, hoping she might have seen someone go in after Sidney.

"He had a drink with him," she said.

"A drink?"

"Our cider. I recognized the cup."

"He carried it into the bathroom with him?" I made a face. I wouldn't even take a glass of water into my own bathroom with me. I'd seen those articles about all the micro-sized particles that got on everything, and in no way wanted anything that came from a bathroom to get into my water. But to take a drink into a public restroom, especially one made of plastic that might not have been cleaned in weeks? No, thank you.

"No," Beth said. "He didn't take it in with him. He gave it to a woman who was with him."

That caused me to perk up. "A woman?"

Beth nodded. "I didn't know who she was at the time. She was with another guy, this one good-looking, that I originally assumed was her boyfriend or husband because they were talking with their heads nearly touching. You know, standing real close, like lovers might."

I nodded, anxious for her to go on.

"After I opened my door, Sidney shoved his drink into the woman's hand. I had to go around her and the guy she was with because they refused to move. All I heard when I passed was the guy urging her to 'do it now.'"

"Do what?"

"I have no idea," Beth said. "But the woman noticed me passing and glared a hole into my back. I felt it all the way back to our booth."

Excitement had me nearly bouncing from foot to foot. "You say you didn't know the woman at the time," I said. "Does that mean you know her now?"

"I do. It's the same woman who has been pasting those flyers on our windows." She glanced toward those same windows, but there were no flyers there now. "And I think she was with the doctor who pronounced Sidney dead."

Maggie Reed touched Sidney's apple cider.
And she was with Darrin.

My stomach churned as I considered the implications. Maggie and Sidney together I could understand. But Darrin? He was supposed to have problems with Sidney. Why would he be hanging around him at the festival if that was the case?

Beth had to be mistaken. I'd pressed her on what the guy looked like, and the description could have been of Darrin Crenshaw, but it could also have been dozens of other attractive men.

You just don't want him to be guilty.

I couldn't stop thinking about it as I helped Beth and Mason clean up for the night. Vicki arrived and distracted me for a few minutes, but as soon as she wandered upstairs to help Mason, I was right back to thinking about Maggie and Darrin and how they fit in to all of this. I even called Paul, hoping he might tell me something that would clear Darrin from suspicion, but all I got was his voicemail and he didn't call me back.

I was mindlessly wiping down a table I feared I'd already wiped down twice before, when the door opened and Rita walked through. Much to my relief, Johan wasn't with her. I didn't think I could deal with *that* right then.

"Can I get you anything?" I asked her, happy for the distraction. My brain was tired from running in circles.

"Oh, I don't know, dear," Rita said, perusing the menu. "I was driving by and saw your vehicle here and thought I'd pop on in and say hi. I'm not sure I want any coffee this late."

"We do have water." And my mom's apple cider, which we'd temporarily put on the menu, but right then, I didn't want to think about it, or how it connected to the murder.

"No, that's all right," Rita said. "Honestly, I'm not sure why I stopped by. I guess I didn't want to go home to an empty house quite yet."

"Is Johan . . . ?" I left it hanging, not quite sure what I was asking.

Rita waved off the question as if she were shooing a fly. "He's fine. Just busy out of town right now, so I can't even phone him." She sighed dramatically. "This is the sort of thing I didn't miss from dating. When you get used to having someone around, it's a lot harder to be by yourself, you know?"

I nodded. Now that Paul was coming around more often, the idea of my empty house wasn't as appealing as it used to be. At least I had Misfit to keep me company. As far as I was aware, Rita didn't have any pets or family she could use to fill the silence.

"I suppose I should tell you that you have a busted taillight while I'm here," she said with a tsk. "There's nothing on the ground out there now, so I guess it happened elsewhere. Did you back into something?" Another tsk, and before I could answer, she added, "You really should get it fixed. It's dangerous to go without those lights."

"I know," I said. "The bulb still works, and I just got the money for the repairs from the guy who did it, so it'll be fixed soon."

"You know who hit you? That's nice. I had a car that got backed into once. It smashed the passenger rear door in so far, it was practically riding shotgun. Whoever did it drove off and they never did find them. And, of course, my insurance company fought me every step of the way when it came to paying for the repairs. I swear, they are nothing but a scam. Who ran into you, dear? Did it happen here?" She glanced out the door like she thought the culprit might walk by.

"No, it happened at the school." And then, because I was feeling rather spiteful and knowing Rita would plaster it all over town, I said, "Irving Barrow was the man who hit me."

Rita clucked her tongue. "Well, that doesn't come as much of a surprise." She shook her head as if incredulous. "He paid you out of pocket, didn't he?"

I nodded.

"That doesn't surprise me one bit. The way I hear it, he's been funneling money from organizations he belongs to for years. No one can prove it, of course. He's too careful for that. I've always thought of him as the type who'd burn down an entire village, just to kill the mosquito who bit him. He's not a pleasant man."

"No, he's not," I said. And after some thought, I asked, "What kind of organizations does he belong to?"

Rita shrugged. "He keeps it hush-hush, which makes me think whatever it is, it isn't something the rest of us would approve of. From what I hear, he's managed to drag a few other people in the deep with him, though I can't say who."

I immediately thought about Tori Carmichael and her big house. How many other people were involved in Irving's schemes? And did it have anything to do with Sidney's death?

Rita stepped closer to me, dropping her voice. "Rumor has it, Irving has been courting that woman who's been running around town causing all sorts of trouble."

"Maggie Reed?" I asked, breath catching.

"That's her, all right. I heard from Andi just yesterday that they were seen together outside the church, though they didn't go in. Andi was about to leave when she saw Maggie pacing outside, and since she didn't want to bother her, she waited by the door instead. Irv eventually showed up, and while Andi didn't get into details on whether or not they acted romantically, she did say that he took Maggie by the arm and led her away."

"Maggie and Irv?" Beth had mentioned a good-looking man who was seen with Maggie. While there were differences between Irv and Darrin, there were quite a few similarities as well. Could the man she had seen actually have been Irving Barrow and *not* Darrin Crenshaw? "Were they at the festival together?" I asked, barely able to contain my excitement.

Rita tapped her chin. I noted her nails were painted pink, a color I'm not sure I'd ever seen her wear. "Now that you mention it, I do believe they were. I believe I saw both Maggie and Irv when I was given my book at the apple-bobbing station." Her eyes widened as the implication settled in. "And they were with Sidney Tewksbury right before he died!"

26

"See you tomorrow," I said as Mason and Vicki headed for the door, arm in arm.

"Tomorrow?" Mason chuckled. "I'm more concerned about seeing you Thursday. It better be a big, honking turkey."

"*You're* a big, honking turkey," Vicki said, tugging on his arm.

The way he looked at her then made me a little jealous. There was no denying that the two of them were deeply in love with one another. And while my own love life had picked up recently, Paul and I were still in the feel-each-other-out stage, despite how long we'd known one another.

And while I was okay with our slower pace, I still sometimes wished we could be as comfortable with one another as my friends were. Of course, I was okay with sitting out back at his place, roasting marshmallows over a fire, while talking about nothing, but sometimes, a little more excitement would be welcome.

Well, romantic excitement; not murder.

"Hey, we do need to get together soon," I said to Vicki. "I was thinking we could start to watch *The Boys*."

Mason made a face. "I heard that's gory."

"Sounds perfect," Vicki said, nudging Mason. "And you're not invited anyway."

"Next weekend?" I asked. It would put it after Thanksgiving, and I hoped to have my living room put back together by then.

"It's a date."

Vicki waved as she and Mason stepped outside, leaving me as the last person in Death by Coffee. We'd officially closed for the night over an hour ago, but we'd stuck around after the register was closed out to talk about the remodel upstairs. We'd settled on Mason's plan, and work would begin in the gap between Thanksgiving and Christmas. The plan was to do it without having to close down the bookstore, which meant having much of the work being done at night when no one would be there. Then, once the new shelves were installed, we'd need a few days to get all the books shelved where they needed to be, and that meant chaos and clutter.

I turned off all the lights, grabbed a thermos of apple cider I planned on drinking at home, and then picked up the deposit bag and hefted it in my hand. Today must have been a pretty good day because I thought it felt heavier than usual. A quick stop at the bank and then I'd be on my way home for a much-deserved rest.

My phone jangled in my purse and I paused before rounding the counter to answer it. I recognized the number, which caused heat to spread from my toes, upward.

"Hey, Paul," I said by way of answer. "I tried to call you earlier."

"Got the message. Is everything okay."

I opened my mouth to tell him about what I'd learned from Rita, but caught myself before it could slip out. I wanted to tell him all about it, of course, but thought it might be far more interesting to do so face-to-face. And maybe after a few pleasantries. It wasn't like he could do anything about it tonight, anyway.

"Everything's fine," I said. "I was just about to head home. Do you think you might be able to stop by?"

There was a brief pause before he answered, "As much as I'd love to, it's been a really long day and I have an early morning."

My spirits drooped, but I refused to give up that easily. "Rita stopped by Death by Coffee earlier. She had some interesting things to say that I'd like to pass on to you. It might help with your case."

"And you can't tell me over the phone?" There was a playfulness to his voice that made my toes more than warm; they were vibrating.

"Nope. You'll have to wrestle it from me face-to-face."

"Sounds fun," he said. "I'll be there in twenty."

"I've got to stop by the bank, so better make it thirty." And I was hoping to have a few minutes to clean up before he showed. I smelled like stale coffee and sweat, which would never be attractive.

"See you then," Paul said and then disconnected.

A small part of me felt a little guilty for not telling him

what I knew, but I was hoping the guilt would be worth it in the end. If everything worked out the way I hoped, he'd find Sidney's killer, but not before a rather pleasant night celebrating.

I returned my phone to my purse, double-checked to make sure the thermos and deposit bag were secure, and then I rounded the counter to head for the door. I stepped out into the brisk evening wind and came face-to-face, not with Paul, but with a brick.

Thankfully, said brick wasn't flying just yet. It was still in the hand of the woman holding it.

"Maggie," I said, jerking to a stop. "What do you think you're doing?"

She lowered her arm and gave me a sweet smile, as if she hadn't been about to throw a brick through the plate glass window that fronted Death by Coffee.

"Justice."

"Justice for what?" I asked, tightening my grip on the money bag. There were a lot of bills in there, but there was quite a bit of change in it too. It wasn't a brick like she was holding, but it would hurt just the same if I were to use it as a weapon.

"For Sidney. For the people of this town corrupted by you and the evil you peddle."

I couldn't help it; I laughed. "For Sidney?" I asked, taking a step to the side so that if she were to throw the brick at me, it wouldn't accidentally take out the store window if she missed. "You and I both know I had nothing to do with his death."

"Kevin—"

"Didn't either," I cut in. "But you? I'm not so sure about." Another step. She turned with me, which was exactly what I wanted.

Down the street, behind Maggie, I noted headlights shining in my direction. The car was parked at the side of the road, and I hoped whoever was there was busy calling the police, and wasn't recording the altercation for social media instead.

"Sidney and I cared about one another."

"You might have once, but I heard his podcasts. It sounded to me like he was getting tired of pandering your venom."

"Sidney believed in the cause," Maggie said. "He died for it."

Something in her tone told me that she truly believed that. I didn't know if that made her loyal, or crazy. Maybe both.

"This doesn't help anything," I said, taking another step as I motioned toward the brick she was holding. My Escape was parked at the side of the road, only a few feet away. With the keyless entry, I wouldn't have to fumble with a fob or key to unlock it, which meant I could be inside and driving away in seconds if she decided to get aggressive.

I just needed to get close enough to the door so that I'd have a chance to make that escape. And no, the pun wasn't lost on me.

Maggie's fingers whitened on the brick. "Sometimes, the only solution to corruption is violence. Change doesn't happen easy. You have to force it, and in doing so, sacrifices must be made."

"Why change anything?" I asked. "I get it; you don't like certain books, or how sciences are taught. It's your right to believe what you want. But other people don't have the same beliefs as you. Why does it matter what they believe? So you can sleep easier at night? Don't you think those of us who like reading books about fictional murders deserve the freedom to read such things?"

"It corrupts. It brings ruin." There was a tremble to her voice. I couldn't tell if it was caused by anger, or if she was struggling to hold on to her hatred. Could I actually be getting to her? "Why should I suffer because you choose to wallow in filth?"

"Isn't it my choice to entertain myself however I see fit?"

Maggie's eyes narrowed. "Choice is an illusion."

I wanted to scream at her. No matter what I said, she would contradict me. No matter what argument I provided, she'd find some way to twist it to her own ends. Arguing with Maggie was useless. Her mind was made up, and nothing I could do or say would ever change it.

Another step. I flexed my fingers in preparation of jerking my car door open. Down the street, the headlights clicked off and a shape emerged from the driver's side, onto the sidewalk. It was too dark to make out who it was, but that didn't really matter. If they were coming to help, it could be Raymond Lawyer or John Buchannan for all I cared.

I kept my focus on Maggie so she wouldn't turn back to look. "We can sit down and talk about this," I said. "There's no need to vandalize my property."

"It's too late for talk."

"Is this what Sidney would want?"

She flinched like I'd struck her, so I pressed on.

"Was all of this Irving Barrow's idea?"

"You know nothing."

I continued to press, as if she hadn't spoken. "Did Irv convince you to poison Sidney? The police know you two were with him at the festival. Someone saw you three together, saw you with the cup in your hand. If Irv is responsible for Sidney's death—"

"Stop it!" Maggie reared back, and with all her might, heaved the brick at my head.

I saw it coming a mile away and ducked even before she'd readied her throw. The brick sailed over my head and with a crash of safety glass, went through the back window of my Escape.

I stared at the hole, mouth agape, when I should have been paying attention to the crazed woman at my back. She hit me in the side full-force as I gawped at the damage. The force of the blow took me down to the pavement, Maggie atop me. I hit the sidewalk with a grunt and my wrist erupted in pain. I tried to buck Maggie off of me, but since I was one-handed and she was fueled by anger, I couldn't so much as budge her.

"You don't know what you're talking about," she hissed into my face. "Sidney was a hero." A shape appeared behind her. My heart leapt, thinking I was saved.

And then I caught a glimpse of the man's face, and those hopes died a horrible, painful death.

"Hello, Ms. Hancock," Irving Barrow said. "It looks like we have ourselves a predicament, now don't we?"

"What are we going to do?" Maggie paced back and forth between two shelves, vanishing and reappearing at either end. "This wasn't the plan."

"We'll think of something." Irv stood towering over me, arms crossed, as he watched her pace. He looked worried, but I don't think it had much to do with me, but rather, at Maggie's agitated reaction to my capture.

I was sitting on the couch upstairs at Death by Coffee.

The lights were still off, which made Maggie's expression hard to see, though I could *feel* it. Anger and worry radiated off of her in waves. She could explode at any moment, and I knew I would be the target of that explosion.

When would I learn not to antagonize murderers?

I no longer had any doubts about her guilt. She all but confirmed it when she'd attacked me.

"We can't let her go," Maggie said, jabbing a finger at me as she emerged from the darkness between the shelves. "She'll tell everyone."

"We won't, which means she won't."

"Then what are we going to do with her?"

As Maggie paced away, Irv turned his attention to me. There was a calmness in his expression that chilled me to the bone. No compassion. No fear. He acted like he was in complete control, and to be honest, I wasn't so sure he wasn't.

"The police know," I said. "I talked to Paul Dalton right before I ran into Maggie. She probably saw me talking on the phone. Hurting me won't help you."

"Now, why don't I believe you?" Irv said, bending over so he could look at me closer. His chiseled jaw looked downright evil in the shadows of the store. "I think you're fibbing."

"Why do this?" I asked. "Why do any of this?" And then, because I needed to know. "Why kill Sidney? He was on your side."

"Your filth killed him!" Maggie shouted before pacing away again.

Irv sighed and shook his head at her outburst. He acted like a father disappointed in a child. It made me wonder if Maggie would be next on his kill list.

After me, of course.

"He's a martyr for the cause," he said. "He served his purpose, and brought attention to our beliefs."

"Did he have a say in it?" I asked.

"In his death? Only in so much that he was the one who gave up his life for the cause. His will was growing weak, and he began to question us. Deep down, he knew he was in the wrong for his shift, but his words were betraying him. He lost his conviction. We gave that conviction back to him."

"He's a hero," Maggie added. She wiped an arm across her brow. She was sweating despite the chill. She didn't look like a leader, not with how nervous she was acting. And now, seeing her with Irv, I realized that she never was.

"You've run everything the whole time," I said, focusing on Irv. "Sidney's podcasts. Maggie's protests. You put them out there, let them take the heat, while you hid behind your job at the school."

"Someone has to be in charge," Irv said. "Why not me?"

"Because your leadership got a man killed?" *And has me trapped in my own store with a crazy woman.* The last was best left unsaid while said crazy woman was pacing a hole in the floor.

"Sidney would understand," Irv said. "He might have been wavering, but that didn't mean he'd abandoned us. His death showed everyone what was at stake. It made people see that these books"—he gestured toward the shelves—"and the lies taught at the school are responsible for all of the evil in the world."

"You *murdered* him," I said, not bothering to hide my incredulousness. They were already trying to decide what to do with me, and I doubted whatever they decided would end up with me going free, so it wasn't like I could make my situation much worse.

"I gave his life a purpose," Irv said. "Maggie cared deeply for him, yet even she understood what needed to be done to cleanse Pine Hills."

I looked past him to Maggie, who had stopped pacing and was leaning against one of the shelves. She didn't look convinced. *Did she doubt him?* And if so, could I use that to save my own skin?

"Did you really love him?" I asked her.

She glanced at me, but didn't answer.

"If you cared so much about Sidney, why meet Kevin after using that dating site? Did Irv put you up to it?"

"I . . . I was weak." She lowered her head.

"Wouldn't using a website like that run counter to your beliefs?" I asked. "Are you sure you're as dedicated to the cause as Irv wants you to believe? He's using you, Maggie. You don't have to listen to him. Help me."

"That'll be quite enough," Irv said, stepping between Maggie and me. "Maggie is the face of our organization. Your pathetic attempts to sway her to your side will have no effect." He glanced back at her. "Right, Maggie?"

She gave him one sharp nod, jaw clenched.

Irv knelt in front of me and I tensed. I wasn't tied up, and I was pretty sure I could knock him over if I were to dive at him, but how far would I get before Maggie caught me? She was closer to the stairs. If I failed to get away now, I doubted I'd get a second chance.

"Now," Irv said. "I think it's time we dealt with this little problem of ours." He straightened. "Maggie, start knocking books off the shelves, but do it quietly. I don't want someone to check on the noise before we're done."

I wanted to bring up the hole in my Escape, and how

someone had to have heard the glass shatter, but that would only make them work faster. I just had to bide my time and stall them until the police arrived.

If they arrived.

Maggie hesitated a moment before she began pulling books from the bookshelves, one by one. They hit the floor with a solid *thump* that sounded loud to my ears, but likely didn't even carry down the stairs into the café.

Irv picked up the deposit bag filled with Death by Coffee's earnings, which he'd taken from me and set on top of a bookshelf along with my thermos and purse. He weighed the bag in his hand, eyes distant, as if considering what to do.

"A robbery," he said. "Poor Ms. Hancock here just so happened to still be in the store when the thief broke in." He smiled at me. It was cold and unfeeling. "This money will come in handy. Thank you for your contribution."

"It doesn't have to be this way," I said, loud enough for Maggie to hear over the sound of books falling. "He made you kill Sidney, a man you cared about. He forced you into these protests, all while hiding safely in his little bubble. He'll kill you next if he thinks it will help him!"

There was a brief pause between one book falling and the next. Since I couldn't see her, I couldn't tell if it was because Maggie was listening, or if she'd simply moved on to another shelf before resuming her destruction of my store.

"You're wasting your breath," Irv said. "Now, how should we go about this?" He smiled. "I know. I—"

In the depths of my purse, my phone buzzed.

Everyone froze, including Maggie. No one made for my purse, though I desperately wanted to make a mad grab for it. It wasn't like I could do much of anything if I did make the attempt. Even if I did manage to find my phone in the mess of my purse before Irv caught me, I doubted I'd be able to swipe *accept*, let alone scream for help before he silenced me.

"It's the cops," I said instead of risking it. "You know I'm dating Officer Dalton, right?" Irv had said as much when we'd dealt with the damage to my Escape. "He knows where I am, and will be here at any moment."

The phone stopped ringing.

Irv regarded my purse for a long moment before sighing. "I guess we'd better hurry this along then."

Before I could object, he grabbed me by my good arm and yanked me up from the couch. He forced me to the stairs, and down into the café portion of Death by Coffee. He glanced through the window and not seeing anyone, forcefully led me back around the counter, toward the door that led into the kitchen.

You know, where the knives were kept.

I dug in my heels and refused to go any further. Irv struggled with me, but I had enough leverage—and enough fear-fueled strength—to make it hard on him.

"There's no sense in making this more difficult than it has to be," Irv said through clenched teeth. "I promise to make it quick, if that helps."

"I'd rather stay out here, thanks." When he tried to shove me through the door, I caught myself on the frame with my sprained wrist. Black spots danced in front of my eyes, and I very nearly passed out from the pain, but darn it, I wasn't going to give up.

Irv must have felt me weaken because he used the opportunity to get a better grip on my arm. Using both hands, he steered me toward the door. Nothing I could do could stop him.

"I've done nothing wrong!" I shouted, vainly hoping someone from outside would hear. "Killing me is far worse than someone reading about it in a book. You're living a lie."

"Your death will prove to the town that something must be done. We've won, Ms. Hancock. You, like Sidney, are a mere piece of the puzzle that will bring Pine Hills back to respectability. And I have a feeling, like Sidney, no one will mourn you when you're gone."

Irv shoved me forward. I hit the doorframe again, but this time, the door popped open. One more shove and I'd be through. Once inside, with the knives, I'd stand no chance.

"You're wrong. *I* mourn him."

The voice came from behind us. It was followed by a loud *thud*. A lukewarm, sticky liquid splashed over me as Irv's hands fell away. I staggered against the wall and nearly fell into the back room before I caught myself. I turned just in time to see Maggie rear back and strike Irv, who'd spun around to face her, in the face with my now-empty thermos of apple cider.

He went down in a heap.

"Go," Maggie said, tears in her eyes as she dropped the thermos to the ground. "Go, now." And then she sank down onto the floor, sobbing over an unconscious Irving Barrow.

27

"Where do you want the pies?"

"The counter works," I said, pointing with my one good arm. Vicki carried the pies—both a pumpkin and a chocolate—from the fridge to where I'd indicated.

"Do you think this looks done? Should I leave it in?" Mason scowled at the oven. "Why can't I tell?"

"The timer will go off and then you can use the meat thermometer to check its internal temp," I said, suppressing a grin.

"They're going to implode, you know?" Paul said from beside me. We were sitting on the stools in my kitchen while Mason and Vicki handled Thanksgiving dinner. Thanks to my injuries and, as Vicki put it, my mental trauma, I was on strict orders to let everyone else handle the cooking.

"It is fun to watch," I said, though a part of me hated not being able to help out at my own party. I turned away so I wouldn't be tempted to chip in. "I was worried you'd be tied up with the case and wouldn't be able to make it."

Paul stretched and then shrugged. "Buchannan can handle it. He *is* the new detective. Or will be once he goes through the rest of the process."

Detective Buchannan. No matter how many times it ran through my head, I couldn't imagine it. "He's going to make my life miserable."

"Actually, I have a feeling it's going to be the other way around."

A squeal from across the room made me think something bad had happened and I half-rose from my seat. Robert picked up Trisha and spun her in a circle before they sloppily kissed. Apparently, he was the source of the squeal.

"She said yes!" he declared once they separated. There was a smattering of applause. Will patted Robert on the back and across the room, Rita jerked out her phone and started talking into it, eyes never leaving the freshly engaged couple.

My house was packed to the gills, and I couldn't be happier. Misfit, as expected, was hiding in the bedroom, but I figured he'd come sniffing around the moment the turkey hit the table. He'd likely eat just as well as my guests.

Much to my surprise, nearly everyone had come. Jules and Lance were talking to Lena and Zay. I noted Zay had his arm around Lena's waist and she kept shooting me warning looks not to say anything. Still, she looked pleased. Johan was here with Rita, but I refused to let my concerns about him ruin the day.

Will's new flame, Deb, was standing near Rita and Johan, and since Rita was now on the phone, conversation had dried up. Will was chatting up Robert and Trisha. It was good to see everyone getting along, even if it felt odd to have both my exes and my current boyfriend under the same roof and soon, sitting at the same dinner table.

And yet, it felt right.

It felt like family.

"It sounds like both Maggie Reed and Irving Barrow are talking," Paul said, drawing my attention back to the conversation. "John said they're trying to blame one another for the murder, as well as a lot of the destruction that happened afterward, but it's pretty clear they were in on it together."

"I can't believe she stayed," I said. After I'd fled Death by Coffee, I fully expected to hear that Maggie was missing, fled into the night like the criminal she was, but when the police arrived, they found her sitting on the floor next to Irv, right where I'd left her.

"She was brainwashed," Paul said. "She, like Sidney Tewksbury, had conservative leanings, but when they met Irving, he manipulated them into becoming fanatics. They wanted to believe in him so badly, they ignored what was right in front of their faces. All that mattered was that they pleased him, even if what he made them do was wrong."

"Hard to imagine living like that," I said. It ended up getting Sidney killed and before that, estranged from his family. And Maggie . . . well, now she was going to be sitting in prison for a long time for a murder she very likely didn't want to commit. "I still don't get why she did it."

"People do strange things when they think they're in the right."

"I suppose." I paused and then said, "I still don't get why Kevin did what he did. Why send the anonymous message to Tori to get her to sign up for the newsletter?" I'd discovered that part of the story was true just yesterday in conversation with Rita. "And why drag Cindy into it at all?"

"I don't know the details, but from what Buchannan has told me, Kevin Tewksbury blamed them for Sidney's death. He thought he could ruin Tori's career through the newsletter, wanted to make Cindy look bad. He's not a killer, thankfully, but he has no problem ruining people's lives from afar. He hides it well, but he's vindictive."

And out of a job. Last I heard, Kevin was fired for what he'd tried to do to Tori Carmichael, and I couldn't say I was sad about it.

The timer dinged. Mason jerked open the oven door and removed the turkey. He set it carefully onto the stove, checked the temperature, and then gave Vicki a pathetic look, which caused her to laugh. She crossed the room and took over.

"Krissy?" Will said, startling me by appearing at my elbow. "Can we talk?" When he asked it, he was looking at Paul.

"Yeah, sure." I rose. "Be right back."

"I'll be here."

Will led me to the hallway, and for a heart-stopping moment, I thought he planned on taking me all the way back to the bedroom. I didn't think he'd try anything, but the thought of what Rita would say if she saw us head that way would be near life-ending. Thankfully, he stopped the moment we were in a semiprivate spot in the hall.

"I just wanted to thank you for inviting me."

"Why wouldn't I? We're still friends."

"I know." His smile was self-deprecating. "But you didn't have to. And, honestly, I wasn't sure if I should come. With Officer Dalton here, and all your friends—"

I stopped him with a hand on his arm. "You belong here," I said. "Anytime you're in town, feel free to stop by."

He nodded. "I will. And again, thank you."

I wasn't sure why he needed to talk to me privately about that, but I was glad he did. Any frustrations I might have had over Will leaving me for a job in Arizona were gone. I liked Deb, I liked that he was happy. And, despite what Rita might think, there was no spark left between us that risked being rekindled, no matter how alone we might find ourselves.

Will reached into his pocket and removed a small jewelry box. When my eyes widened, he laughed. "It's not what you think." He held it out to me.

"What is it?" I asked, taking it from him. Will only nodded toward it, so I opened it. Inside, a gold chain with a tiny book charm rested on velvet.

"I found this," he said, "and immediately thought of you. Think of it as a gift for accepting me after how I acted."

"Will . . ." My first instinct was to refuse it, but realized that would be wrong of me. "Thank you."

I removed the chain and put it on. Will looked like he

wanted to help, but that would have been a little *too* intimate.

"It looks good on you," he said once I let the charm fall. "Like it was made for you."

"Now I just need a coffee one to complete the set."

Will laughed. "I'll keep an eye out."

I stepped forward and wrapped Will in a hug. Let Rita see us. He was my friend and I wasn't going to pretend otherwise, just because we'd once dated.

Once we parted, we returned to the living room in time to see Mason throw his hands up into the air, while Vicki and Paul laughed. Paul took the turkey carver from him and took over, while Vicki put an arm around her husband in mock comfort.

"Ms. Hancock? Krissy?" Lena approached as Will took his leave to rejoin Deb, who was now talking to Trisha and Robert. Zay was hovering nearby, watching us, but wasn't joining the conversation.

Somehow, that made me nervous.

"Hi, Lena. Having a good time?"

"Yeah, it's great." She took a deep breath. "Smells good too."

There was a knock at the door. Jules answered it for me with a boisterous hello. A moment later, Beth and Jeff walked through the door, but with how they entered, I had a feeling their mutual arrival was coincidence, not a date.

"I'm leaving," Lena said, drawing my attention back to her.

"Now? We're about to eat."

"No, I mean, the store. Pine Hills." She closed her eyes and a tear formed. Another deep breath; this one releasing in a huff. "I'm finally going to college. Zay and I are. It's out of town, and it's a good one, and I really want to go and . . ."

Happiness warred with sadness inside of me. Happiness won out. "That's great!" I said. "I'm happy for you, Lena."

"I can't stay at Death by Coffee." It sounded like a lament. "It's too far away."

"I completely understand." I pulled her into a hug when it looked like she might burst into tears. "I really am happy for you. That's not a lie." I let her step back and was forced to wipe away a tear of my own. "I'll miss you, but that's all right. You're moving on to bigger and better things."

"Yeah, I guess." Zay approached and Lena took his hand when he offered it. "Thanks for understanding. I still have a couple of months before I've got to go, so there's no rush to replace me."

"Oh, I'm already mentally lining up a whole list of prospects," I joked, before adding in a serious tone, "No one will be able to replace you. You'll always be a part of the Death by Coffee family. And if ever you come back and need a job, even for a summer, feel free to stop by. You'll have it."

"Thanks, Krissy. That means a lot." She breathed a heavy sigh of relief. "I'd better let Mrs. Lawyer know."

Lena hurried off with Zay in tow to give Vicki the bittersweet news. I took a deep, trembling breath to calm myself, and then I headed over to Robert and Trisha.

"Congratulations," I said, going in for the hug. Surprisingly, Robert didn't hold on any longer than he should, and actually released me first. "The both of you."

"Thanks!" Robert was bouncing from foot to foot. "I was really starting to worry."

"You had nothing to worry about," Trisha said. Her blond hair was pulled back from her face, which was flush with excitement. "You know that."

"Yeah, I did. I knew all along that you couldn't resist me." Robert winked, but I could see the insecure man hidden beneath the bluster. If he hadn't annoyed me so much, I might have seen his insecurities long ago.

"Well, I'm glad for you. You'll have to let me know when you set the date."

My pocket vibrated. As I checked the screen—a *Happy Thanksgiving!* text from Dad—Robert and Trisha were assaulted by Jules, who was asking them if they would need any chocolates for the wedding.

I stepped back and let them discuss it and simply took in the festivities. I had all my friends in one place. Everyone was alive and healthy, and moving forward with their lives. A part of me couldn't stop thinking about Sidney and Kevin and Maggie and everyone else involved in the murder. Their homes were either empty, or had holes in them where loved ones once were.

I never wanted to experience that kind of pain; not again. Losing my mom had been hard enough, but I still had my memories of her to patch the wound. It wasn't perfect, but what is?

I shot Dad a return text, wishing both him and Laura good health. The turkey was carved and ready. The food hot and waiting.

"Everyone!" I shouted over the cacophony. The murmur died down slowly as all eyes turned toward me. "Thank you for coming," I said. "There's not a lot of space, but that's all right. We're all friends here."

"Hear! Hear!" Lance called, raising a glass of wine someone had opened. Everyone responded with a cheer of their own. Glasses clinked and someone sniffed loudly.

I'm not one for speeches. Anything I might have said would have come out sounding like I'd rehearsed it. Badly. So, instead of making a fool out of myself in front of the people who mattered to me most, I spread my arms wide and grinned.

"Let's eat!"